DEEP
INTO THE
AMAZON
JUNGLE

Also in the
Fabien Cousteau Expeditions

GREAT WHITE SHARK ADVENTURE

JOURNEY UNDER THE ARCTIC

FABIEN COUSTEAU EXPEDITIONS

DEEP INTO THE AMAZON JUNGLE

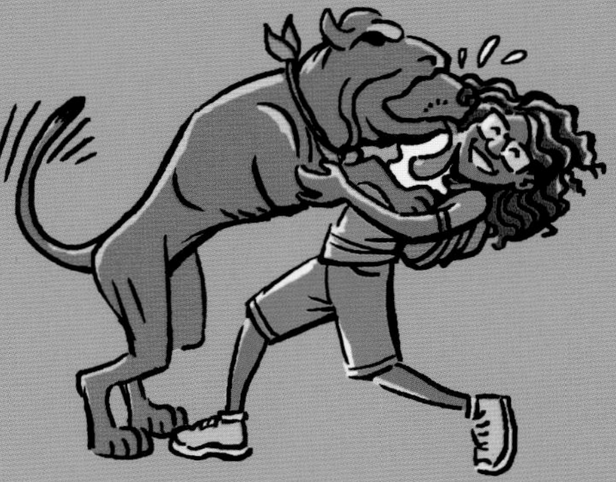

WRITTEN BY

JAMES O. FRAIOLI

ILLUSTRATED BY

JOE ST.PIERRE

MARGARET K. McELDERRY BOOKS

NEW YORK LONDON TORONTO SYDNEY NEW DELHI

AUTHORS' NOTE

Deep into the Amazon Jungle is a work of fiction
based on actual expeditions and accepted ideas
about the Amazon and its inhabitants.

MARGARET K. McELDERRY BOOKS
An imprint of Simon & Schuster Children's Publishing Division
1230 Avenue of the Americas, New York, New York 10020
Text © 2021 by Fabien Cousteau and James O. Fraioli
Illustrations © 2021 by Joseph St.Pierre
Case design by Tom Daly © 2021 by Simon & Schuster, Inc.
MARGARET K. McELDERRY BOOKS is a trademark of Simon & Schuster, Inc.
For information about special discounts for bulk purchases, please contact Simon & Schuster
Special Sales at 1-866-506-1949 or business@simonandschuster.com.
The Simon & Schuster Speakers Bureau can bring authors to your live event.
For more information or to book an event, contact the Simon & Schuster Speakers
Bureau at 1-866-248-3049 or visit our website at www.simonspeakers.com.
Also available in a Margaret K. McElderry Books hardcover edition
Interior design by Tom Daly
The text for this book was set in Chaparral Pro.
The illustrations for this book were rendered digitally.
Manufactured in China
1220 SCP
First Margaret K. McElderry Books paper-over-board edition March 2021
10 9 8 7 6 5 4 3 2 1
CIP data for this book is available from the Library of Congress.
ISBN 978-1-5344-2093-9 (paper over board)
ISBN 978-1-5344-2094-6 (hardcover)
ISBN 978-1-5344-2095-3 (eBook)

TO THE EFFORTS AND INDIVIDUALS WHO WORK DILIGENTLY
TO PROTECT AND PRESERVE THE AMAZON RAINFOREST
AND ITS DIVERSE ECOSYSTEMS.

DEEP INTO THE AMAZON JUNGLE

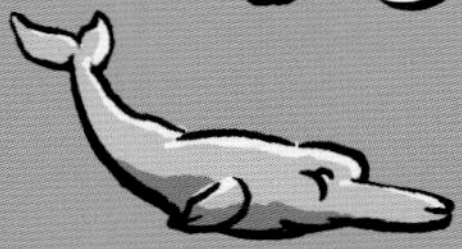

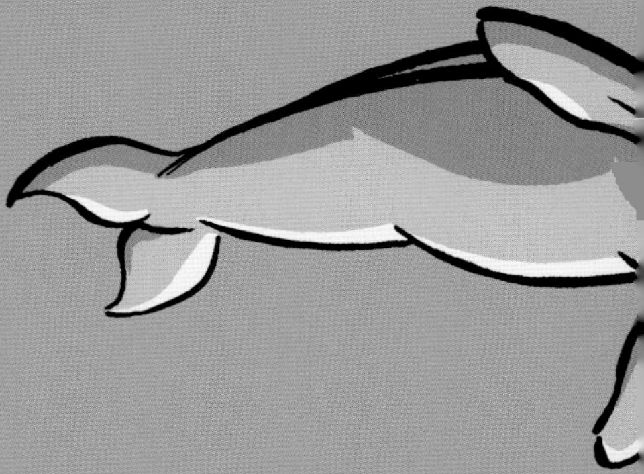

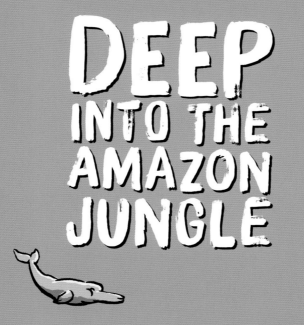

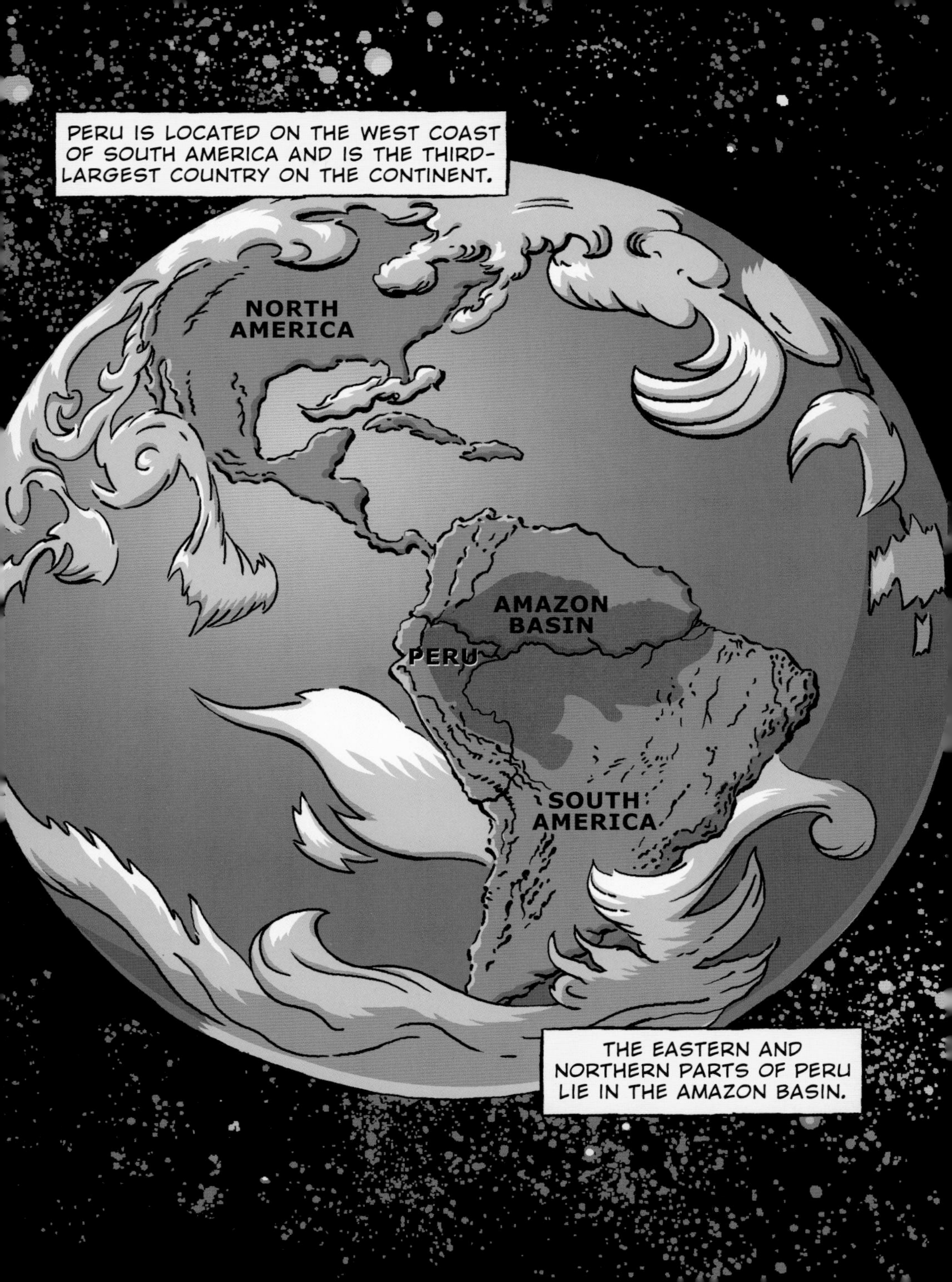
PERU IS LOCATED ON THE WEST COAST OF SOUTH AMERICA AND IS THE THIRD-LARGEST COUNTRY ON THE CONTINENT.
NORTH AMERICA
AMAZON BASIN
PERU
SOUTH AMERICA
THE EASTERN AND NORTHERN PARTS OF PERU LIE IN THE AMAZON BASIN.

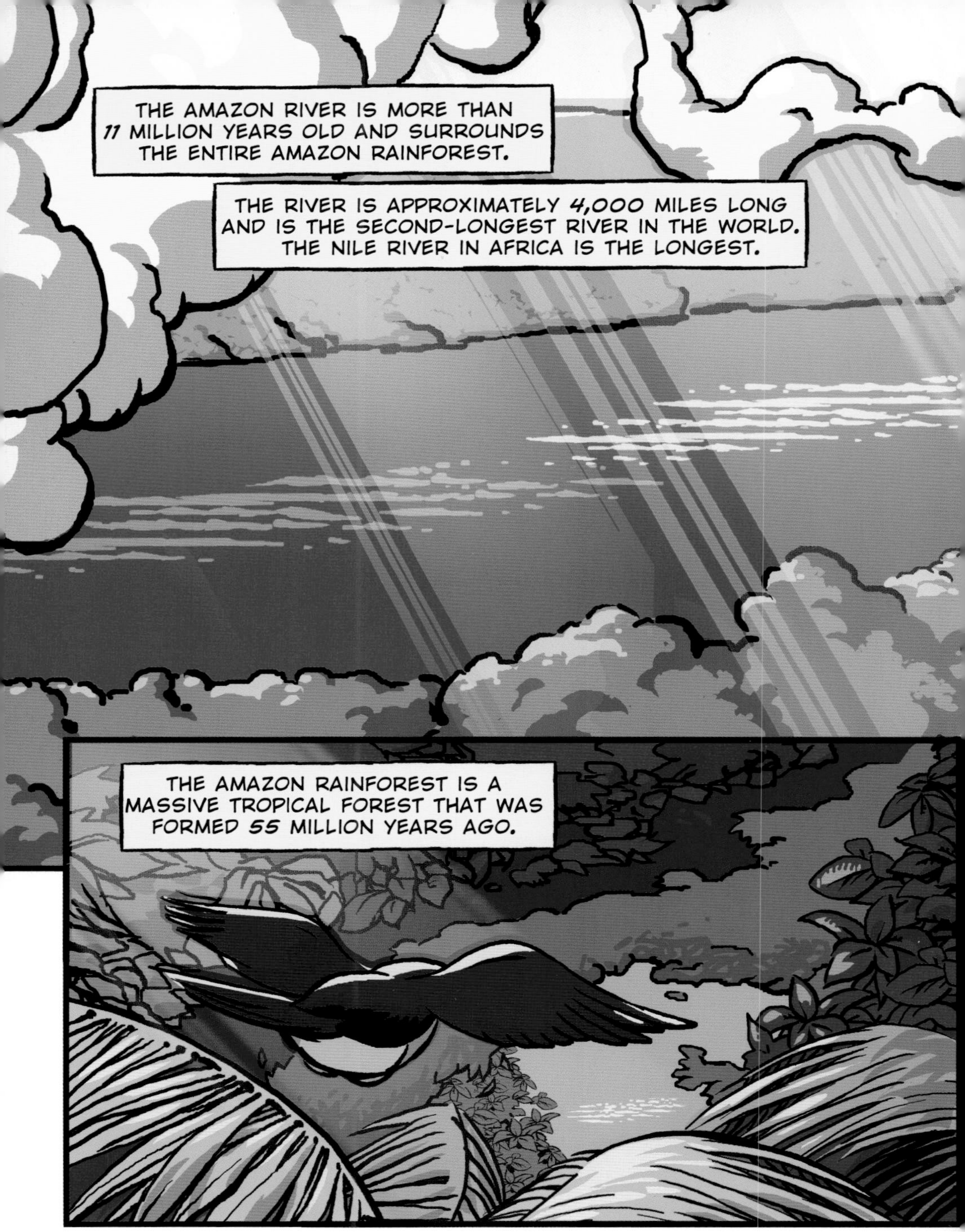
THE AMAZON RIVER IS MORE THAN 11 MILLION YEARS OLD AND SURROUNDS THE ENTIRE AMAZON RAINFOREST.
THE RIVER IS APPROXIMATELY 4,000 MILES LONG AND IS THE SECOND-LONGEST RIVER IN THE WORLD. THE NILE RIVER IN AFRICA IS THE LONGEST.
THE AMAZON RAINFOREST IS A MASSIVE TROPICAL FOREST THAT WAS FORMED 55 MILLION YEARS AGO.

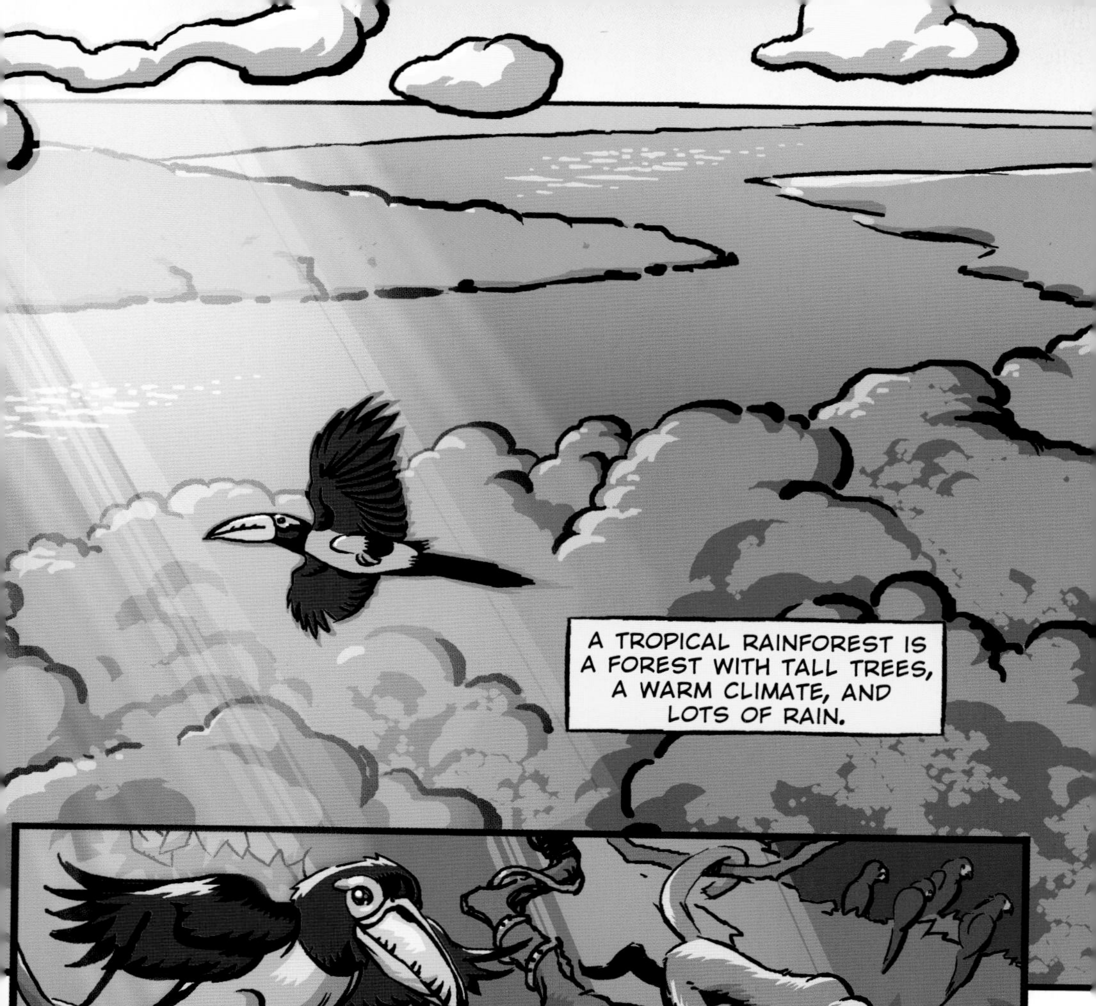
A TROPICAL RAINFOREST IS A FOREST WITH TALL TREES, A WARM CLIMATE, AND LOTS OF RAIN.

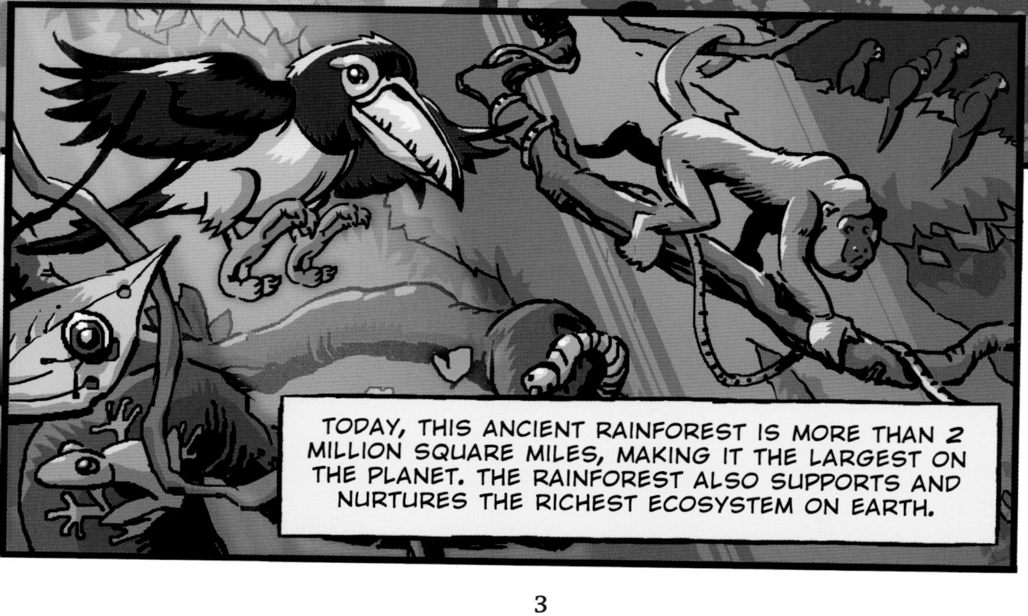
TODAY, THIS ANCIENT RAINFOREST IS MORE THAN 2 MILLION SQUARE MILES, MAKING IT THE LARGEST ON THE PLANET. THE RAINFOREST ALSO SUPPORTS AND NURTURES THE RICHEST ECOSYSTEM ON EARTH.

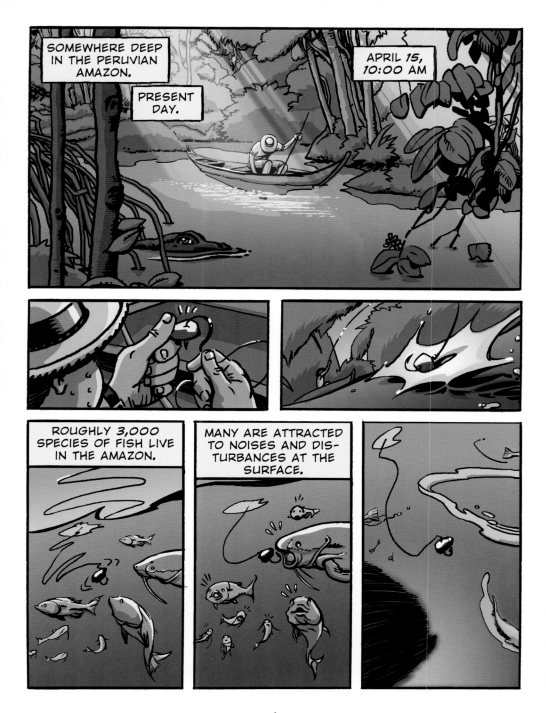

SOMEWHERE DEEP IN THE PERUVIAN AMAZON.

PRESENT DAY.

APRIL 15, 10:00 AM

ROUGHLY 3,000 SPECIES OF FISH LIVE IN THE AMAZON.

MANY ARE ATTRACTED TO NOISES AND DISTURBANCES AT THE SURFACE.

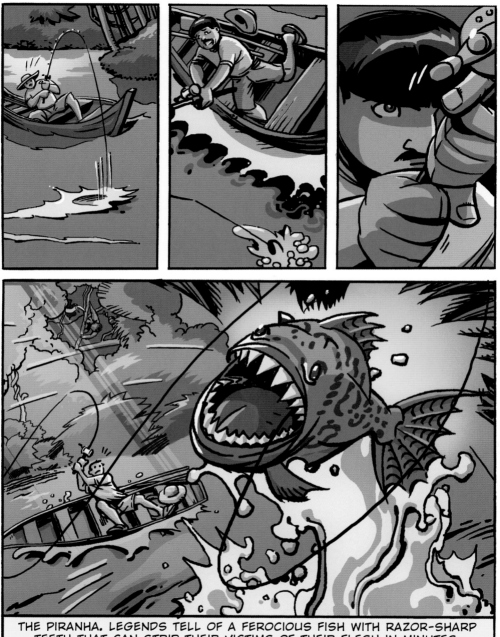

THE PIRANHA. LEGENDS TELL OF A FEROCIOUS FISH WITH RAZOR-SHARP TEETH THAT CAN STRIP THEIR VICTIMS OF THEIR FLESH IN MINUTES, TAKING APART THEIR PREY PIECE BY PIECE.

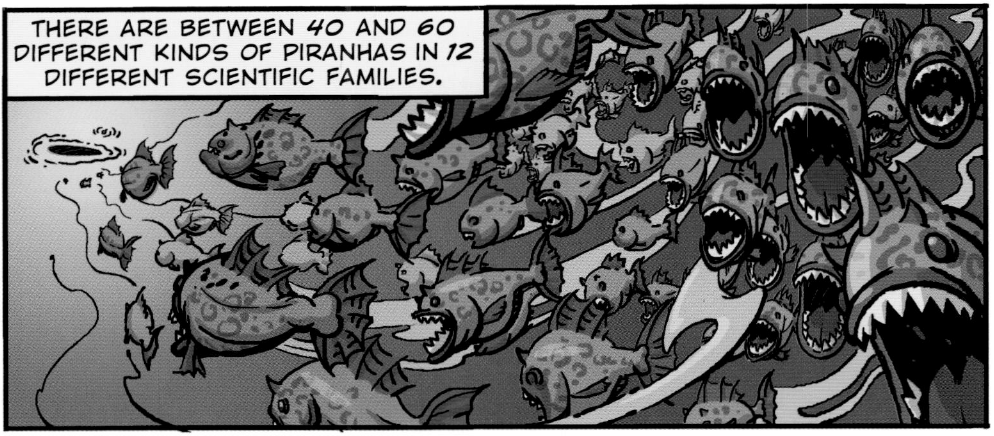
THERE ARE BETWEEN 40 AND 60 DIFFERENT KINDS OF PIRANHAS IN 12 DIFFERENT SCIENTIFIC FAMILIES.

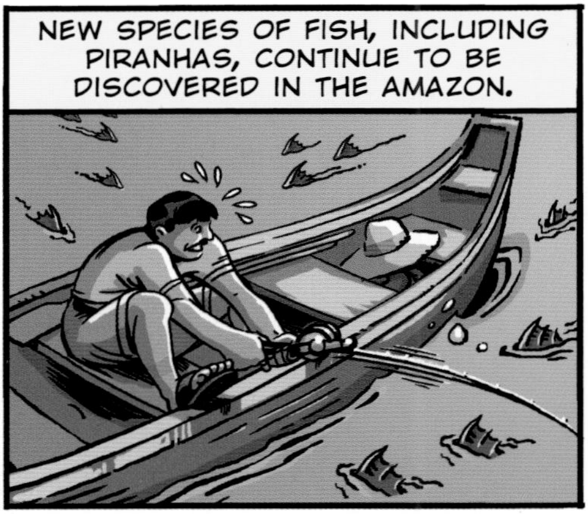
NEW SPECIES OF FISH, INCLUDING PIRANHAS, CONTINUE TO BE DISCOVERED IN THE AMAZON.

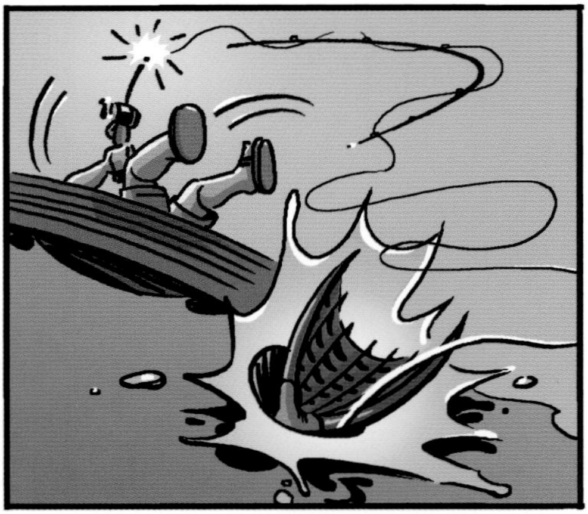

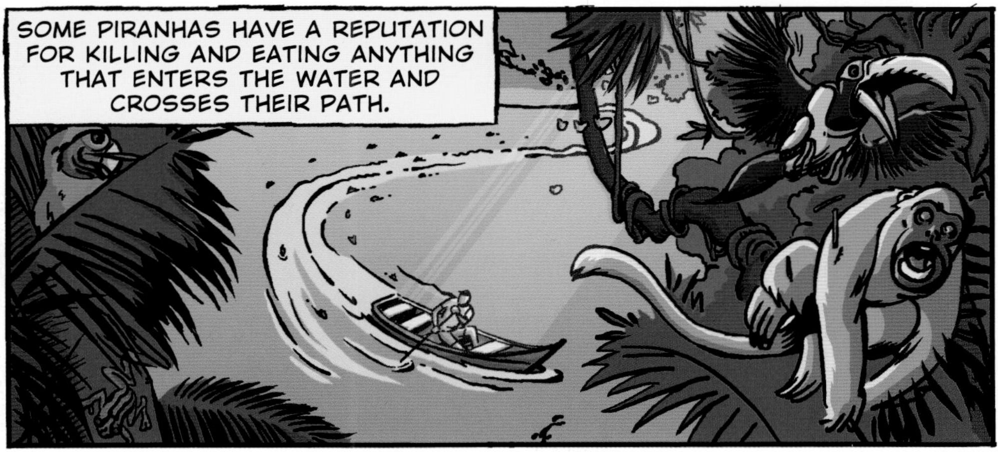
SOME PIRANHAS HAVE A REPUTATION FOR KILLING AND EATING ANYTHING THAT ENTERS THE WATER AND CROSSES THEIR PATH.

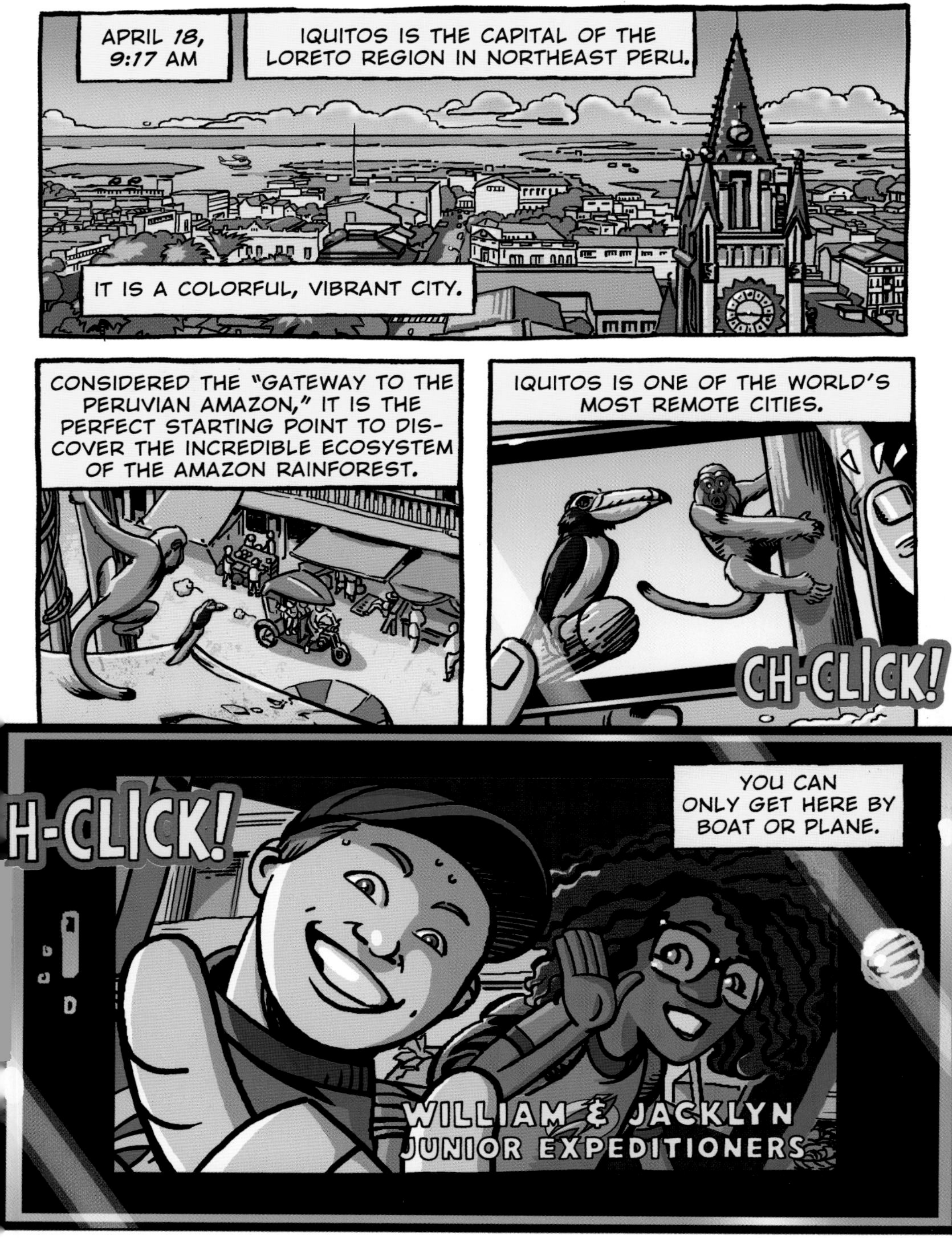
APRIL 18, 9:17 AM
IQUITOS IS THE CAPITAL OF THE LORETO REGION IN NORTHEAST PERU.
IT IS A COLORFUL, VIBRANT CITY.
CONSIDERED THE "GATEWAY TO THE PERUVIAN AMAZON," IT IS THE PERFECT STARTING POINT TO DISCOVER THE INCREDIBLE ECOSYSTEM OF THE AMAZON RAINFOREST.
IQUITOS IS ONE OF THE WORLD'S MOST REMOTE CITIES.
CH-CLICK!
H-CLICK!
YOU CAN ONLY GET HERE BY BOAT OR PLANE.
WILLIAM & JACKLYN
JUNIOR EXPEDITIONERS

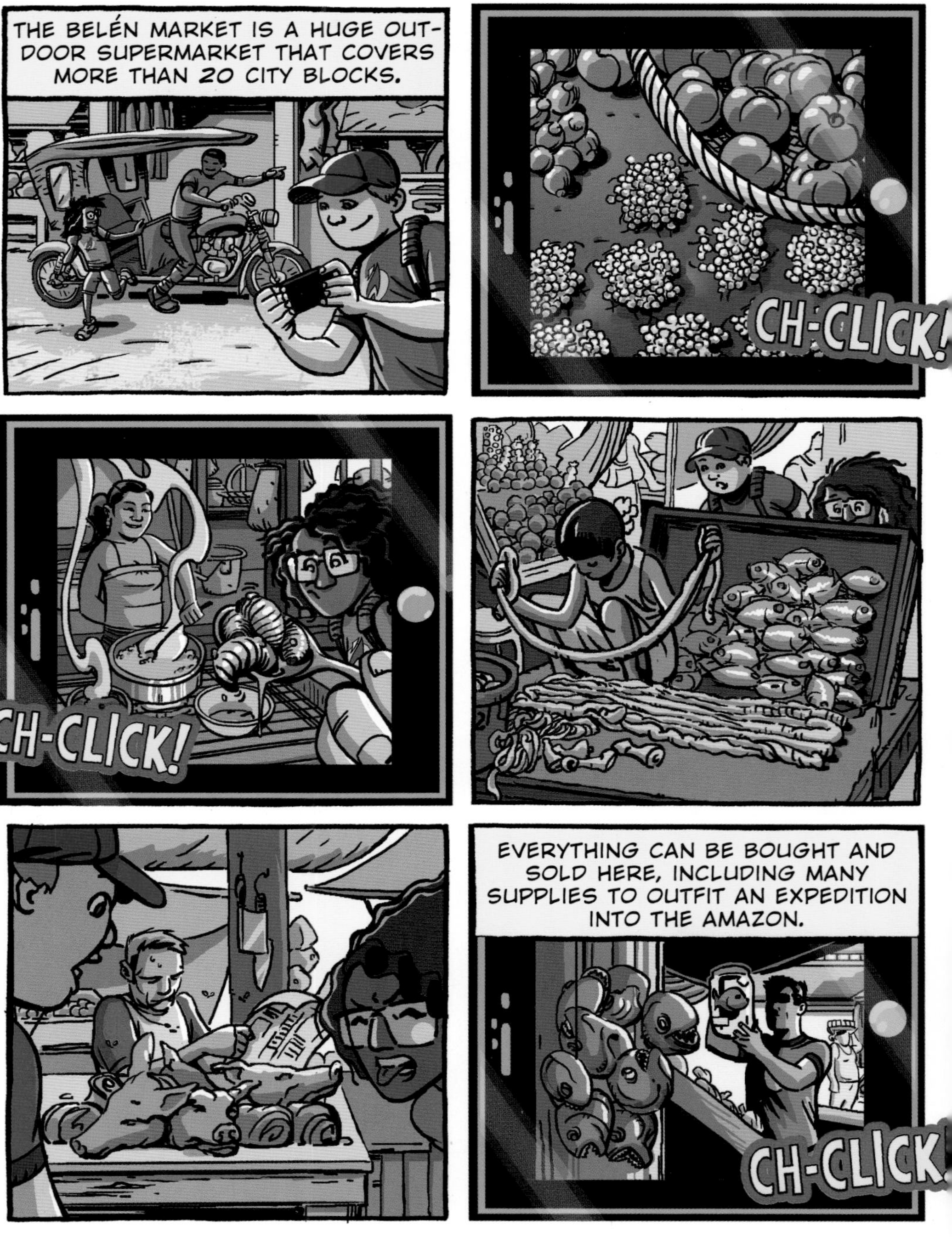
THE BELÉN MARKET IS A HUGE OUT-DOOR SUPERMARKET THAT COVERS MORE THAN 20 CITY BLOCKS.
CH-CLICK!
CH-CLICK!
EVERYTHING CAN BE BOUGHT AND SOLD HERE, INCLUDING MANY SUPPLIES TO OUTFIT AN EXPEDITION INTO THE AMAZON.
CH-CLICK!

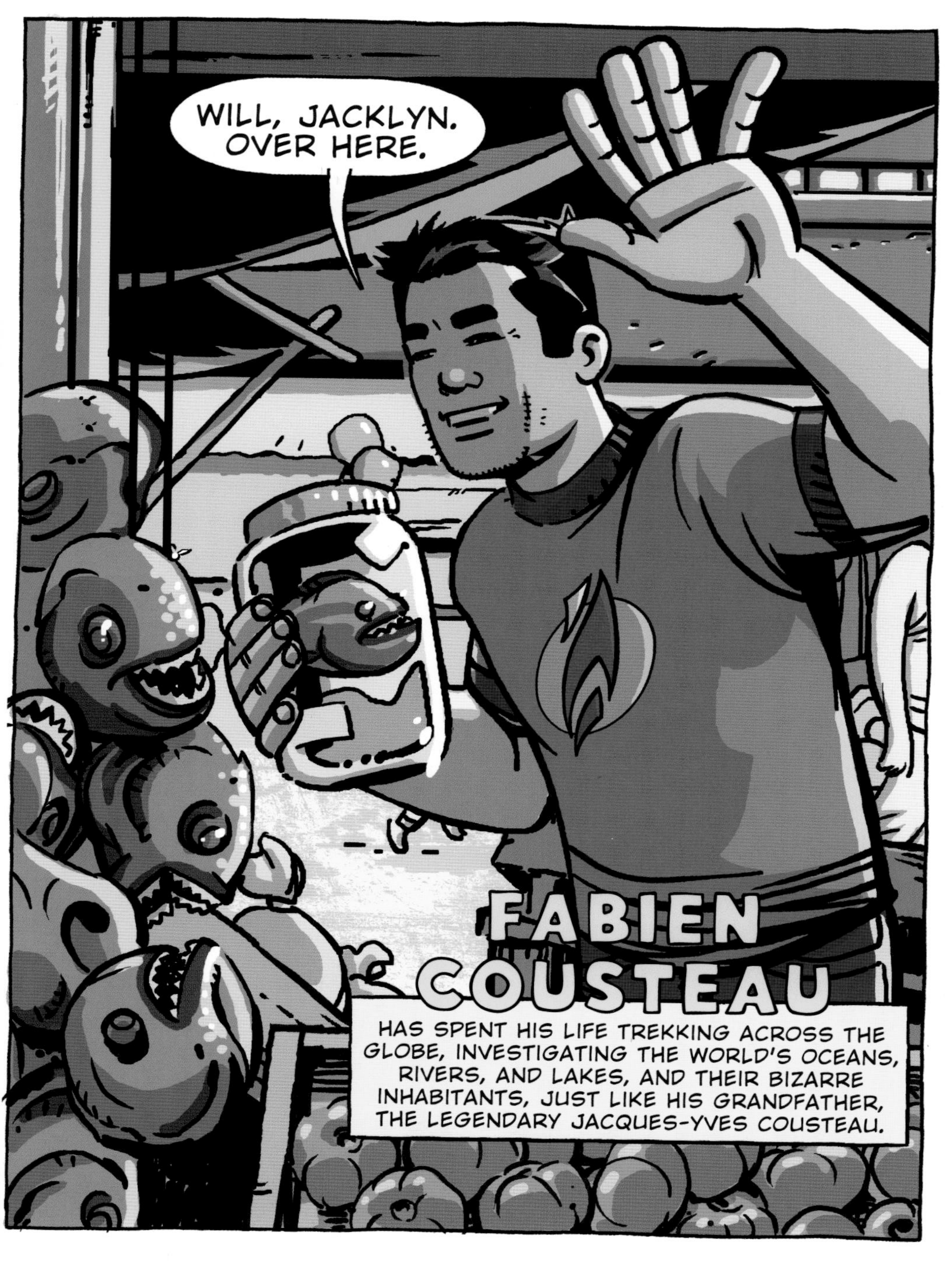
WILL, JACKLYN. OVER HERE.
FABIEN COUSTEAU
HAS SPENT HIS LIFE TREKKING ACROSS THE GLOBE, INVESTIGATING THE WORLD'S OCEANS, RIVERS, AND LAKES, AND THEIR BIZARRE INHABITANTS, JUST LIKE HIS GRANDFATHER, THE LEGENDARY JACQUES-YVES COUSTEAU.

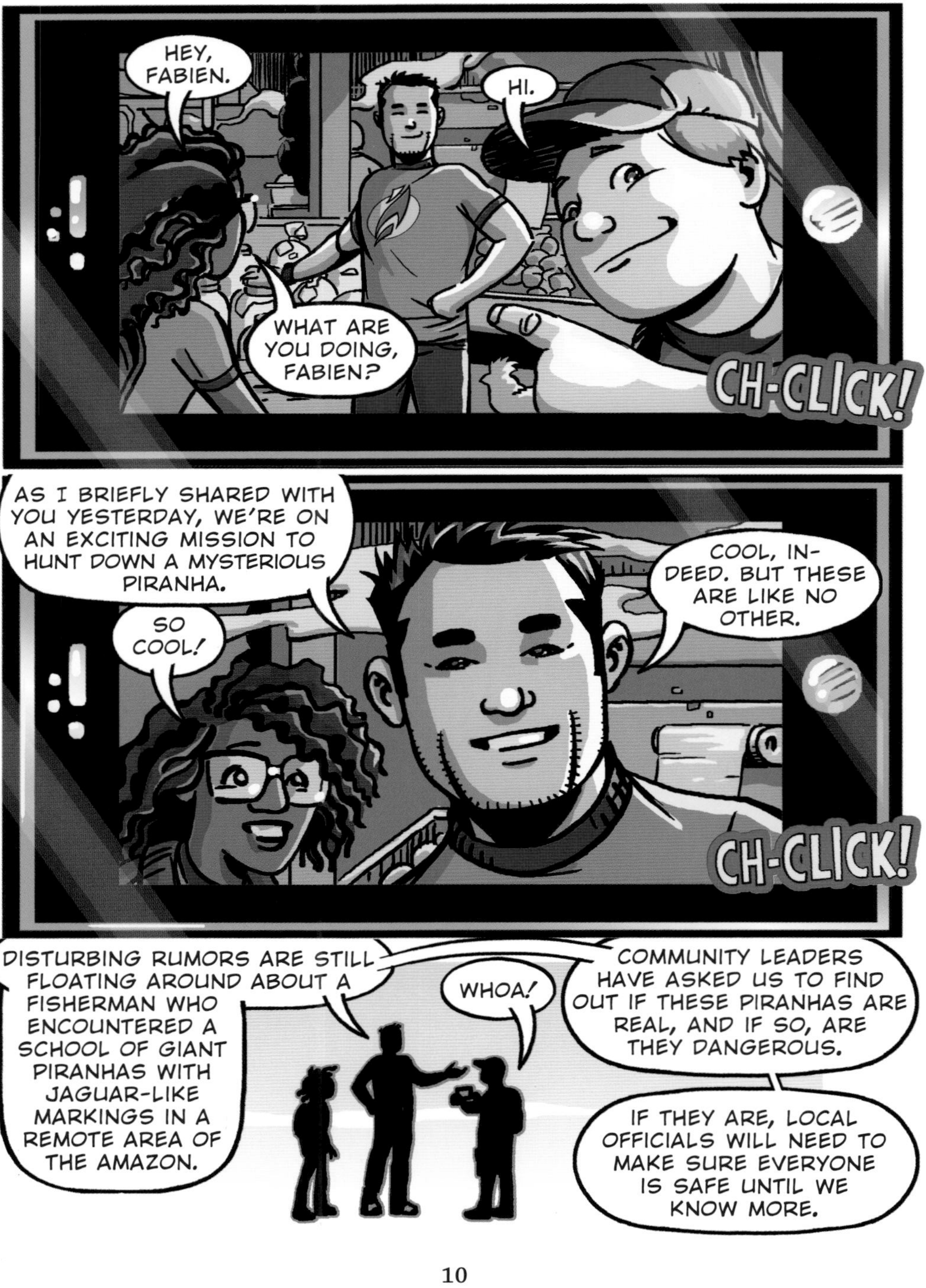
HEY, FABIEN.
HI.
WHAT ARE YOU DOING, FABIEN?
CH-CLICK!
AS I BRIEFLY SHARED WITH YOU YESTERDAY, WE'RE ON AN EXCITING MISSION TO HUNT DOWN A MYSTERIOUS PIRANHA.
SO COOL!
COOL, IN-DEED. BUT THESE ARE LIKE NO OTHER.
CH-CLICK!
DISTURBING RUMORS ARE STILL FLOATING AROUND ABOUT A FISHERMAN WHO ENCOUNTERED A SCHOOL OF GIANT PIRANHAS WITH JAGUAR-LIKE MARKINGS IN A REMOTE AREA OF THE AMAZON.
WHOA!
COMMUNITY LEADERS HAVE ASKED US TO FIND OUT IF THESE PIRANHAS ARE REAL, AND IF SO, ARE THEY DANGEROUS.
IF THEY ARE, LOCAL OFFICIALS WILL NEED TO MAKE SURE EVERYONE IS SAFE UNTIL WE KNOW MORE.

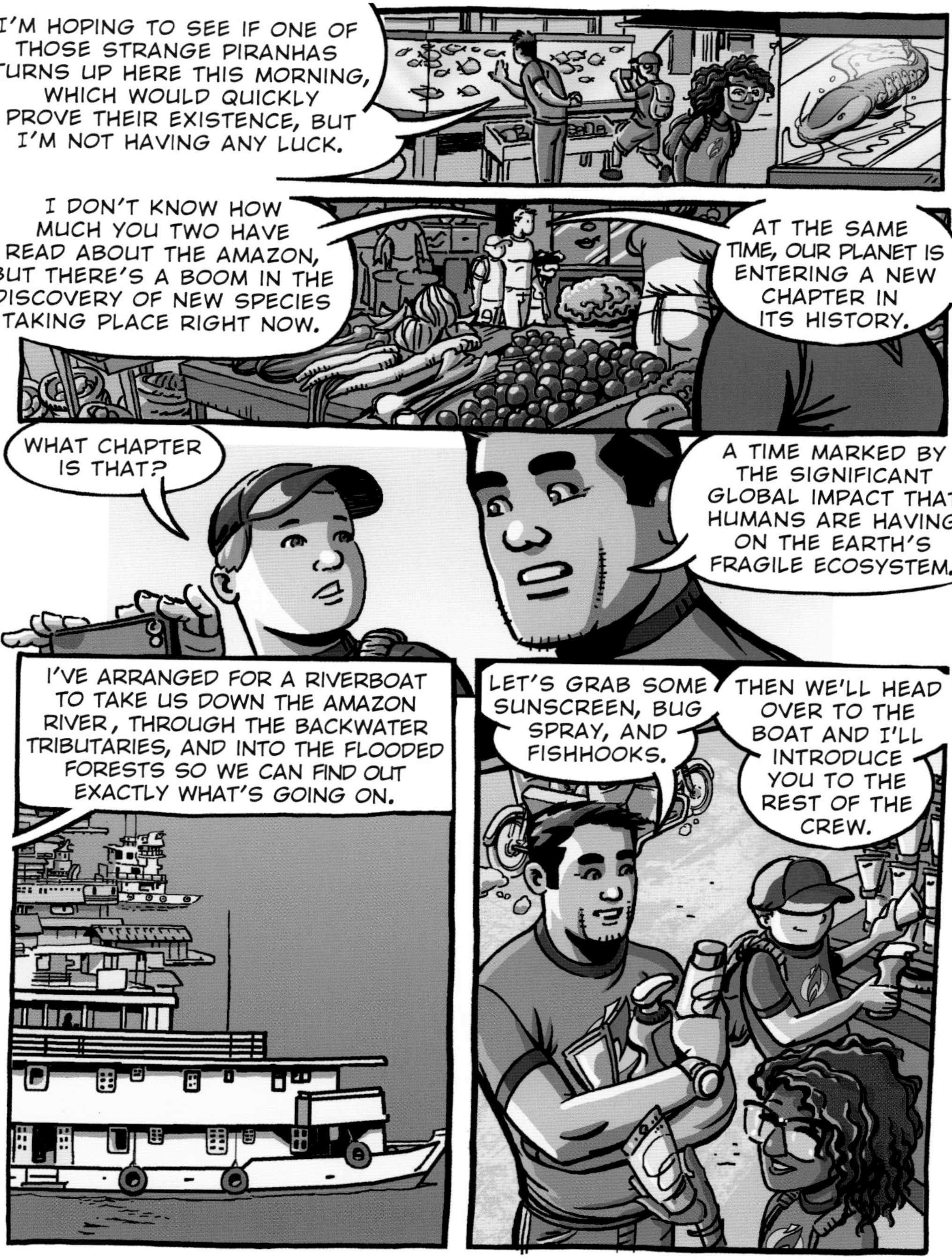
I'M HOPING TO SEE IF ONE OF THOSE STRANGE PIRANHAS TURNS UP HERE THIS MORNING, WHICH WOULD QUICKLY PROVE THEIR EXISTENCE, BUT I'M NOT HAVING ANY LUCK.
I DON'T KNOW HOW MUCH YOU TWO HAVE READ ABOUT THE AMAZON, BUT THERE'S A BOOM IN THE DISCOVERY OF NEW SPECIES TAKING PLACE RIGHT NOW.
AT THE SAME TIME, OUR PLANET IS ENTERING A NEW CHAPTER IN ITS HISTORY.
WHAT CHAPTER IS THAT?
A TIME MARKED BY THE SIGNIFICANT GLOBAL IMPACT THAT HUMANS ARE HAVING ON THE EARTH'S FRAGILE ECOSYSTEM.
I'VE ARRANGED FOR A RIVERBOAT TO TAKE US DOWN THE AMAZON RIVER, THROUGH THE BACKWATER TRIBUTARIES, AND INTO THE FLOODED FORESTS SO WE CAN FIND OUT EXACTLY WHAT'S GOING ON.
LET'S GRAB SOME SUNSCREEN, BUG SPRAY, AND FISHHOOKS.
THEN WE'LL HEAD OVER TO THE BOAT AND I'LL INTRODUCE YOU TO THE REST OF THE CREW.

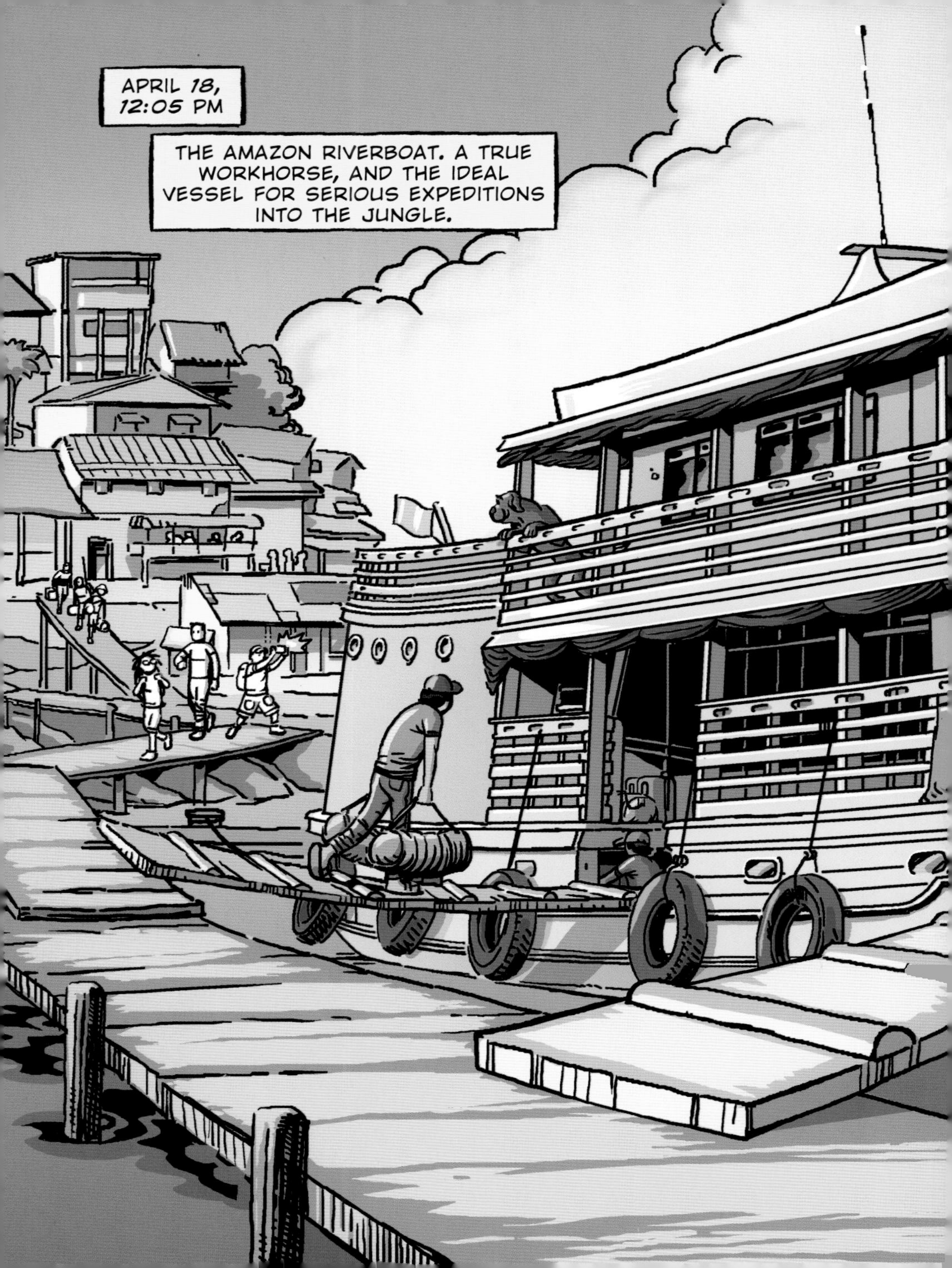
APRIL 18, 12:05 PM
THE AMAZON RIVERBOAT. A TRUE WORKHORSE, AND THE IDEAL VESSEL FOR SERIOUS EXPEDITIONS INTO THE JUNGLE.

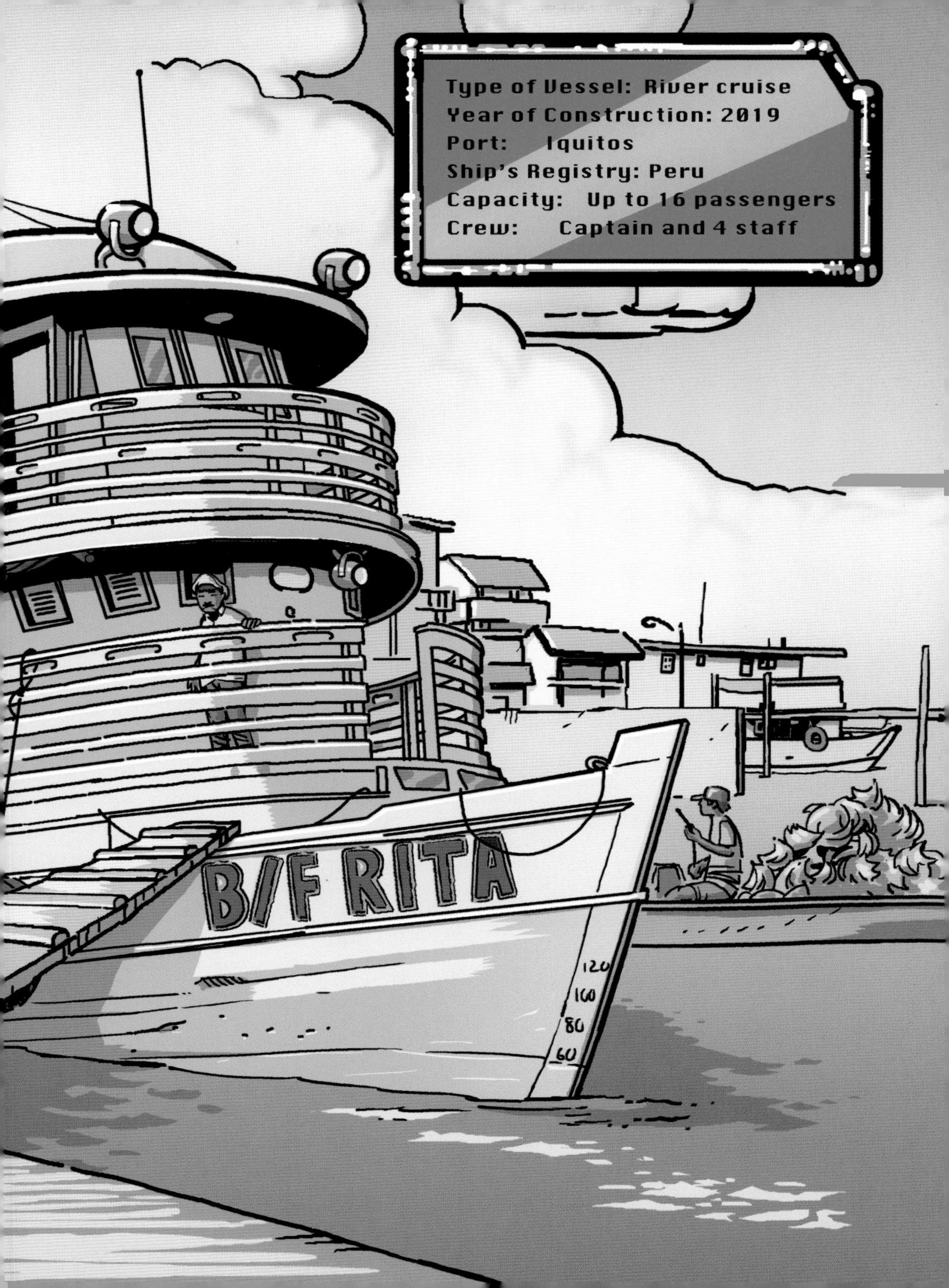
Type of Vessel: River cruise
Year of Construction: 2019
Port: Iquitos
Ship's Registry: Peru
Capacity: Up to 16 passengers
Crew: Captain and 4 staff
B/F RITA
120
100
80
60

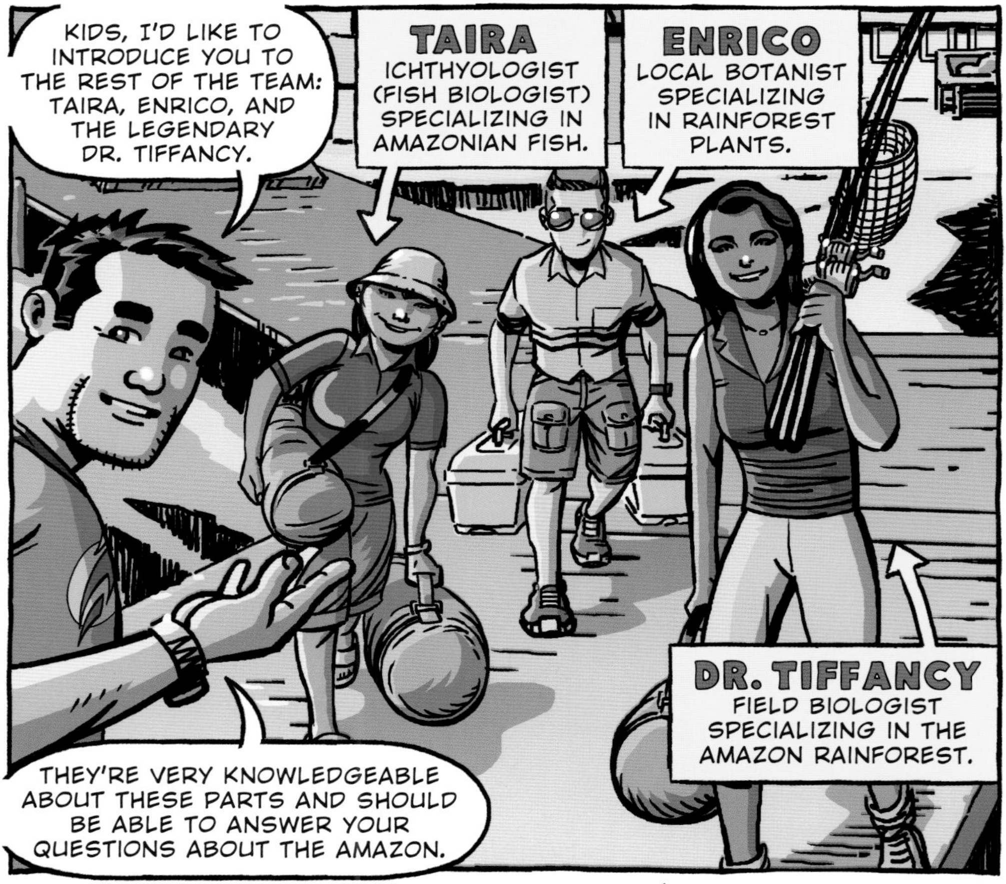
KIDS, I'D LIKE TO INTRODUCE YOU TO THE REST OF THE TEAM: TAIRA, ENRICO, AND THE LEGENDARY DR. TIFFANCY.
TAIRA
ICHTHYOLOGIST (FISH BIOLOGIST) SPECIALIZING IN AMAZONIAN FISH.
ENRICO
LOCAL BOTANIST SPECIALIZING IN RAINFOREST PLANTS.
DR. TIFFANCY
FIELD BIOLOGIST SPECIALIZING IN THE AMAZON RAINFOREST.
THEY'RE VERY KNOWLEDGEABLE ABOUT THESE PARTS AND SHOULD BE ABLE TO ANSWER YOUR QUESTIONS ABOUT THE AMAZON.

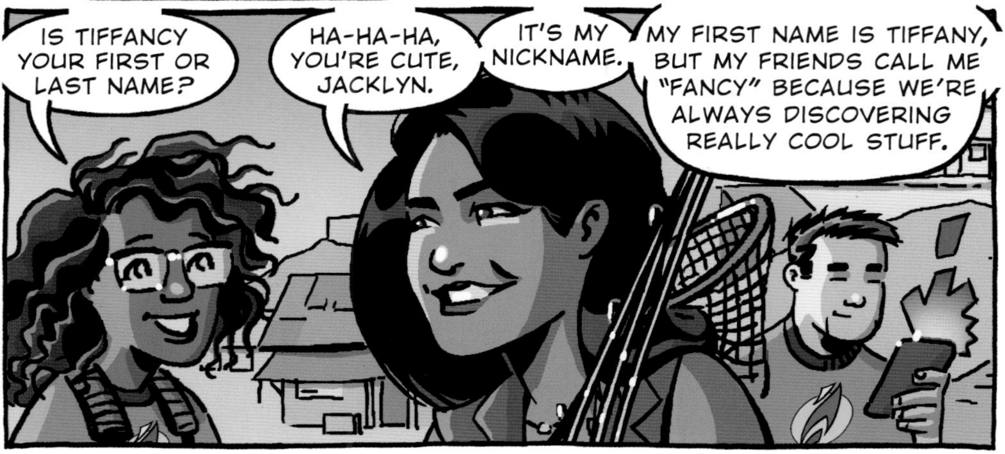
IS TIFFANCY YOUR FIRST OR LAST NAME?
HA-HA-HA, YOU'RE CUTE, JACKLYN.
IT'S MY NICKNAME.
MY FIRST NAME IS TIFFANY, BUT MY FRIENDS CALL ME "FANCY" BECAUSE WE'RE ALWAYS DISCOVERING REALLY COOL STUFF.

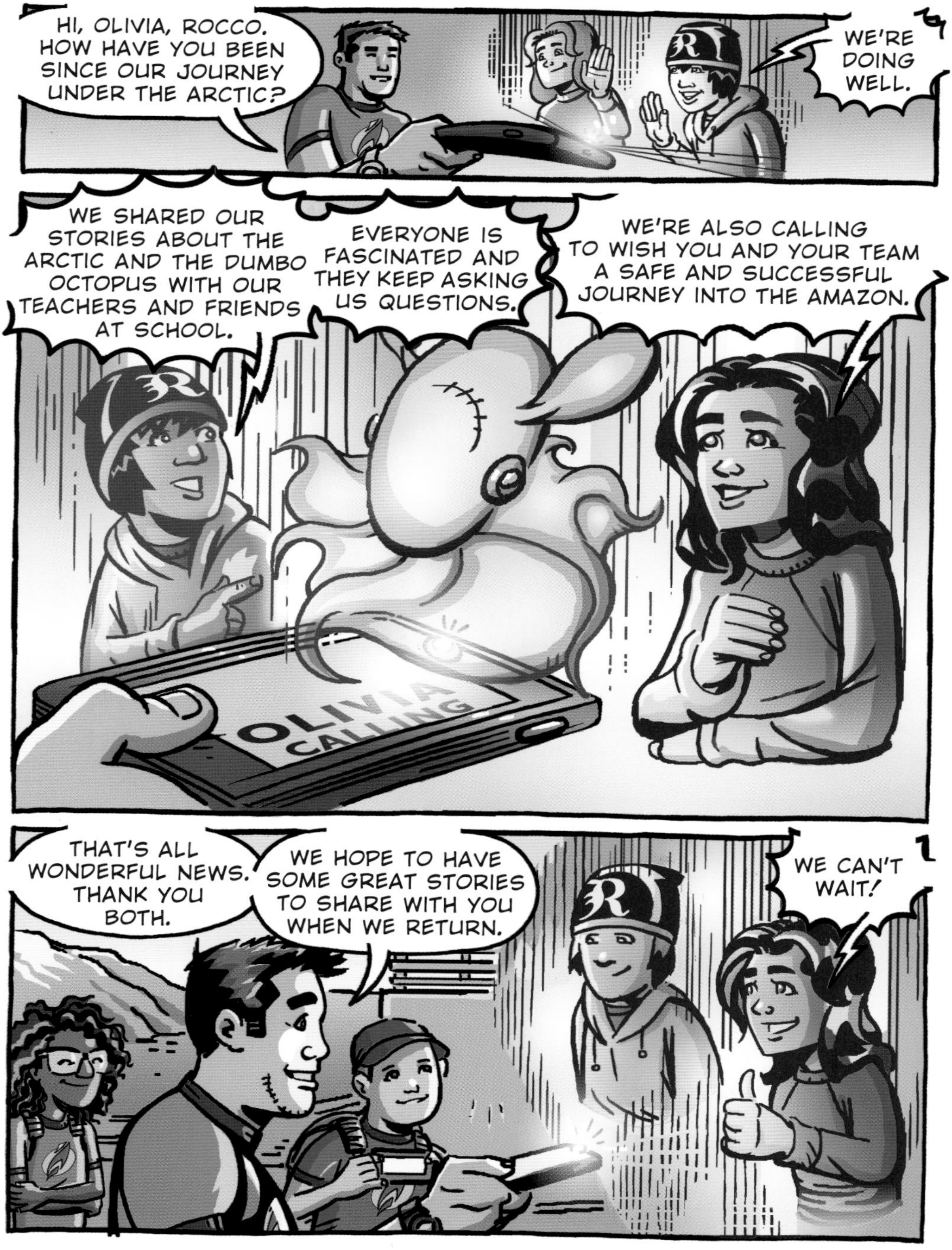
HI, OLIVIA, ROCCO. HOW HAVE YOU BEEN SINCE OUR JOURNEY UNDER THE ARCTIC?
WE'RE DOING WELL.
WE SHARED OUR STORIES ABOUT THE ARCTIC AND THE DUMBO OCTOPUS WITH OUR TEACHERS AND FRIENDS AT SCHOOL.
EVERYONE IS FASCINATED AND THEY KEEP ASKING US QUESTIONS.
WE'RE ALSO CALLING TO WISH YOU AND YOUR TEAM A SAFE AND SUCCESSFUL JOURNEY INTO THE AMAZON.
OLIVIA CALLING
THAT'S ALL WONDERFUL NEWS. THANK YOU BOTH.
WE HOPE TO HAVE SOME GREAT STORIES TO SHARE WITH YOU WHEN WE RETURN.
WE CAN'T WAIT!

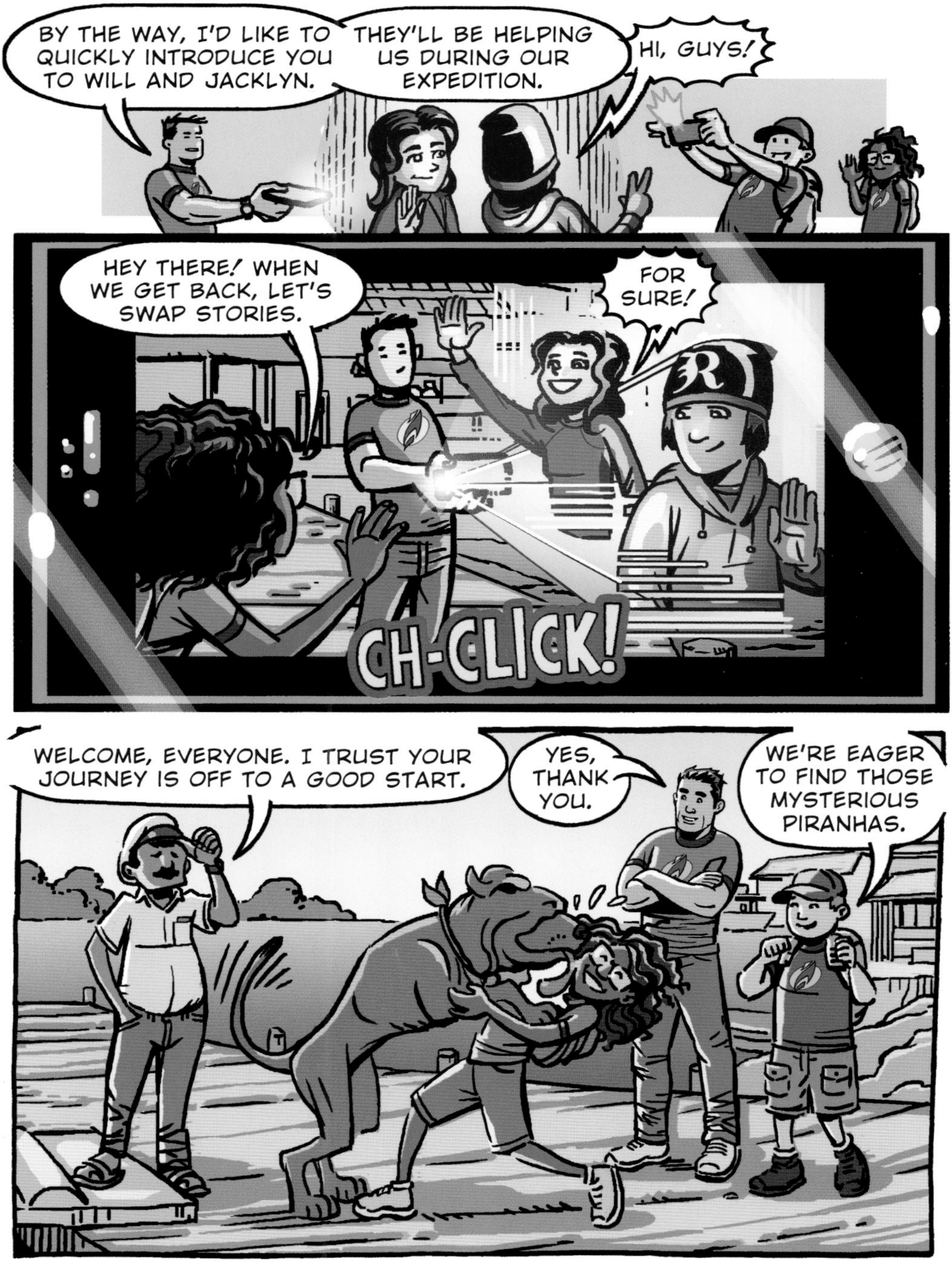
BY THE WAY, I'D LIKE TO QUICKLY INTRODUCE YOU TO WILL AND JACKLYN.
THEY'LL BE HELPING US DURING OUR EXPEDITION.
HI, GUYS!
HEY THERE! WHEN WE GET BACK, LET'S SWAP STORIES.
FOR SURE!
CH-CLICK!
WELCOME, EVERYONE. I TRUST YOUR JOURNEY IS OFF TO A GOOD START.
YES, THANK YOU.
WE'RE EAGER TO FIND THOSE MYSTERIOUS PIRANHAS.

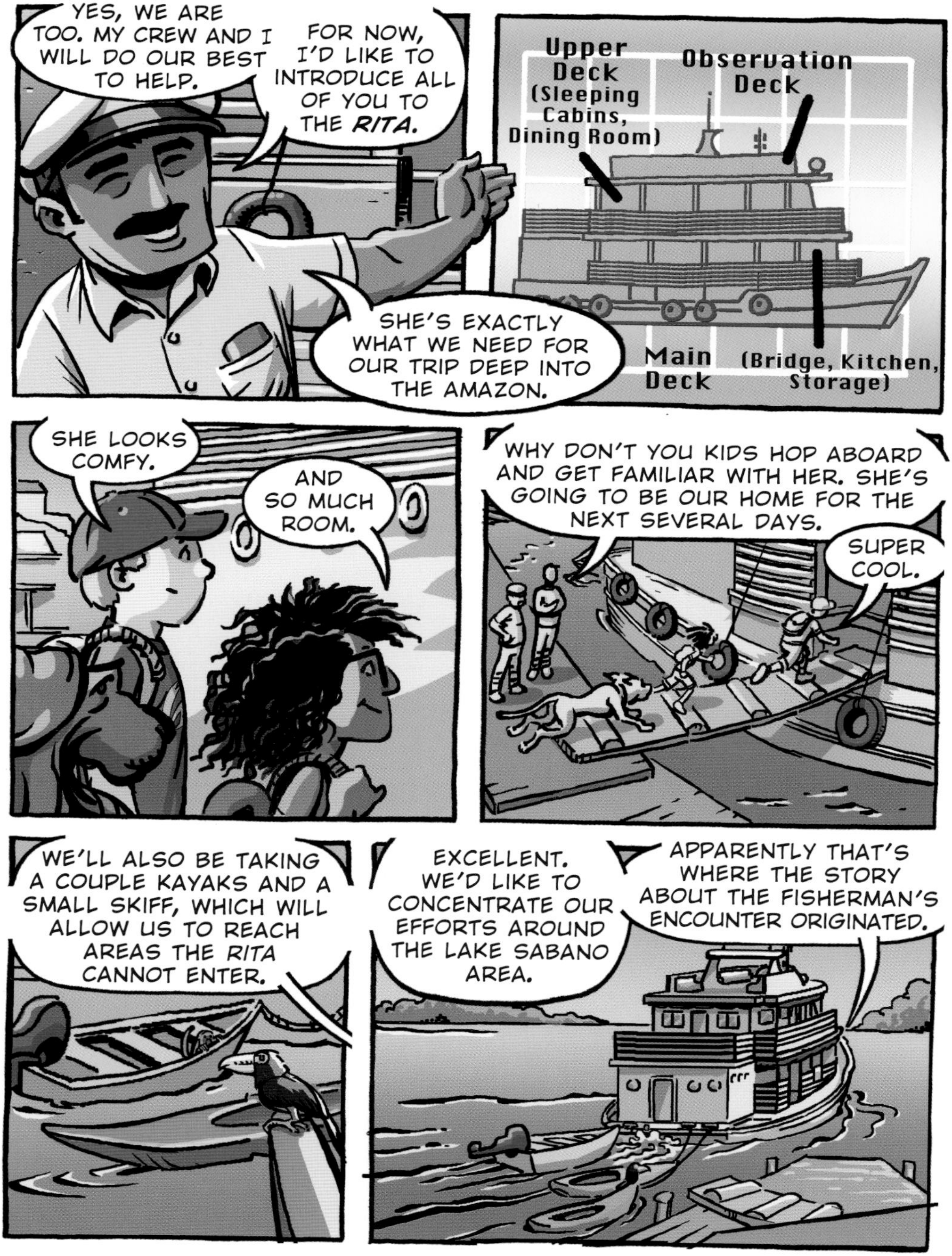
YES, WE ARE TOO. MY CREW AND I WILL DO OUR BEST TO HELP.
FOR NOW, I'D LIKE TO INTRODUCE ALL OF YOU TO THE *RITA*.
SHE'S EXACTLY WHAT WE NEED FOR OUR TRIP DEEP INTO THE AMAZON.
Upper Deck (Sleeping Cabins, Dining Room)
Observation Deck
Main Deck
(Bridge, Kitchen, Storage)
SHE LOOKS COMFY.
AND SO MUCH ROOM.
WHY DON'T YOU KIDS HOP ABOARD AND GET FAMILIAR WITH HER. SHE'S GOING TO BE OUR HOME FOR THE NEXT SEVERAL DAYS.
SUPER COOL.
WE'LL ALSO BE TAKING A COUPLE KAYAKS AND A SMALL SKIFF, WHICH WILL ALLOW US TO REACH AREAS THE *RITA* CANNOT ENTER.
EXCELLENT. WE'D LIKE TO CONCENTRATE OUR EFFORTS AROUND THE LAKE SABANO AREA.
APPARENTLY THAT'S WHERE THE STORY ABOUT THE FISHERMAN'S ENCOUNTER ORIGINATED.

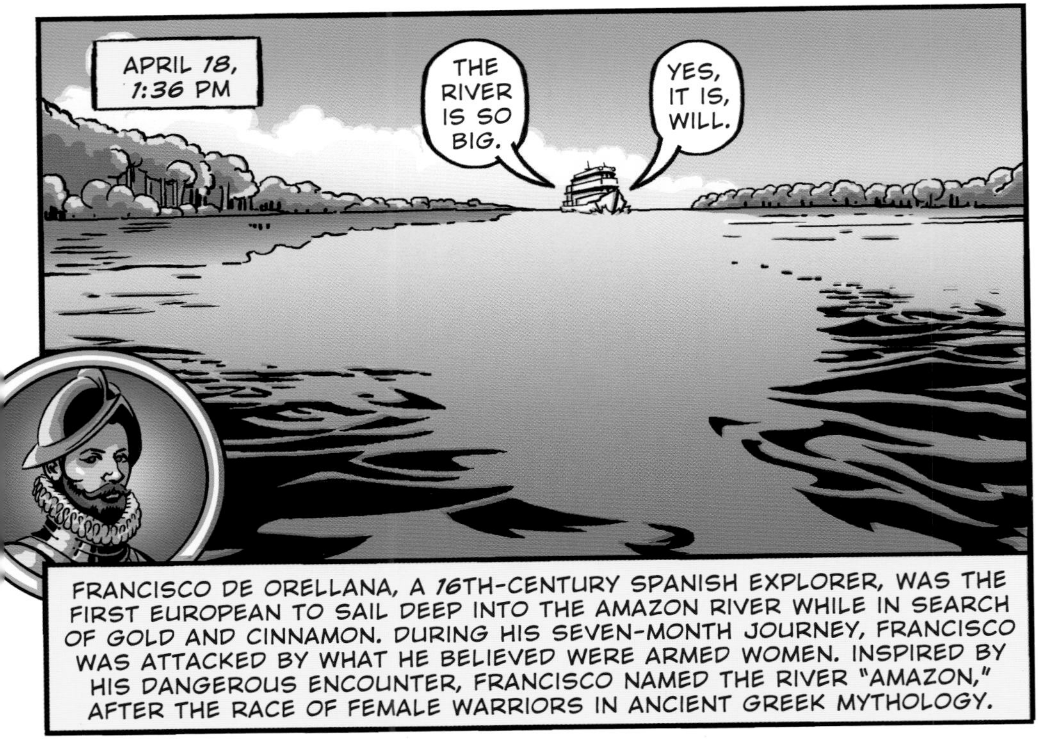

APRIL 18, 1:36 PM
THE RIVER IS SO BIG.
YES, IT IS, WILL.
FRANCISCO DE ORELLANA, A 16TH-CENTURY SPANISH EXPLORER, WAS THE FIRST EUROPEAN TO SAIL DEEP INTO THE AMAZON RIVER WHILE IN SEARCH OF GOLD AND CINNAMON. DURING HIS SEVEN-MONTH JOURNEY, FRANCISCO WAS ATTACKED BY WHAT HE BELIEVED WERE ARMED WOMEN. INSPIRED BY HIS DANGEROUS ENCOUNTER, FRANCISCO NAMED THE RIVER "AMAZON," AFTER THE RACE OF FEMALE WARRIORS IN ANCIENT GREEK MYTHOLOGY.

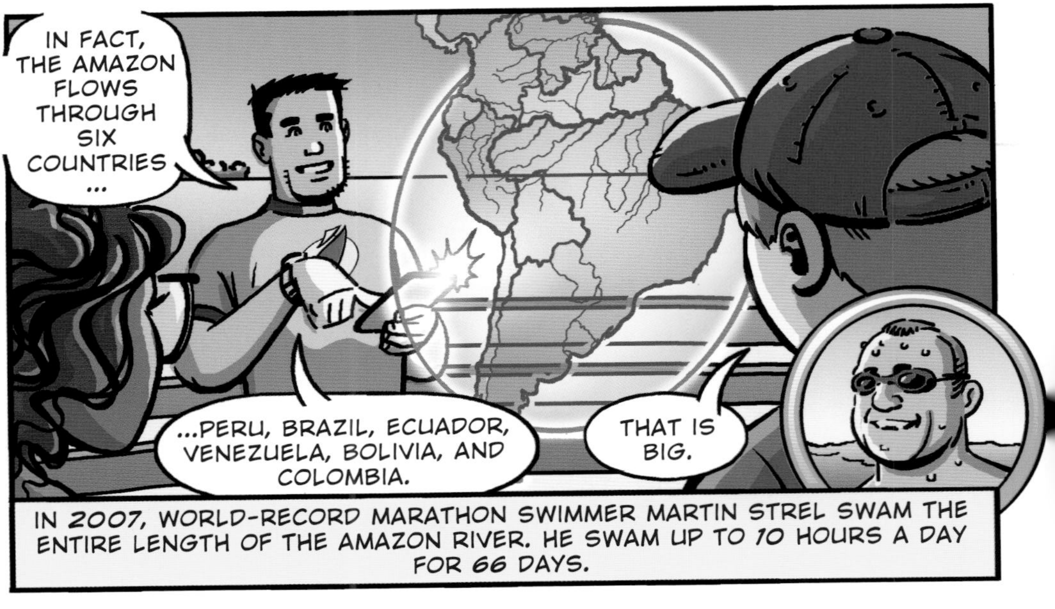

IN FACT, THE AMAZON FLOWS THROUGH SIX COUNTRIES ...
...PERU, BRAZIL, ECUADOR, VENEZUELA, BOLIVIA, AND COLOMBIA.
THAT IS BIG.
IN 2007, WORLD-RECORD MARATHON SWIMMER MARTIN STREL SWAM THE ENTIRE LENGTH OF THE AMAZON RIVER. HE SWAM UP TO 10 HOURS A DAY FOR 66 DAYS.

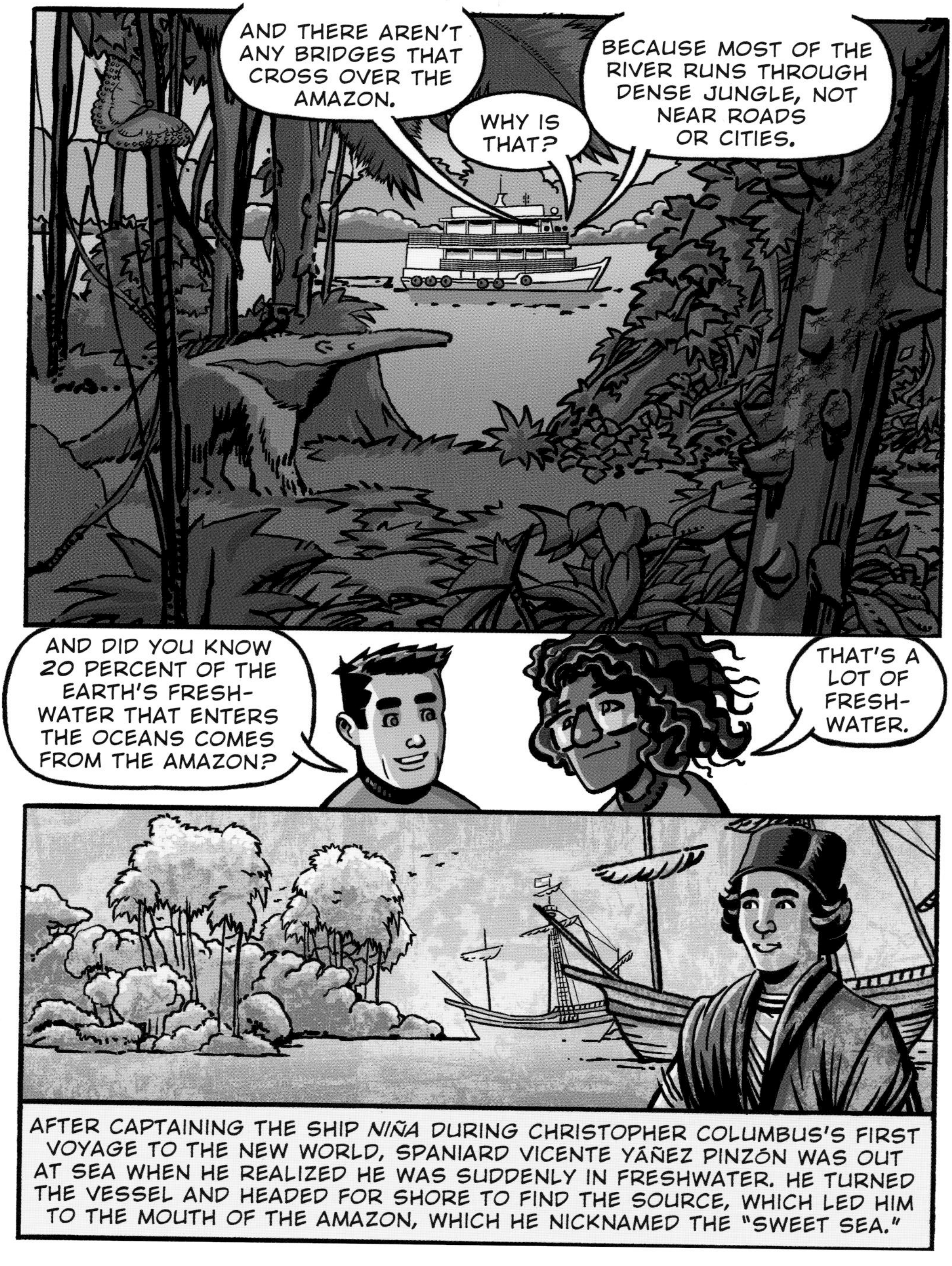
AND THERE AREN'T ANY BRIDGES THAT CROSS OVER THE AMAZON.
WHY IS THAT?
BECAUSE MOST OF THE RIVER RUNS THROUGH DENSE JUNGLE, NOT NEAR ROADS OR CITIES.
AND DID YOU KNOW 20 PERCENT OF THE EARTH'S FRESH-WATER THAT ENTERS THE OCEANS COMES FROM THE AMAZON?
THAT'S A LOT OF FRESH-WATER.
AFTER CAPTAINING THE SHIP *NIÑA* DURING CHRISTOPHER COLUMBUS'S FIRST VOYAGE TO THE NEW WORLD, SPANIARD VICENTE YÁÑEZ PINZÓN WAS OUT AT SEA WHEN HE REALIZED HE WAS SUDDENLY IN FRESHWATER. HE TURNED THE VESSEL AND HEADED FOR SHORE TO FIND THE SOURCE, WHICH LED HIM TO THE MOUTH OF THE AMAZON, WHICH HE NICKNAMED THE "SWEET SEA."

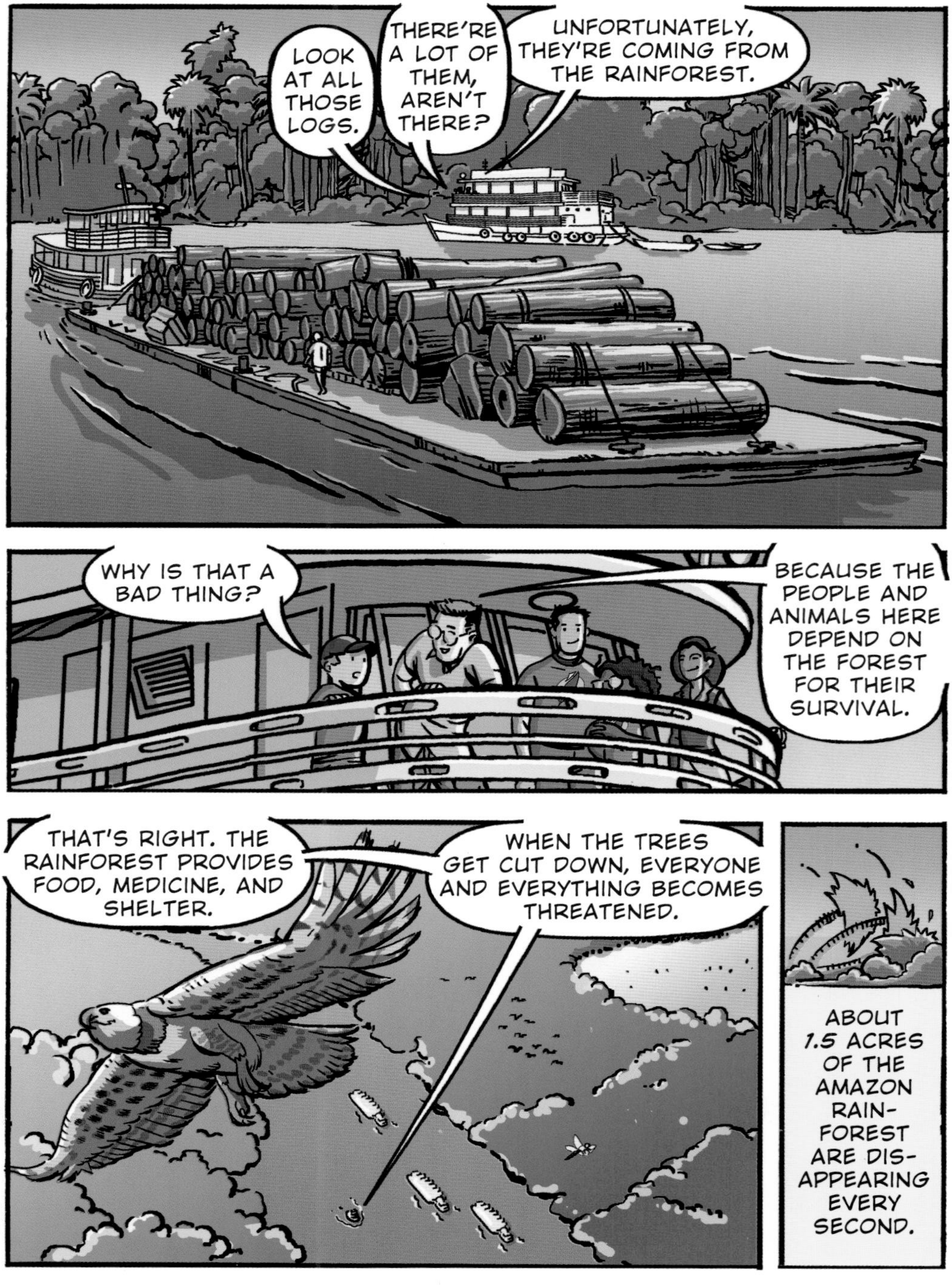
LOOK AT ALL THOSE LOGS.
THERE'RE A LOT OF THEM, AREN'T THERE?
UNFORTUNATELY, THEY'RE COMING FROM THE RAINFOREST.
WHY IS THAT A BAD THING?
BECAUSE THE PEOPLE AND ANIMALS HERE DEPEND ON THE FOREST FOR THEIR SURVIVAL.
THAT'S RIGHT. THE RAINFOREST PROVIDES FOOD, MEDICINE, AND SHELTER.
WHEN THE TREES GET CUT DOWN, EVERYONE AND EVERYTHING BECOMES THREATENED.
ABOUT *1.5* ACRES OF THE AMAZON RAIN-FOREST ARE DIS-APPEARING EVERY SECOND.

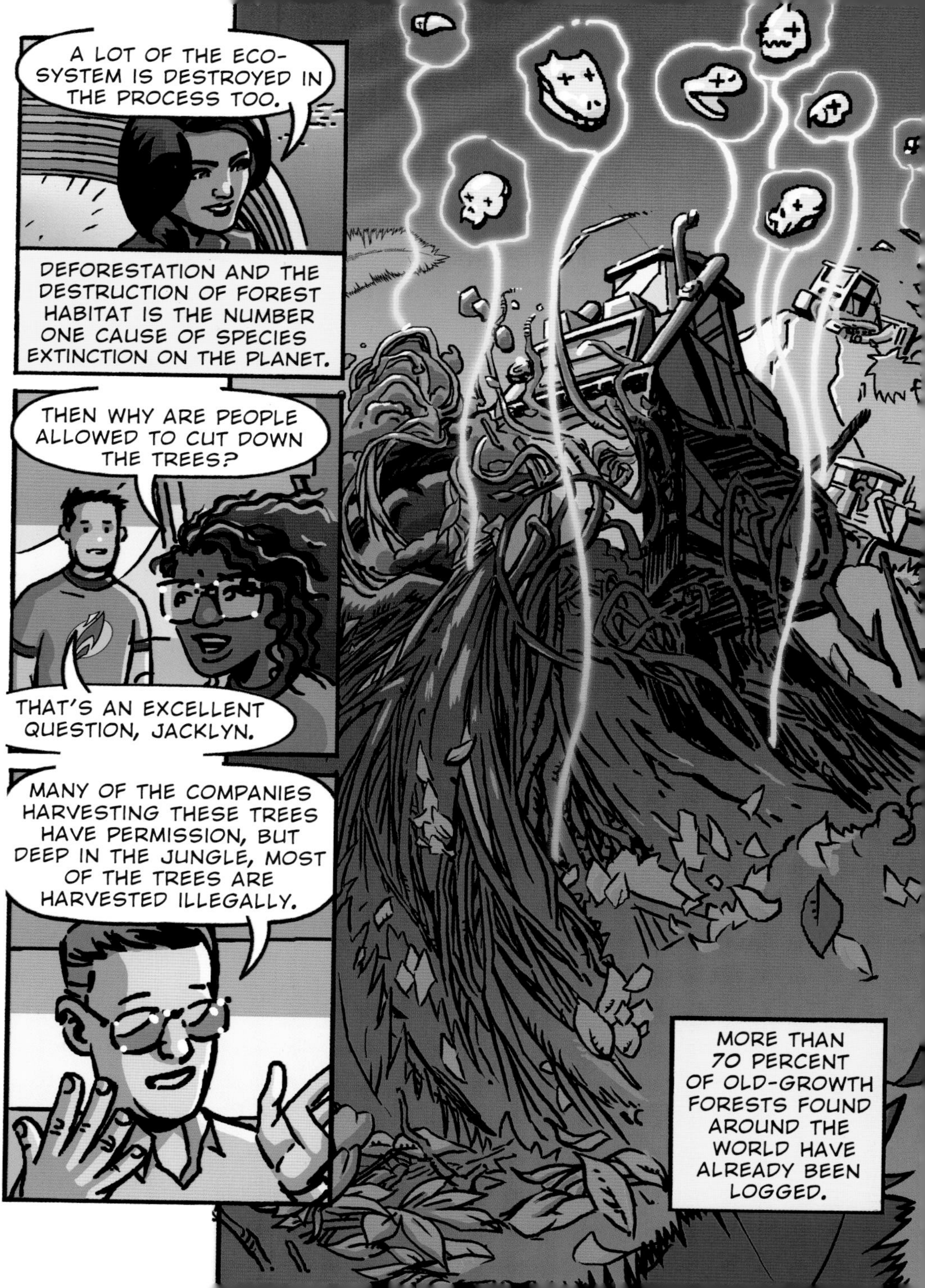
A LOT OF THE ECO-SYSTEM IS DESTROYED IN THE PROCESS TOO.
DEFORESTATION AND THE DESTRUCTION OF FOREST HABITAT IS THE NUMBER ONE CAUSE OF SPECIES EXTINCTION ON THE PLANET.
THEN WHY ARE PEOPLE ALLOWED TO CUT DOWN THE TREES?
THAT'S AN EXCELLENT QUESTION, JACKLYN.
MANY OF THE COMPANIES HARVESTING THESE TREES HAVE PERMISSION, BUT DEEP IN THE JUNGLE, MOST OF THE TREES ARE HARVESTED ILLEGALLY.
MORE THAN 70 PERCENT OF OLD-GROWTH FORESTS FOUND AROUND THE WORLD HAVE ALREADY BEEN LOGGED.

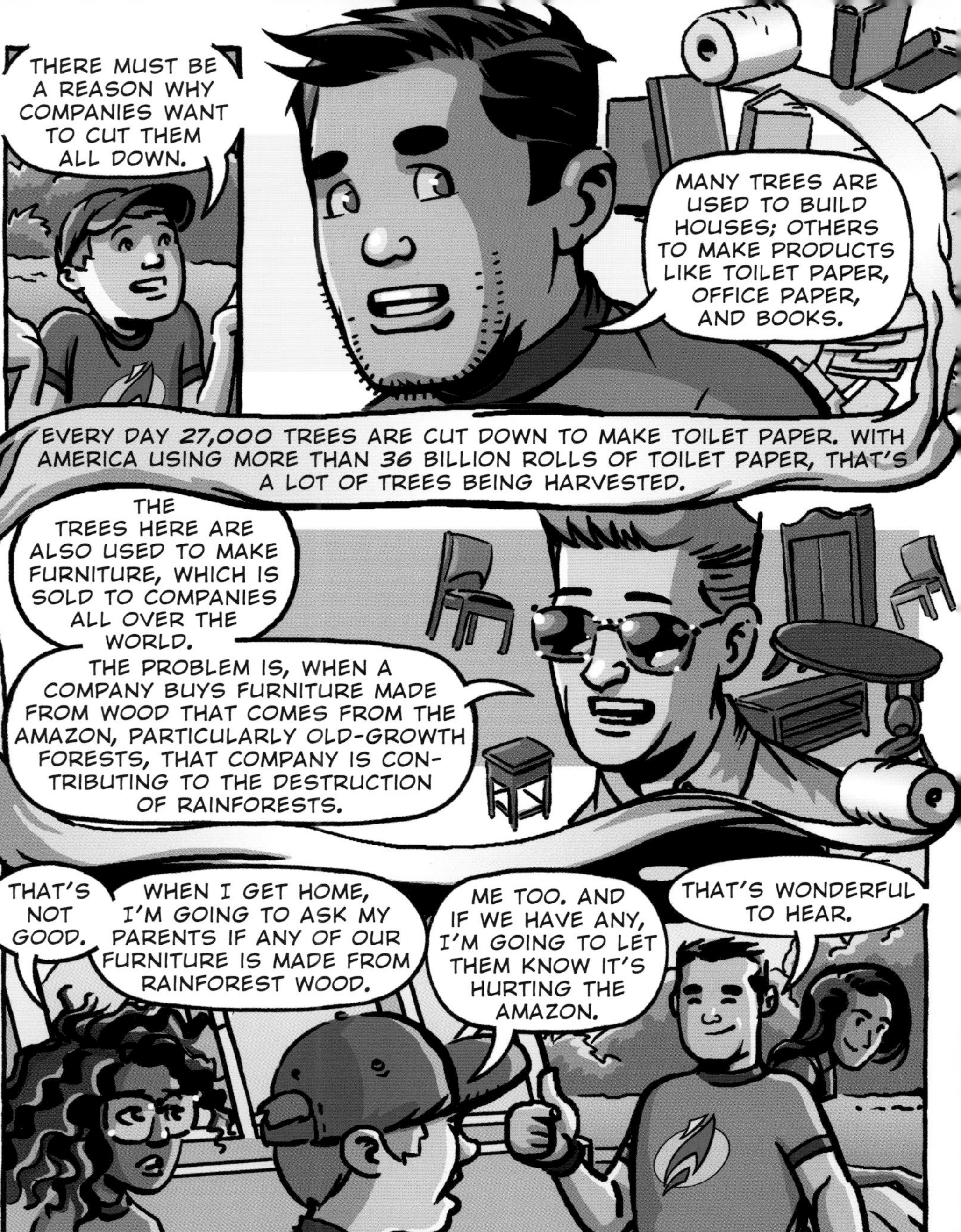
THERE MUST BE A REASON WHY COMPANIES WANT TO CUT THEM ALL DOWN.
MANY TREES ARE USED TO BUILD HOUSES; OTHERS TO MAKE PRODUCTS LIKE TOILET PAPER, OFFICE PAPER, AND BOOKS.
EVERY DAY 27,000 TREES ARE CUT DOWN TO MAKE TOILET PAPER. WITH AMERICA USING MORE THAN 36 BILLION ROLLS OF TOILET PAPER, THAT'S A LOT OF TREES BEING HARVESTED.
THE TREES HERE ARE ALSO USED TO MAKE FURNITURE, WHICH IS SOLD TO COMPANIES ALL OVER THE WORLD.
THE PROBLEM IS, WHEN A COMPANY BUYS FURNITURE MADE FROM WOOD THAT COMES FROM THE AMAZON, PARTICULARLY OLD-GROWTH FORESTS, THAT COMPANY IS CONTRIBUTING TO THE DESTRUCTION OF RAINFORESTS.
THAT'S NOT GOOD.
WHEN I GET HOME, I'M GOING TO ASK MY PARENTS IF ANY OF OUR FURNITURE IS MADE FROM RAINFOREST WOOD.
ME TOO. AND IF WE HAVE ANY, I'M GOING TO LET THEM KNOW IT'S HURTING THE AMAZON.
THAT'S WONDERFUL TO HEAR.

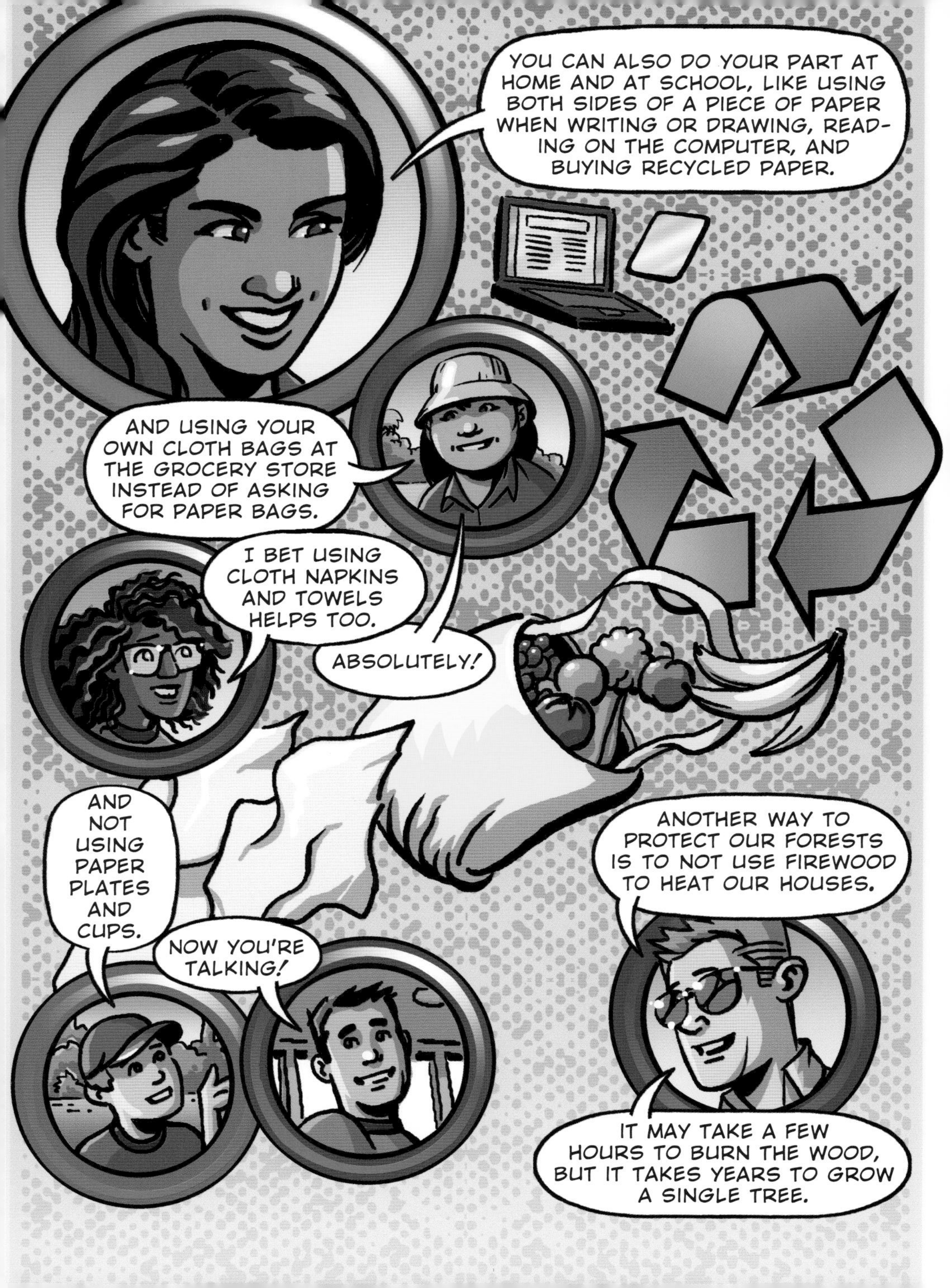
YOU CAN ALSO DO YOUR PART AT HOME AND AT SCHOOL, LIKE USING BOTH SIDES OF A PIECE OF PAPER WHEN WRITING OR DRAWING, READ-ING ON THE COMPUTER, AND BUYING RECYCLED PAPER.
AND USING YOUR OWN CLOTH BAGS AT THE GROCERY STORE INSTEAD OF ASKING FOR PAPER BAGS.
I BET USING CLOTH NAPKINS AND TOWELS HELPS TOO.
ABSOLUTELY!
AND NOT USING PAPER PLATES AND CUPS.
NOW YOU'RE TALKING!
ANOTHER WAY TO PROTECT OUR FORESTS IS TO NOT USE FIREWOOD TO HEAT OUR HOUSES.
IT MAY TAKE A FEW HOURS TO BURN THE WOOD, BUT IT TAKES YEARS TO GROW A SINGLE TREE.

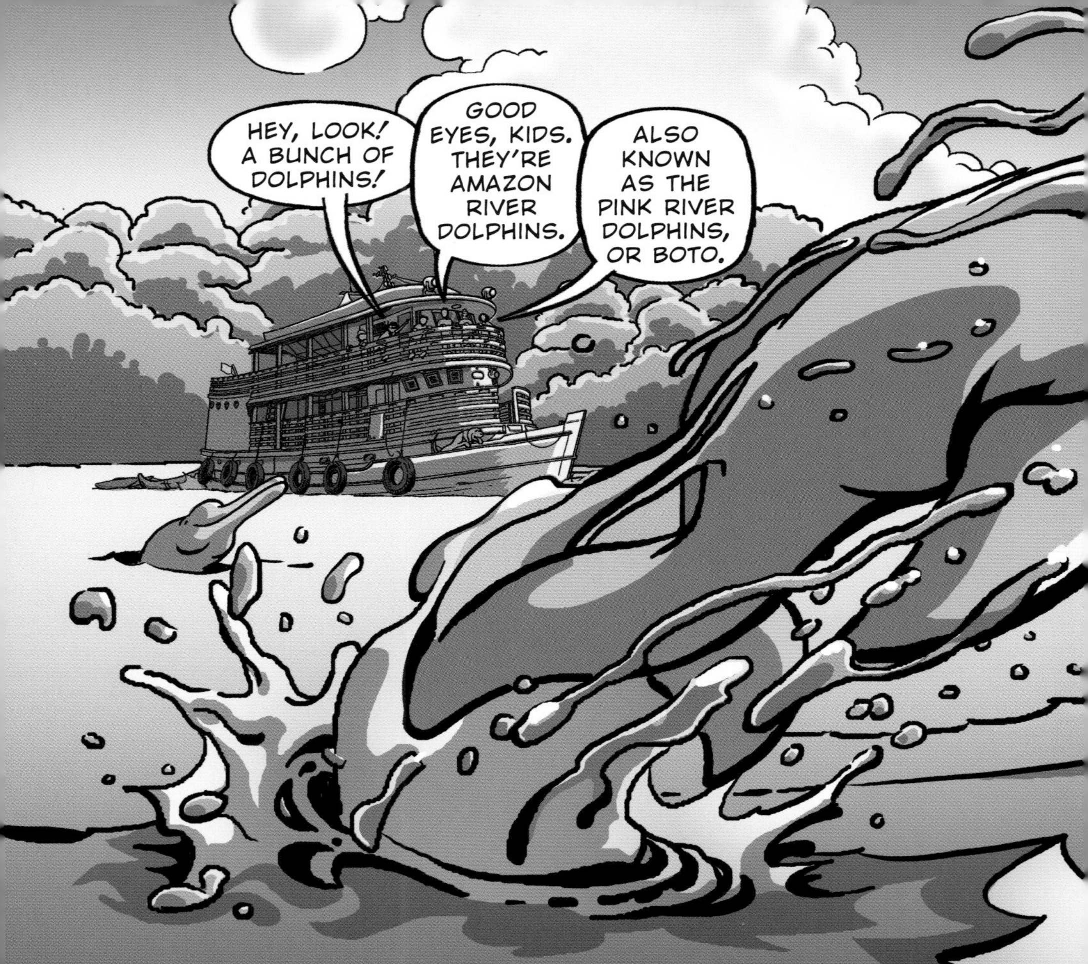
HEY, LOOK! A BUNCH OF DOLPHINS!
GOOD EYES, KIDS. THEY'RE AMAZON RIVER DOLPHINS.
ALSO KNOWN AS THE PINK RIVER DOLPHINS, OR BOTO.

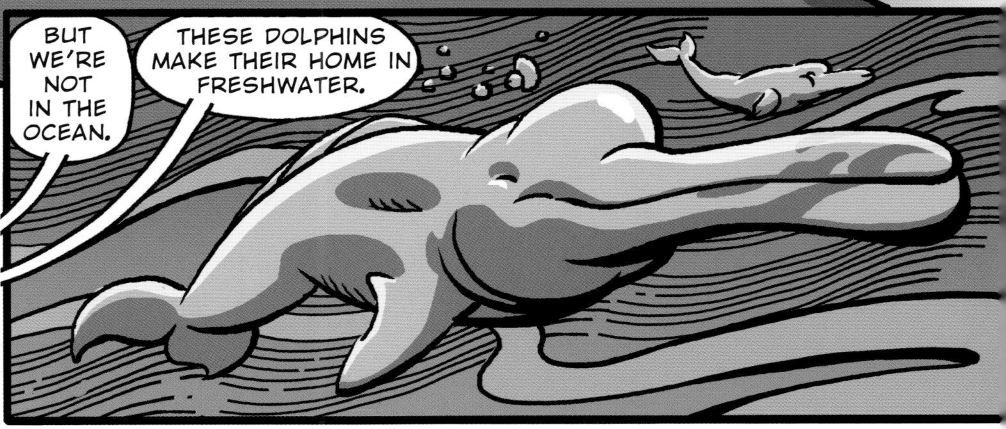
BUT WE'RE NOT IN THE OCEAN.
THESE DOLPHINS MAKE THEIR HOME IN FRESHWATER.

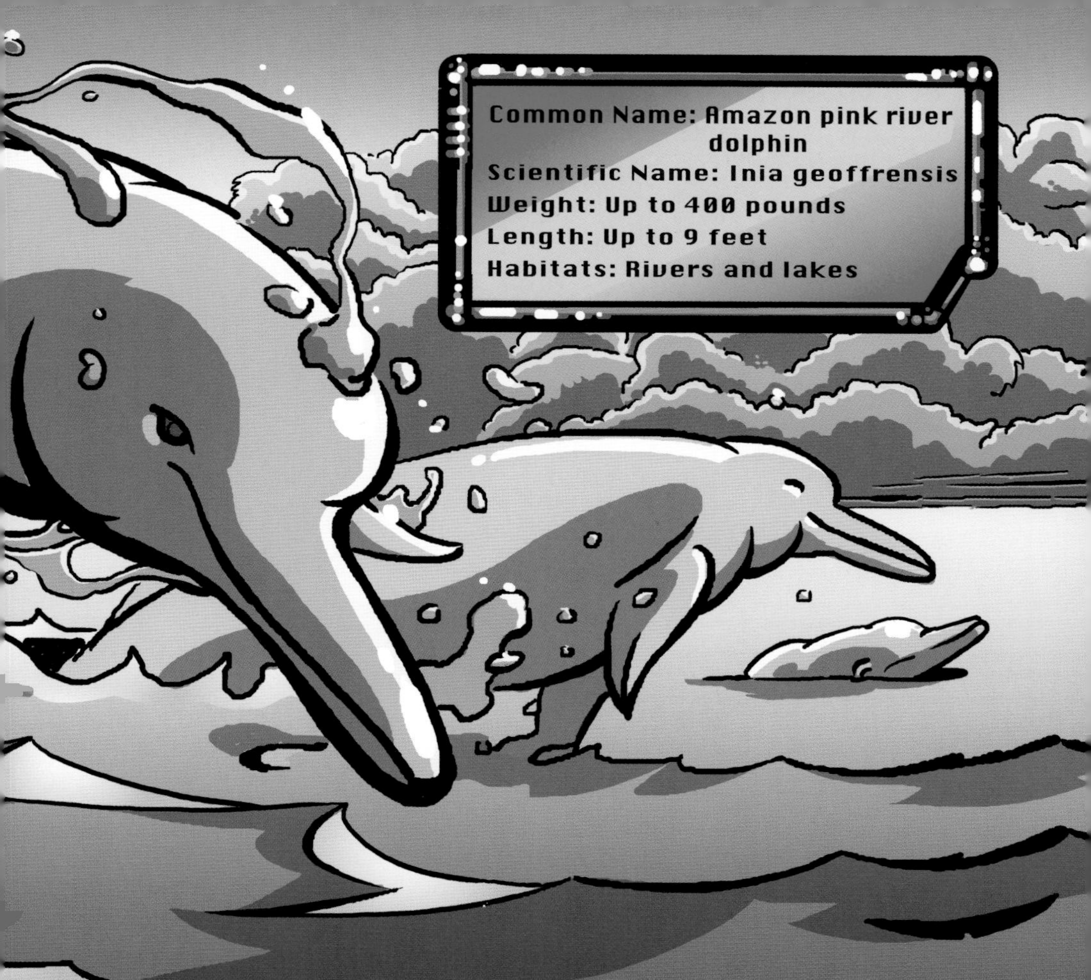
Common Name: Amazon pink river dolphin
Scientific Name: Inia geoffrensis
Weight: Up to 400 pounds
Length: Up to 9 feet
Habitats: Rivers and lakes

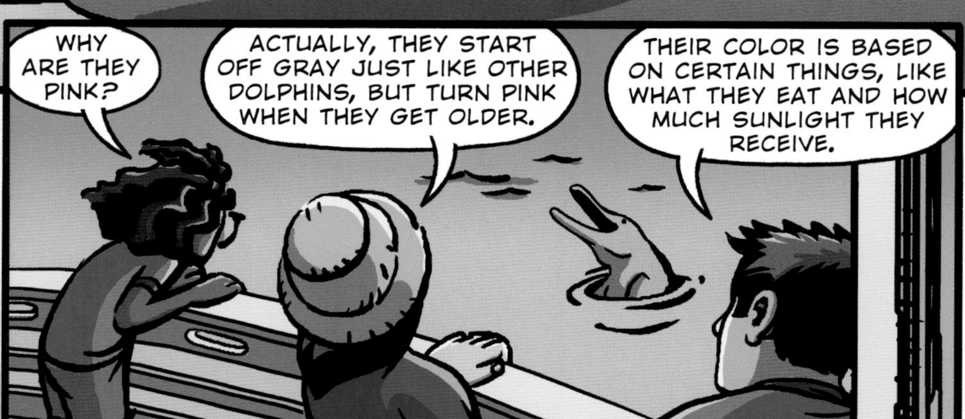
WHY ARE THEY PINK?
ACTUALLY, THEY START OFF GRAY JUST LIKE OTHER DOLPHINS, BUT TURN PINK WHEN THEY GET OLDER.
THEIR COLOR IS BASED ON CERTAIN THINGS, LIKE WHAT THEY EAT AND HOW MUCH SUNLIGHT THEY RECEIVE.

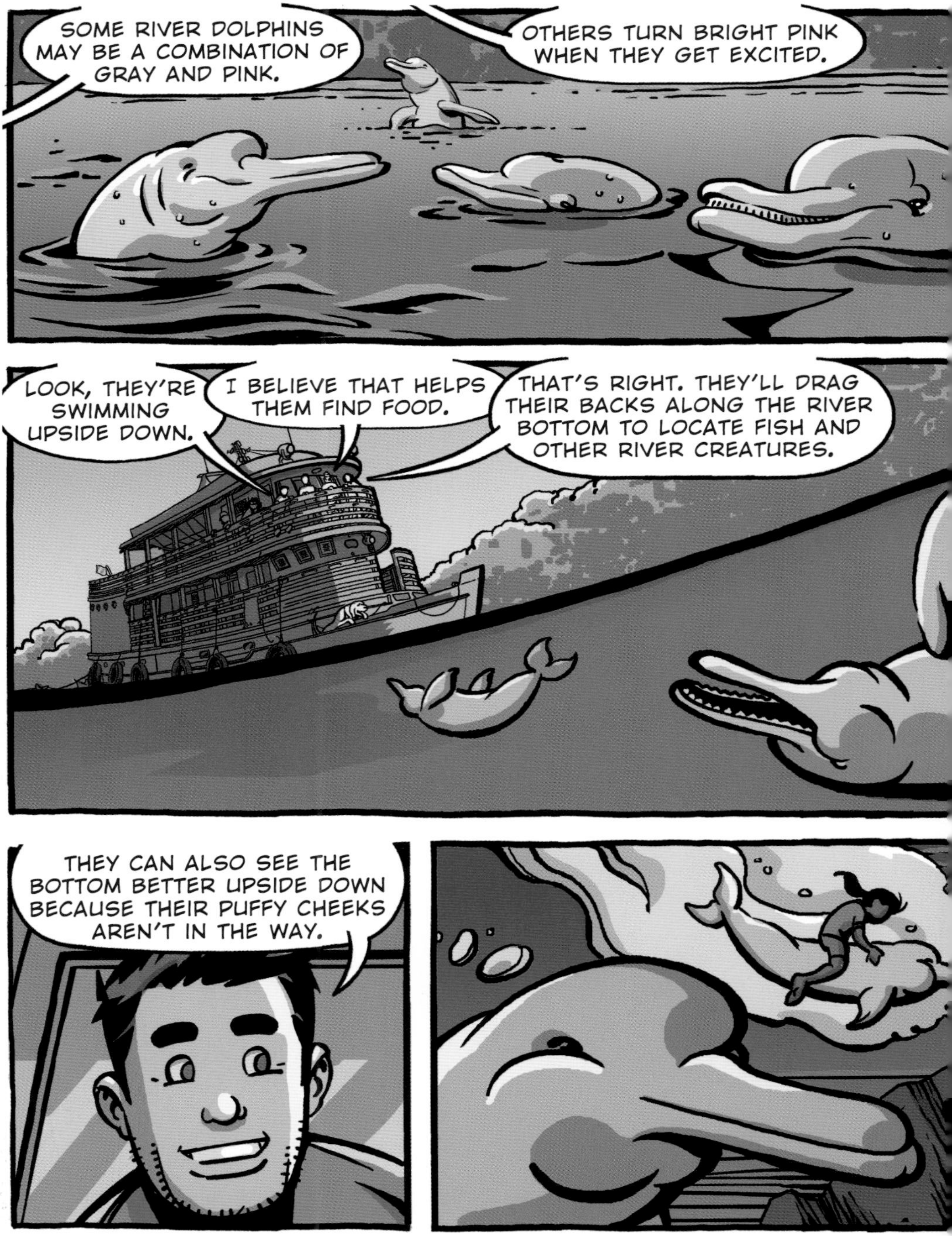
SOME RIVER DOLPHINS MAY BE A COMBINATION OF GRAY AND PINK.
OTHERS TURN BRIGHT PINK WHEN THEY GET EXCITED.
LOOK, THEY'RE SWIMMING UPSIDE DOWN.
I BELIEVE THAT HELPS THEM FIND FOOD.
THAT'S RIGHT. THEY'LL DRAG THEIR BACKS ALONG THE RIVER BOTTOM TO LOCATE FISH AND OTHER RIVER CREATURES.
THEY CAN ALSO SEE THE BOTTOM BETTER UPSIDE DOWN BECAUSE THEIR PUFFY CHEEKS AREN'T IN THE WAY.

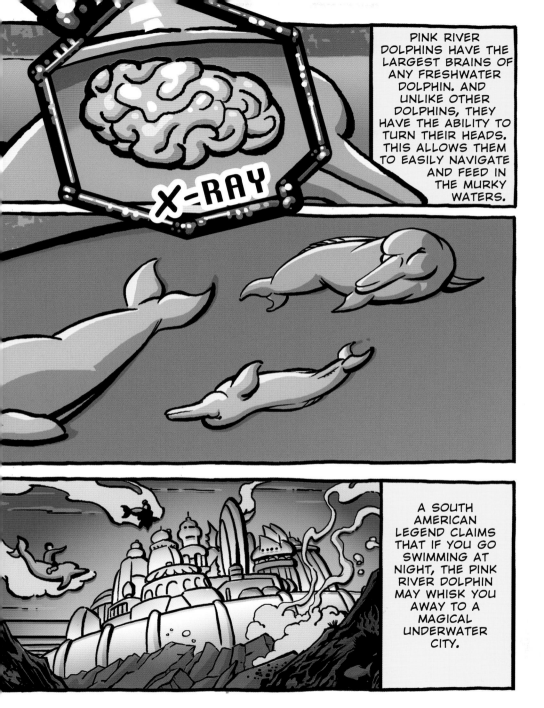

PINK RIVER DOLPHINS HAVE THE LARGEST BRAINS OF ANY FRESHWATER DOLPHIN. AND UNLIKE OTHER DOLPHINS, THEY HAVE THE ABILITY TO TURN THEIR HEADS. THIS ALLOWS THEM TO EASILY NAVIGATE AND FEED IN THE MURKY WATERS.

X-RAY

A SOUTH AMERICAN LEGEND CLAIMS THAT IF YOU GO SWIMMING AT NIGHT, THE PINK RIVER DOLPHIN MAY WHISK YOU AWAY TO A MAGICAL UNDERWATER CITY.

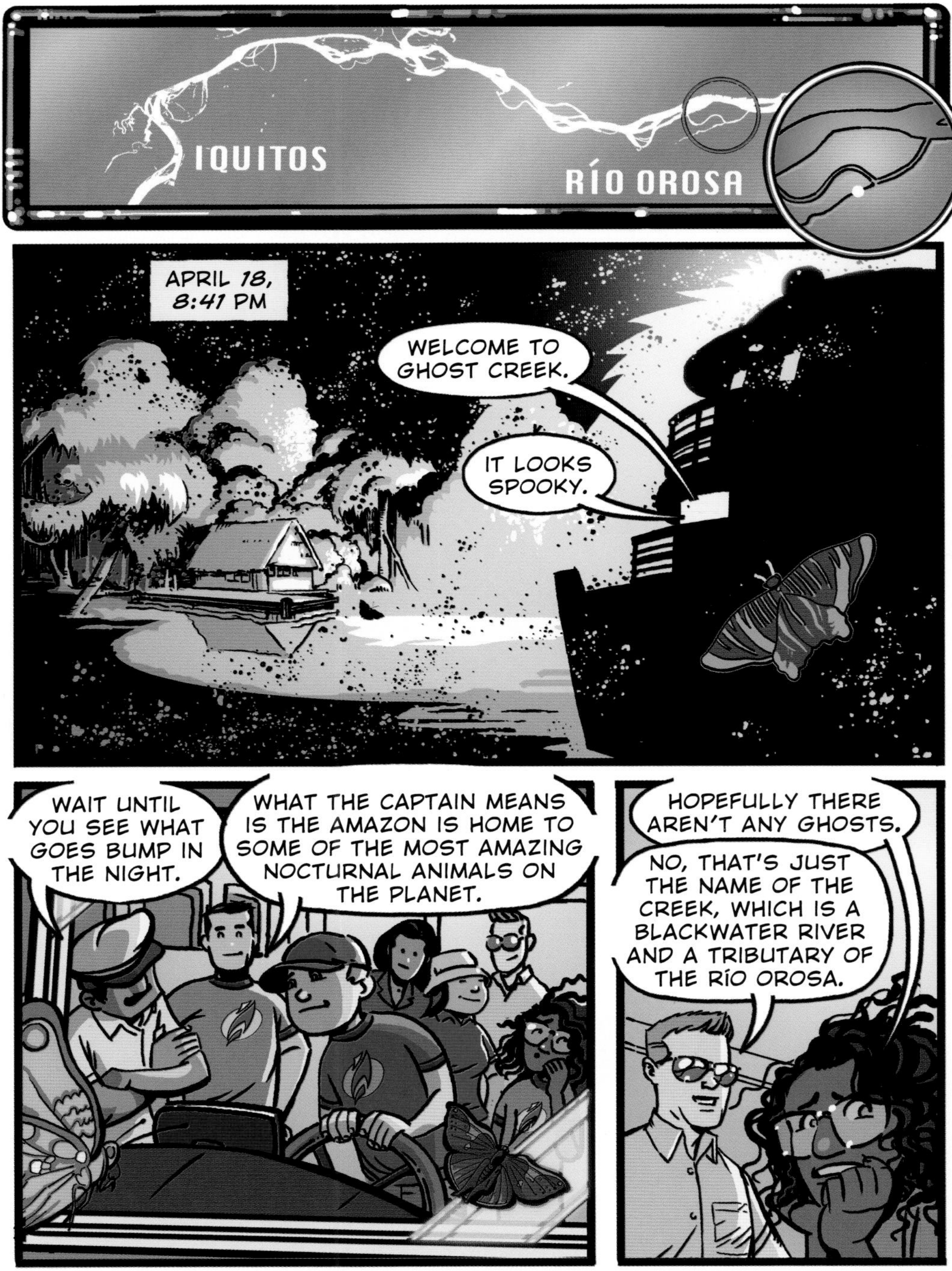
IQUITOS
RÍO OROSA
APRIL 18, 8:41 PM
WELCOME TO GHOST CREEK.
IT LOOKS SPOOKY.
WAIT UNTIL YOU SEE WHAT GOES BUMP IN THE NIGHT.
WHAT THE CAPTAIN MEANS IS THE AMAZON IS HOME TO SOME OF THE MOST AMAZING NOCTURNAL ANIMALS ON THE PLANET.
HOPEFULLY THERE AREN'T ANY GHOSTS.
NO, THAT'S JUST THE NAME OF THE CREEK, WHICH IS A BLACKWATER RIVER AND A TRIBUTARY OF THE RÍO OROSA.

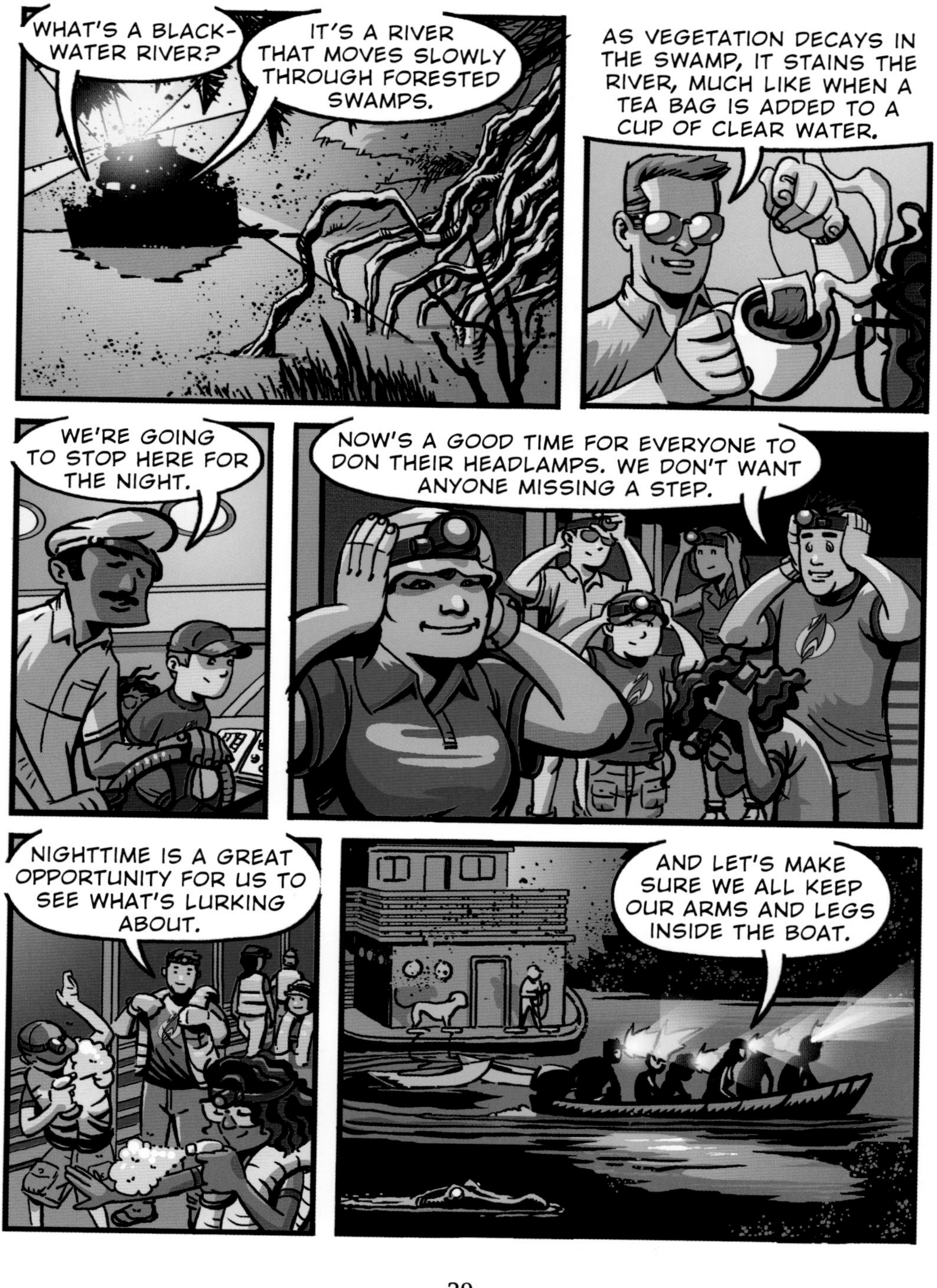
WHAT'S A BLACK-WATER RIVER?
IT'S A RIVER THAT MOVES SLOWLY THROUGH FORESTED SWAMPS.
AS VEGETATION DECAYS IN THE SWAMP, IT STAINS THE RIVER, MUCH LIKE WHEN A TEA BAG IS ADDED TO A CUP OF CLEAR WATER.
WE'RE GOING TO STOP HERE FOR THE NIGHT.
NOW'S A GOOD TIME FOR EVERYONE TO DON THEIR HEADLAMPS. WE DON'T WANT ANYONE MISSING A STEP.
NIGHTTIME IS A GREAT OPPORTUNITY FOR US TO SEE WHAT'S LURKING ABOUT.
AND LET'S MAKE SURE WE ALL KEEP OUR ARMS AND LEGS INSIDE THE BOAT.

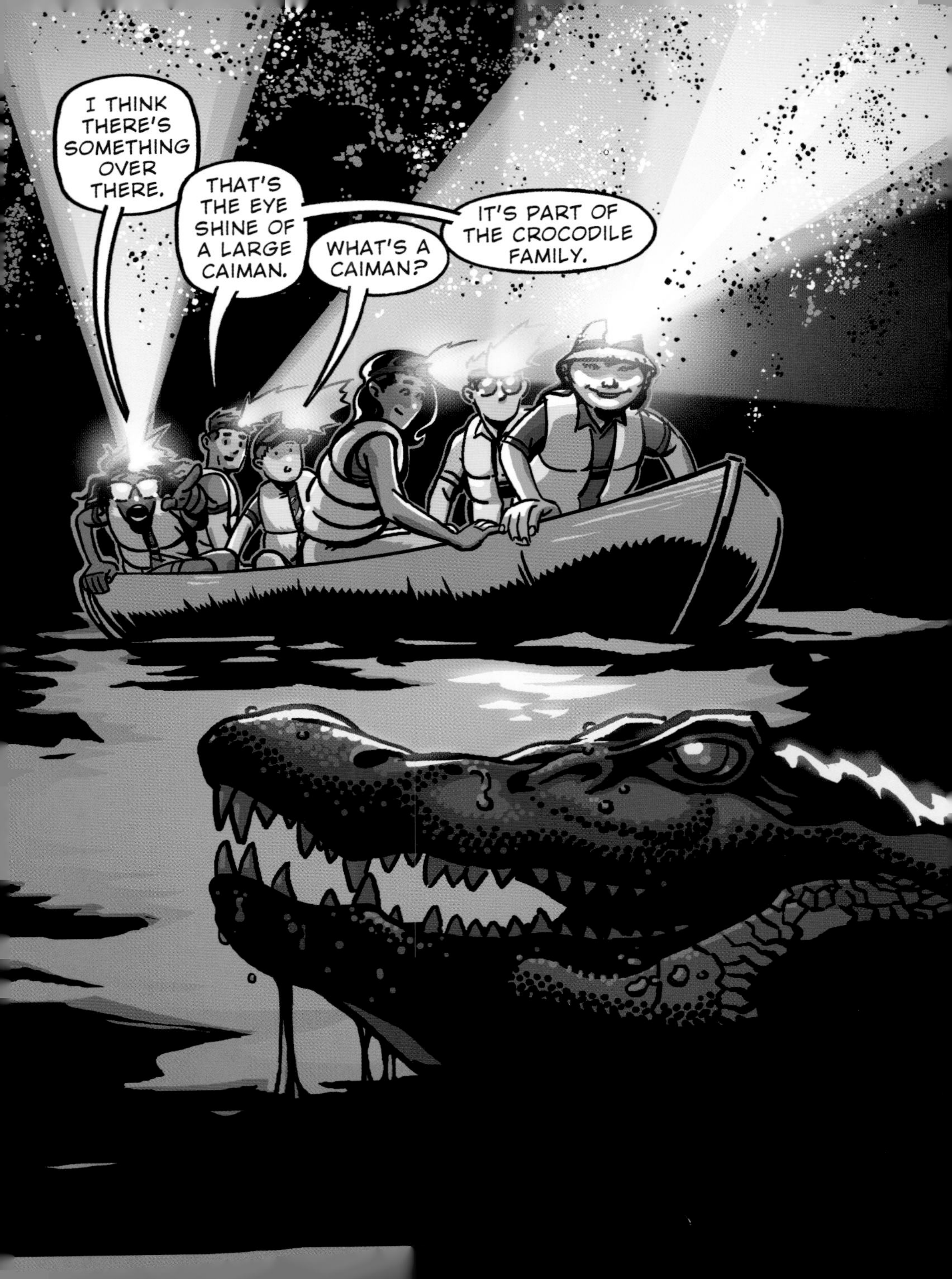
I THINK THERE'S SOMETHING OVER THERE.
THAT'S THE EYE SHINE OF A LARGE CAIMAN.
WHAT'S A CAIMAN?
IT'S PART OF THE CROCODILE FAMILY.

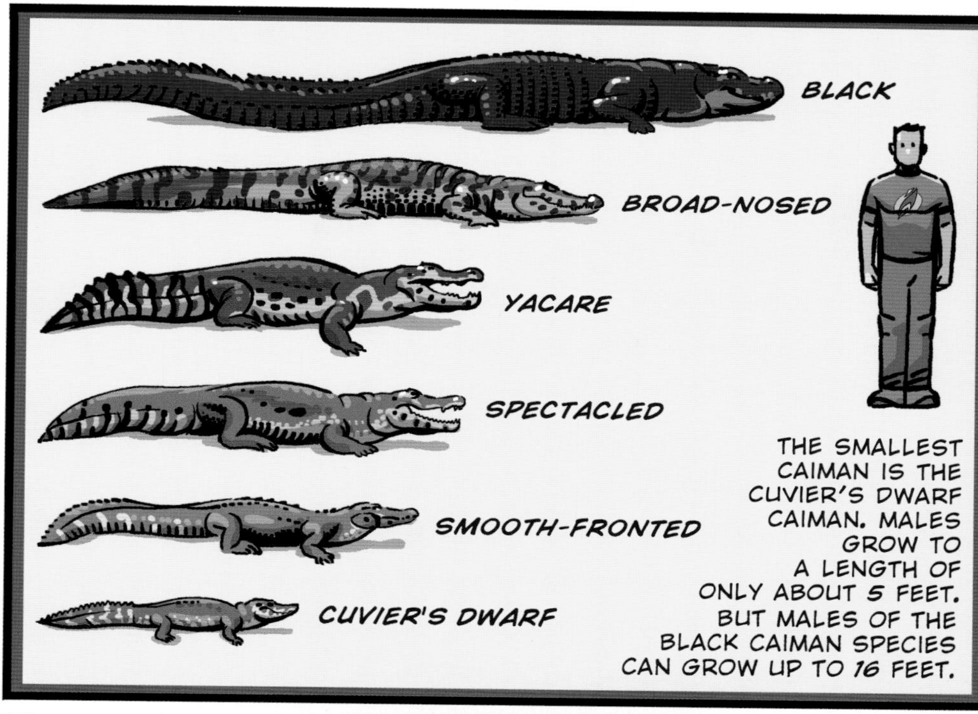
BLACK
BROAD-NOSED
YACARE
SPECTACLED
SMOOTH-FRONTED
CUVIER'S DWARF
THE SMALLEST CAIMAN IS THE CUVIER'S DWARF CAIMAN. MALES GROW TO A LENGTH OF ONLY ABOUT 5 FEET. BUT MALES OF THE BLACK CAIMAN SPECIES CAN GROW UP TO 16 FEET.

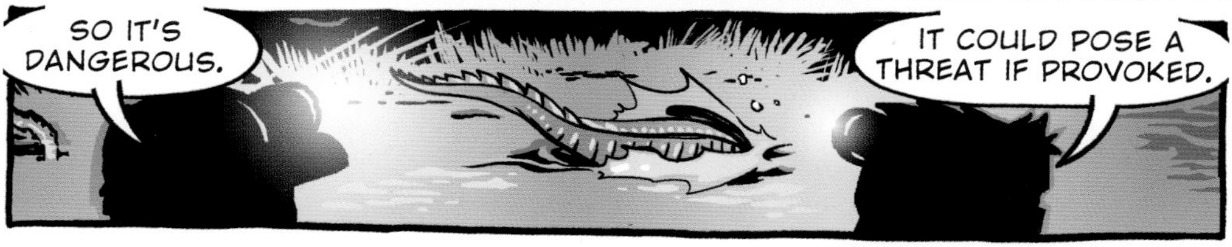
SO IT'S DANGEROUS.
IT COULD POSE A THREAT IF PROVOKED.

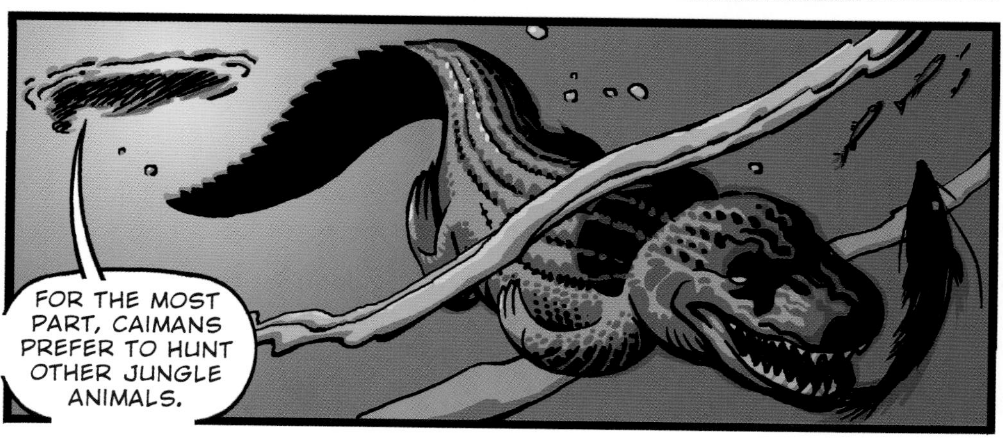
FOR THE MOST PART, CAIMANS PREFER TO HUNT OTHER JUNGLE ANIMALS.

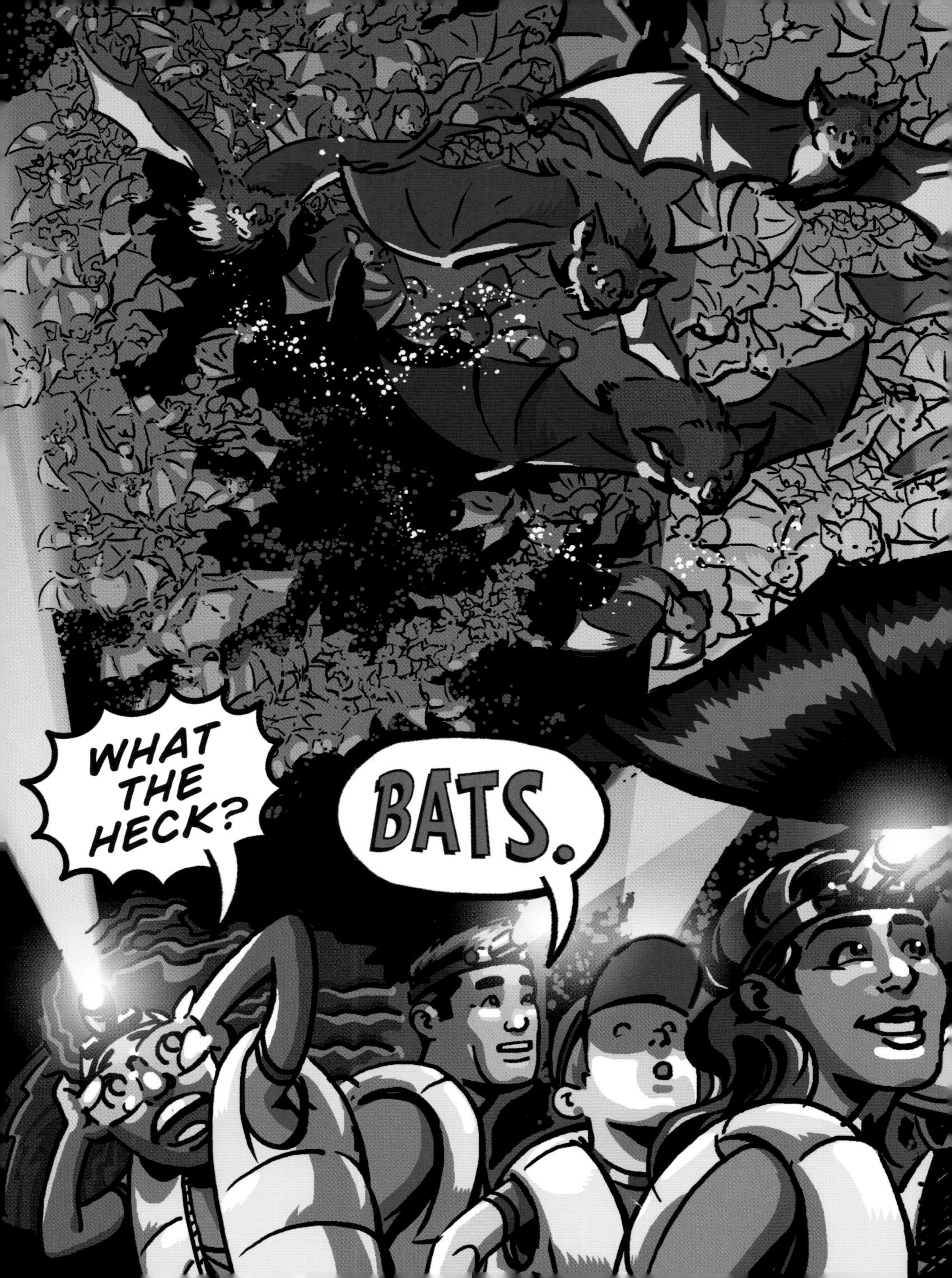
WHAT THE HECK?
BATS.

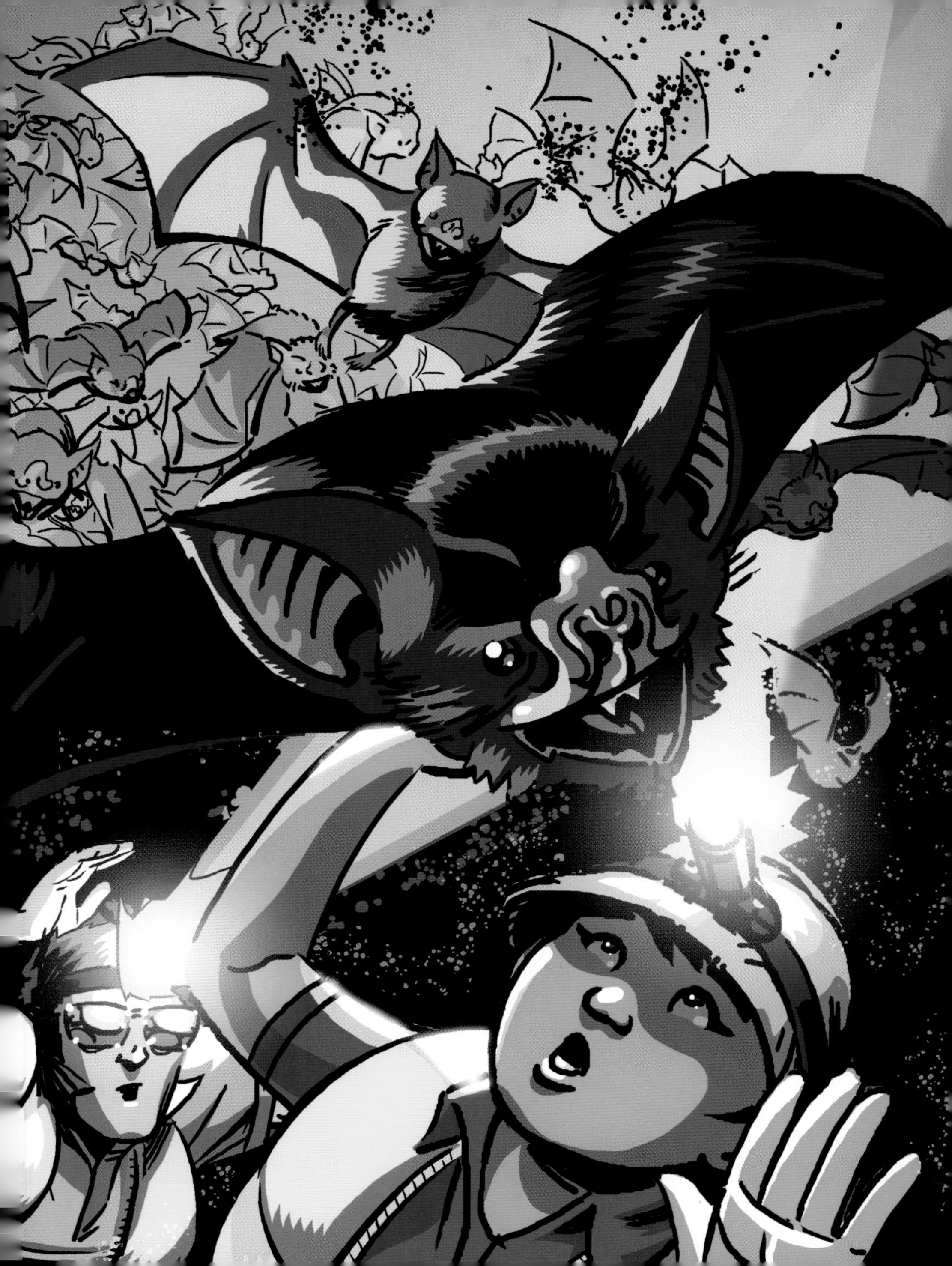

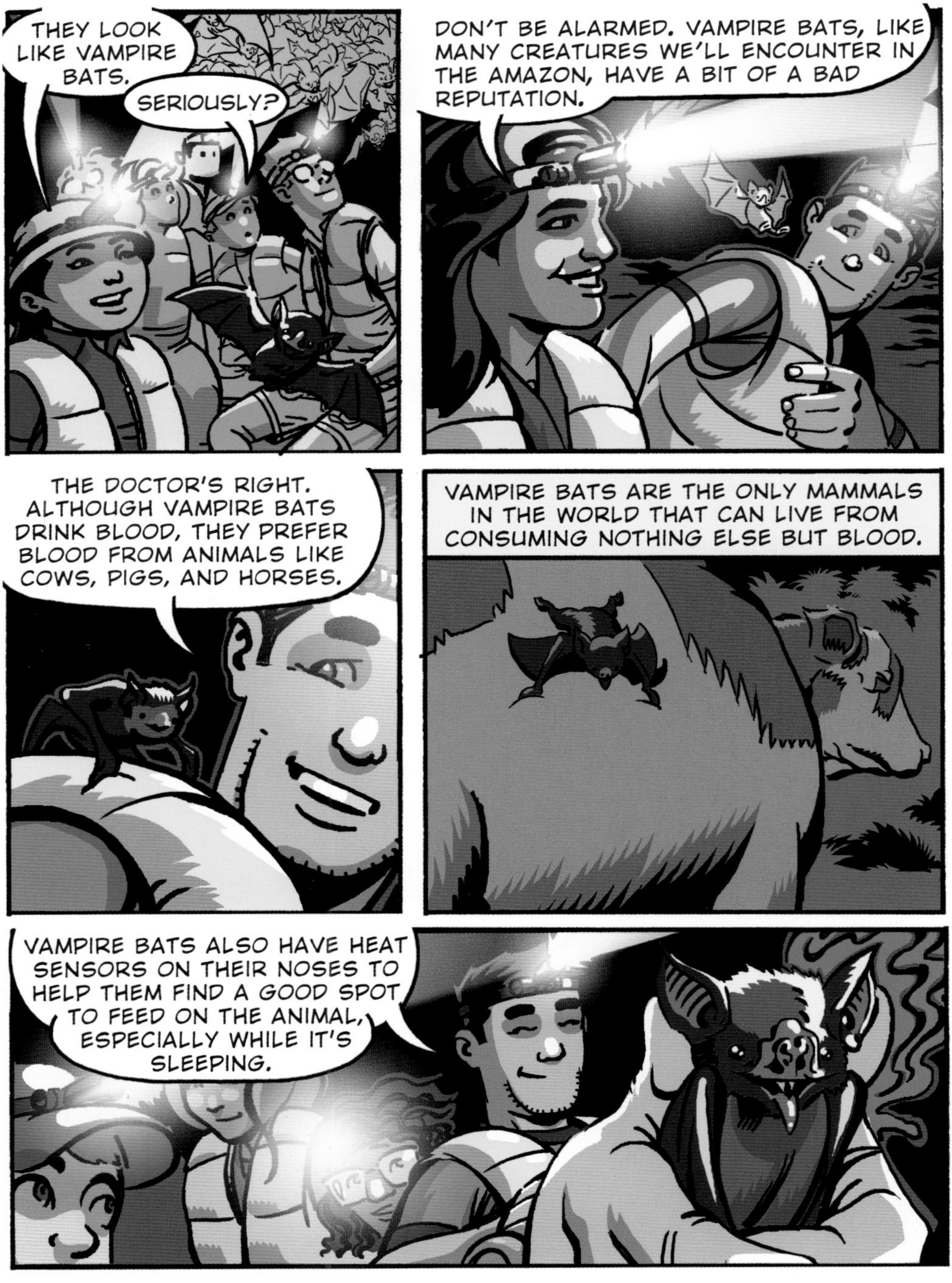
THEY LOOK LIKE VAMPIRE BATS.
SERIOUSLY?
DON'T BE ALARMED. VAMPIRE BATS, LIKE MANY CREATURES WE'LL ENCOUNTER IN THE AMAZON, HAVE A BIT OF A BAD REPUTATION.
THE DOCTOR'S RIGHT. ALTHOUGH VAMPIRE BATS DRINK BLOOD, THEY PREFER BLOOD FROM ANIMALS LIKE COWS, PIGS, AND HORSES.
VAMPIRE BATS ARE THE ONLY MAMMALS IN THE WORLD THAT CAN LIVE FROM CONSUMING NOTHING ELSE BUT BLOOD.
VAMPIRE BATS ALSO HAVE HEAT SENSORS ON THEIR NOSES TO HELP THEM FIND A GOOD SPOT TO FEED ON THE ANIMAL, ESPECIALLY WHILE IT'S SLEEPING.

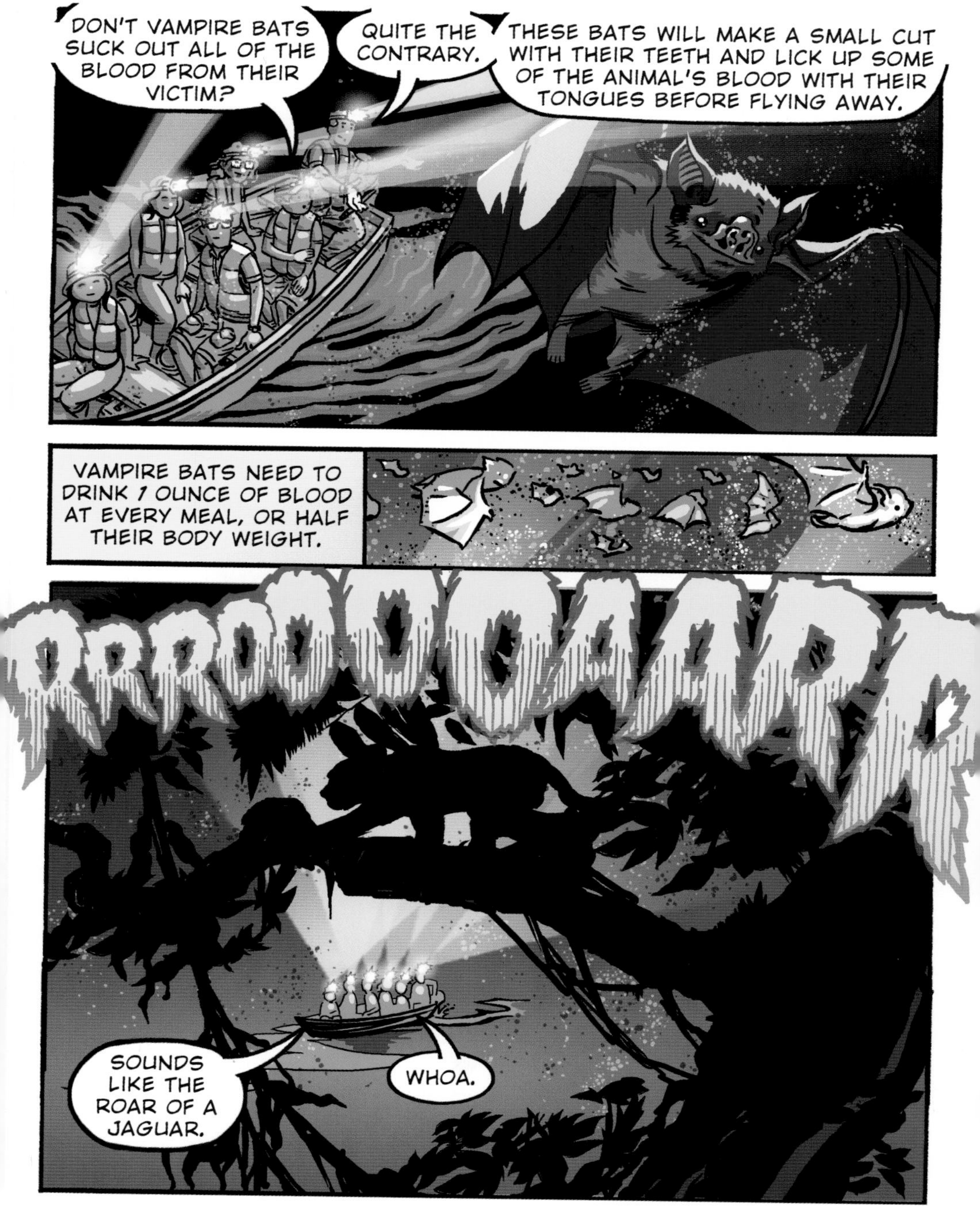
DON'T VAMPIRE BATS SUCK OUT ALL OF THE BLOOD FROM THEIR VICTIM?
QUITE THE CONTRARY.
THESE BATS WILL MAKE A SMALL CUT WITH THEIR TEETH AND LICK UP SOME OF THE ANIMAL'S BLOOD WITH THEIR TONGUES BEFORE FLYING AWAY.
VAMPIRE BATS NEED TO DRINK 1 OUNCE OF BLOOD AT EVERY MEAL, OR HALF THEIR BODY WEIGHT.
RRROOOOAAR
SOUNDS LIKE THE ROAR OF A JAGUAR.
WHOA.

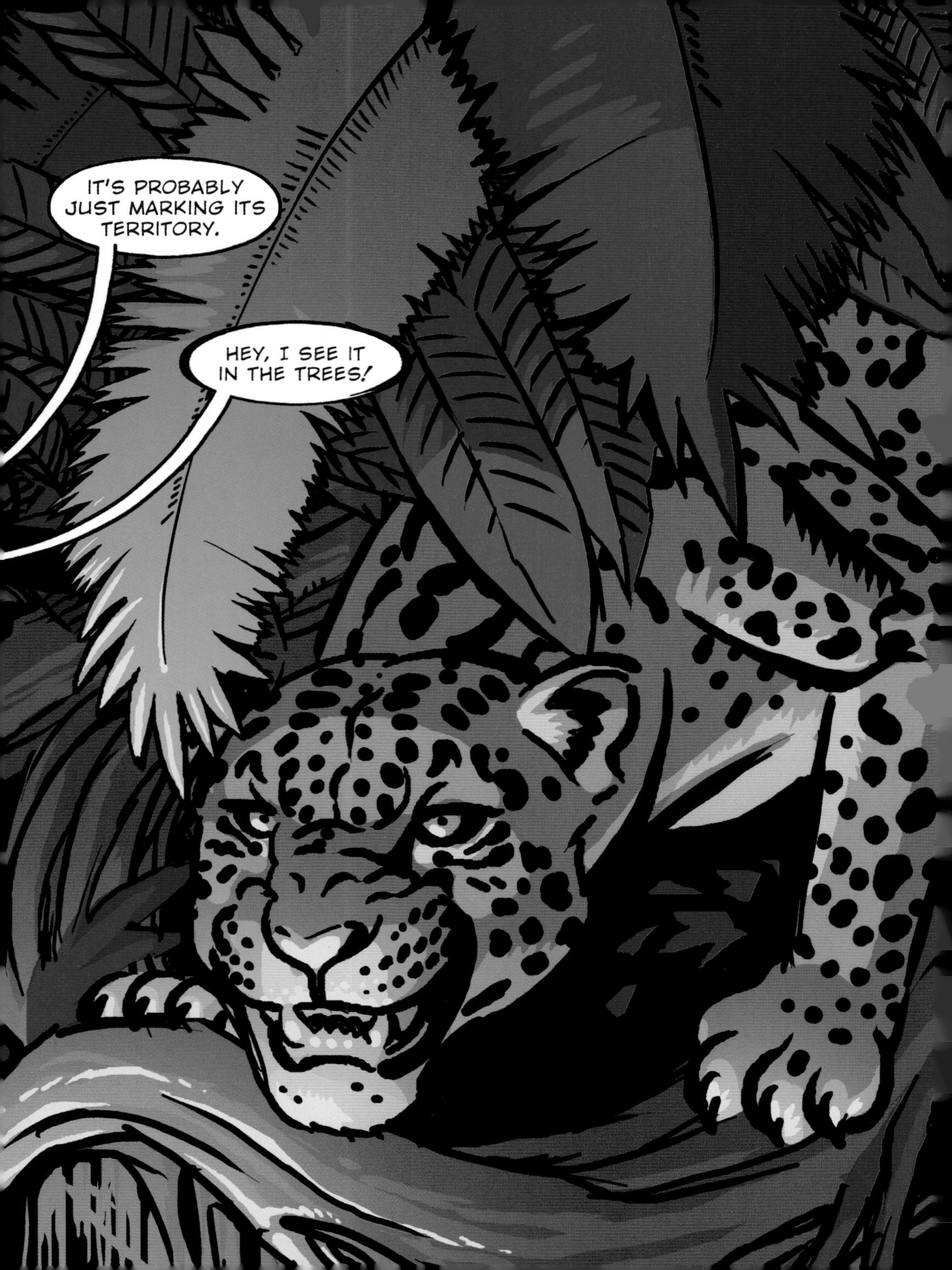
IT'S PROBABLY JUST MARKING ITS TERRITORY.
HEY, I SEE IT IN THE TREES!

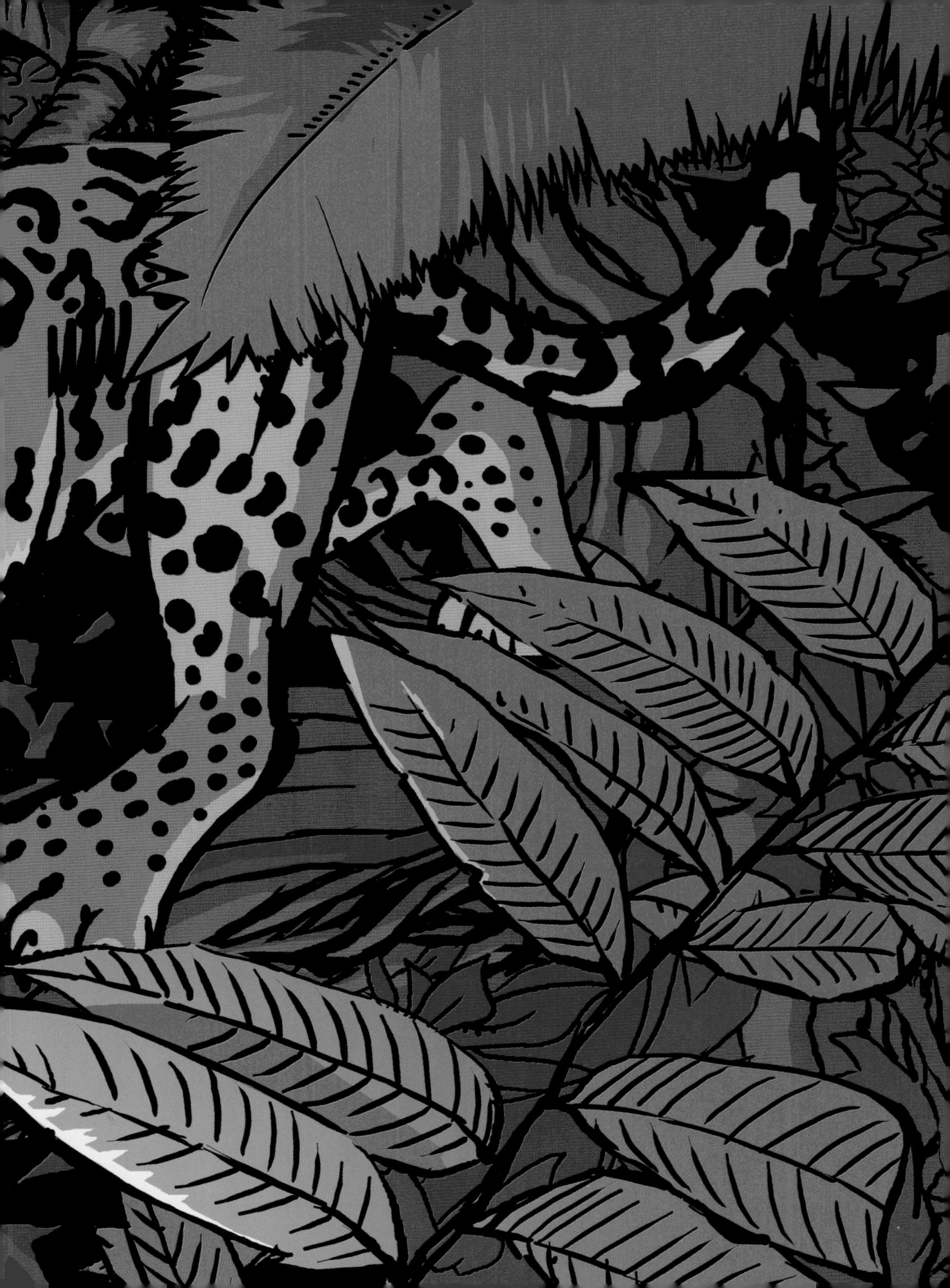

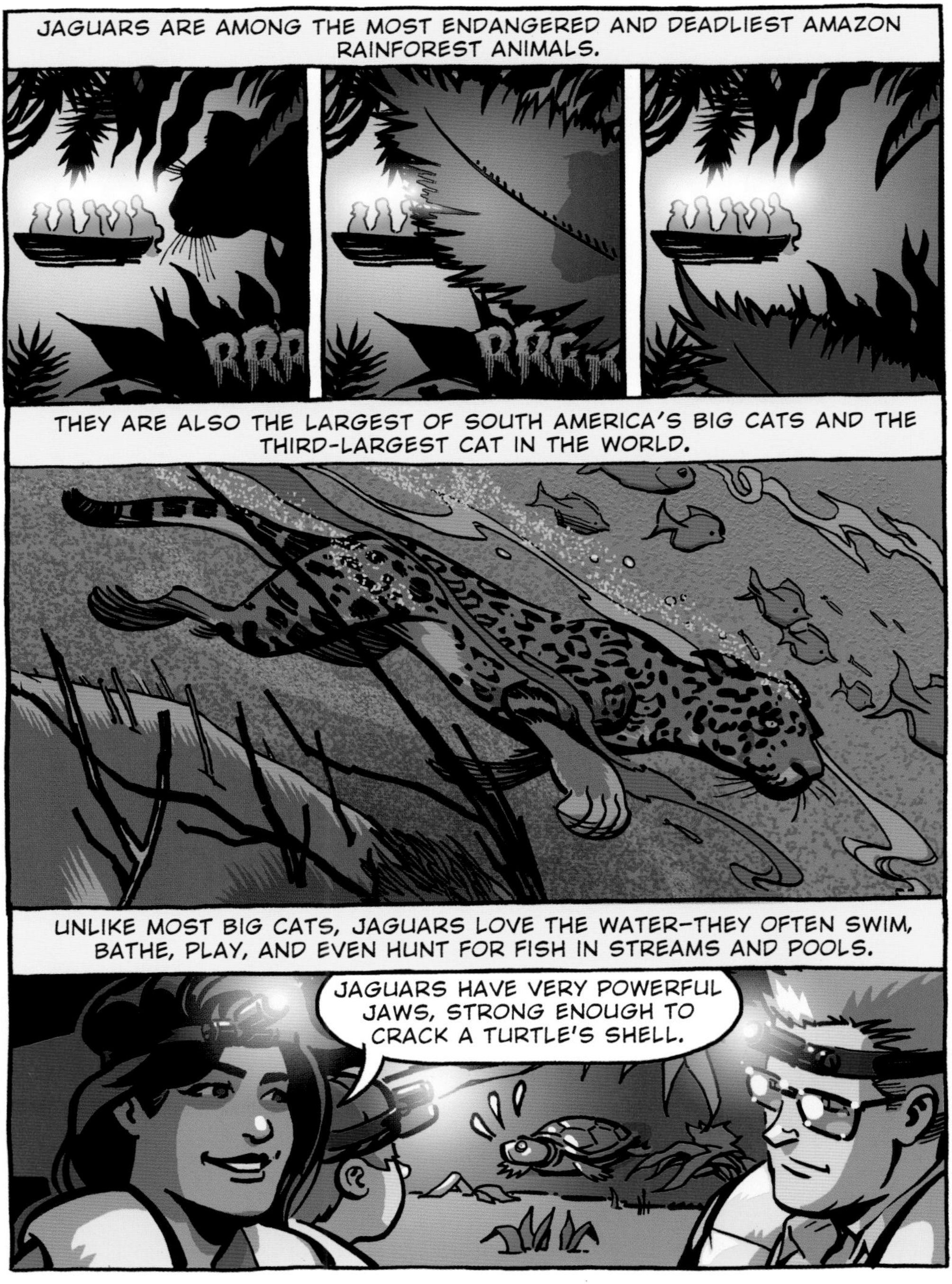
JAGUARS ARE AMONG THE MOST ENDANGERED AND DEADLIEST AMAZON RAINFOREST ANIMALS.
THEY ARE ALSO THE LARGEST OF SOUTH AMERICA'S BIG CATS AND THE THIRD-LARGEST CAT IN THE WORLD.
UNLIKE MOST BIG CATS, JAGUARS LOVE THE WATER—THEY OFTEN SWIM, BATHE, PLAY, AND EVEN HUNT FOR FISH IN STREAMS AND POOLS.
JAGUARS HAVE VERY POWERFUL JAWS, STRONG ENOUGH TO CRACK A TURTLE'S SHELL.

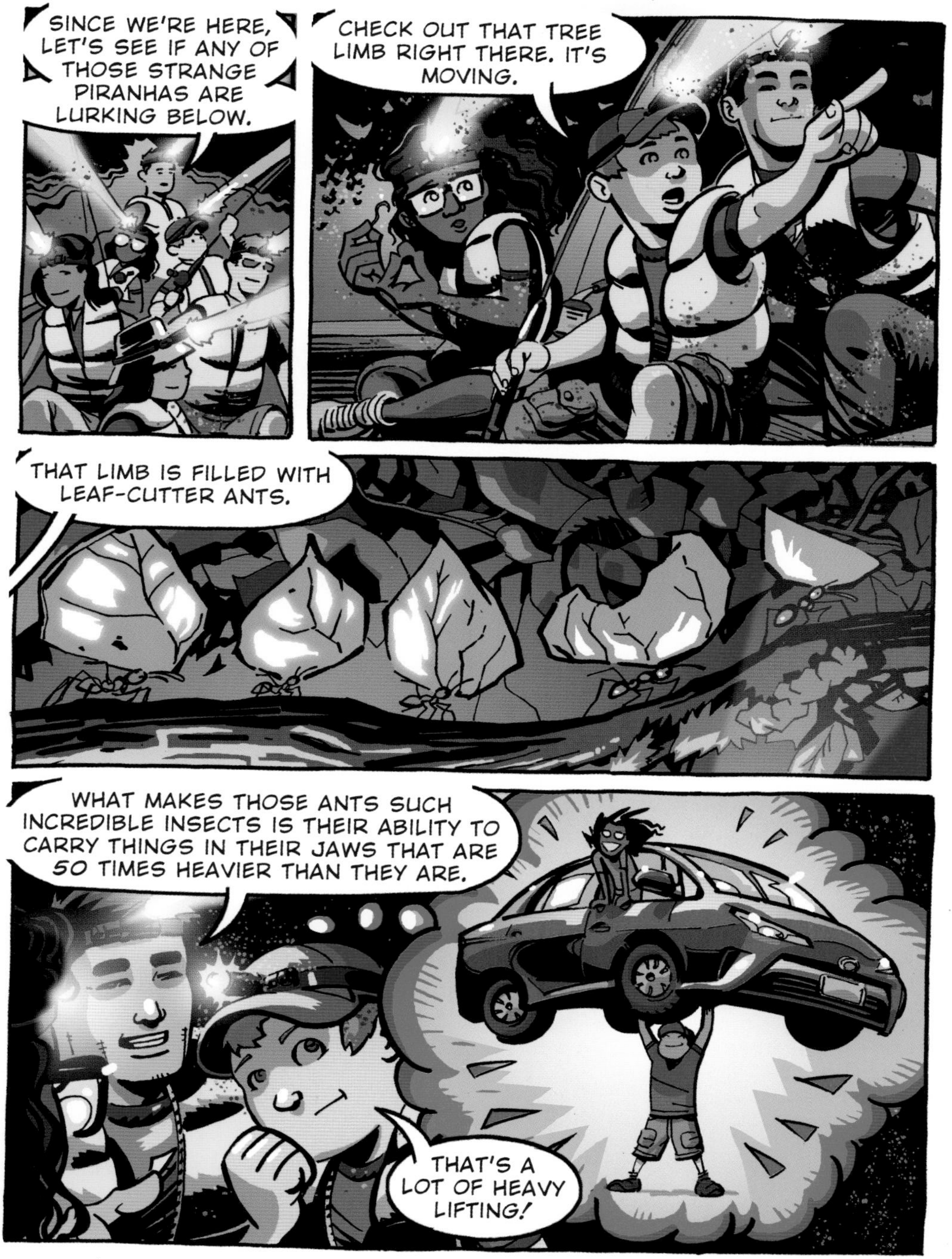
SINCE WE'RE HERE, LET'S SEE IF ANY OF THOSE STRANGE PIRANHAS ARE LURKING BELOW.
CHECK OUT THAT TREE LIMB RIGHT THERE. IT'S MOVING.
THAT LIMB IS FILLED WITH LEAF-CUTTER ANTS.
WHAT MAKES THOSE ANTS SUCH INCREDIBLE INSECTS IS THEIR ABILITY TO CARRY THINGS IN THEIR JAWS THAT ARE 50 TIMES HEAVIER THAN THEY ARE.
THAT'S A LOT OF HEAVY LIFTING!

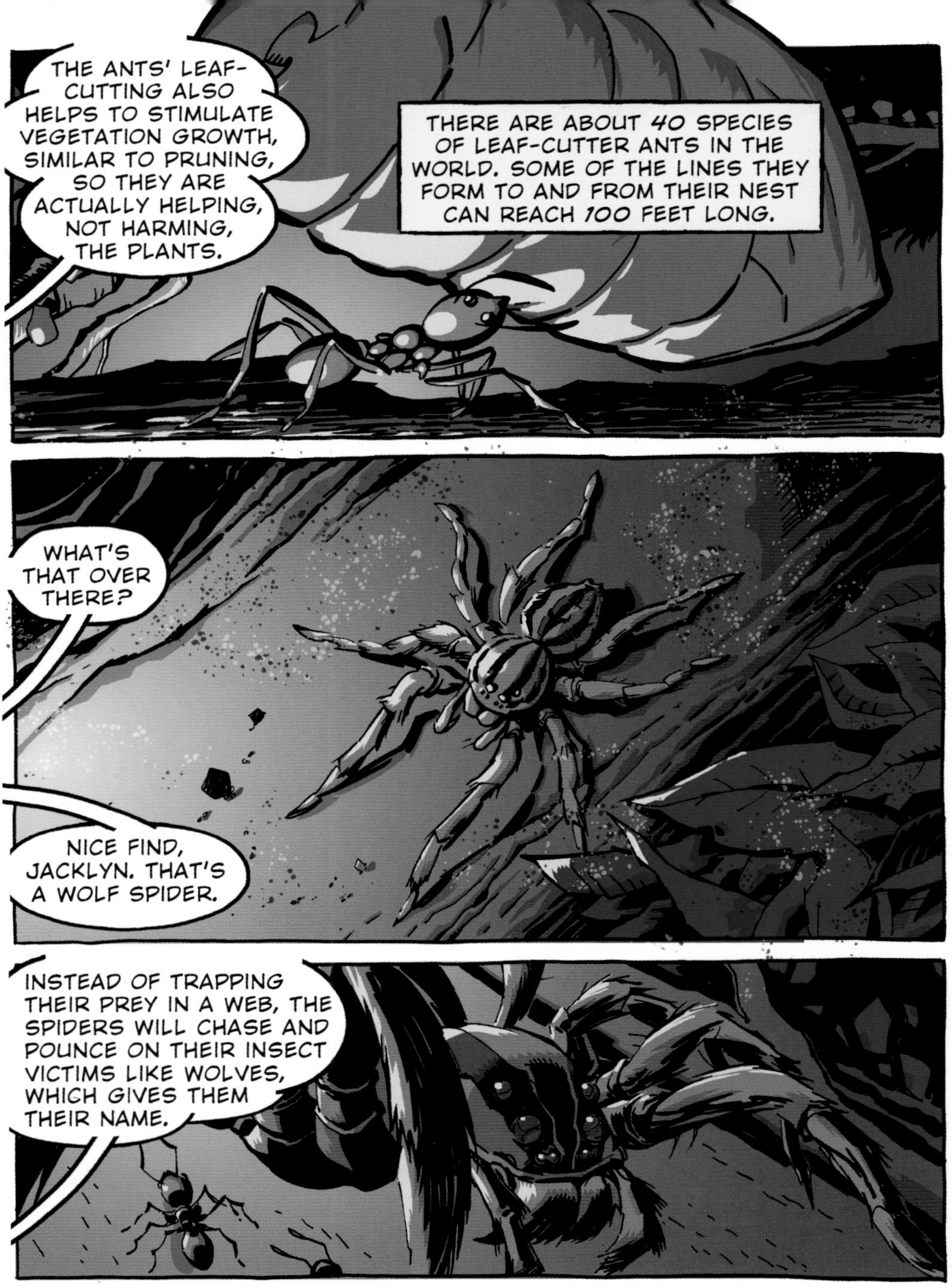
THE ANTS' LEAF-CUTTING ALSO HELPS TO STIMULATE VEGETATION GROWTH, SIMILAR TO PRUNING, SO THEY ARE ACTUALLY HELPING, NOT HARMING, THE PLANTS.
THERE ARE ABOUT 40 SPECIES OF LEAF-CUTTER ANTS IN THE WORLD. SOME OF THE LINES THEY FORM TO AND FROM THEIR NEST CAN REACH 100 FEET LONG.
WHAT'S THAT OVER THERE?
NICE FIND, JACKLYN. THAT'S A WOLF SPIDER.
INSTEAD OF TRAPPING THEIR PREY IN A WEB, THE SPIDERS WILL CHASE AND POUNCE ON THEIR INSECT VICTIMS LIKE WOLVES, WHICH GIVES THEM THEIR NAME.

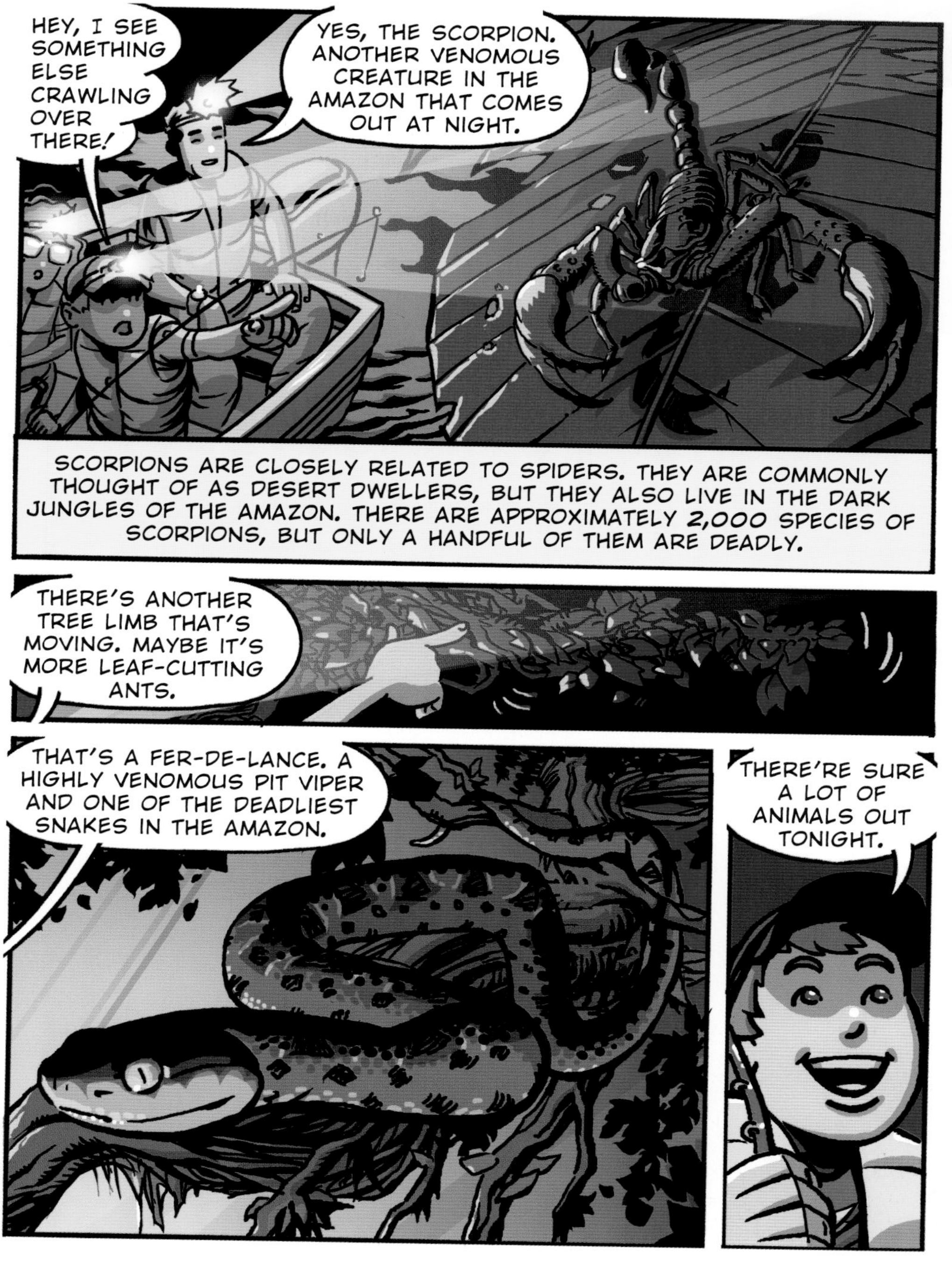
HEY, I SEE SOMETHING ELSE CRAWLING OVER THERE!
YES, THE SCORPION. ANOTHER VENOMOUS CREATURE IN THE AMAZON THAT COMES OUT AT NIGHT.
SCORPIONS ARE CLOSELY RELATED TO SPIDERS. THEY ARE COMMONLY THOUGHT OF AS DESERT DWELLERS, BUT THEY ALSO LIVE IN THE DARK JUNGLES OF THE AMAZON. THERE ARE APPROXIMATELY 2,000 SPECIES OF SCORPIONS, BUT ONLY A HANDFUL OF THEM ARE DEADLY.
THERE'S ANOTHER TREE LIMB THAT'S MOVING. MAYBE IT'S MORE LEAF-CUTTING ANTS.
THAT'S A FER-DE-LANCE. A HIGHLY VENOMOUS PIT VIPER AND ONE OF THE DEADLIEST SNAKES IN THE AMAZON.
THERE'RE SURE A LOT OF ANIMALS OUT TONIGHT.

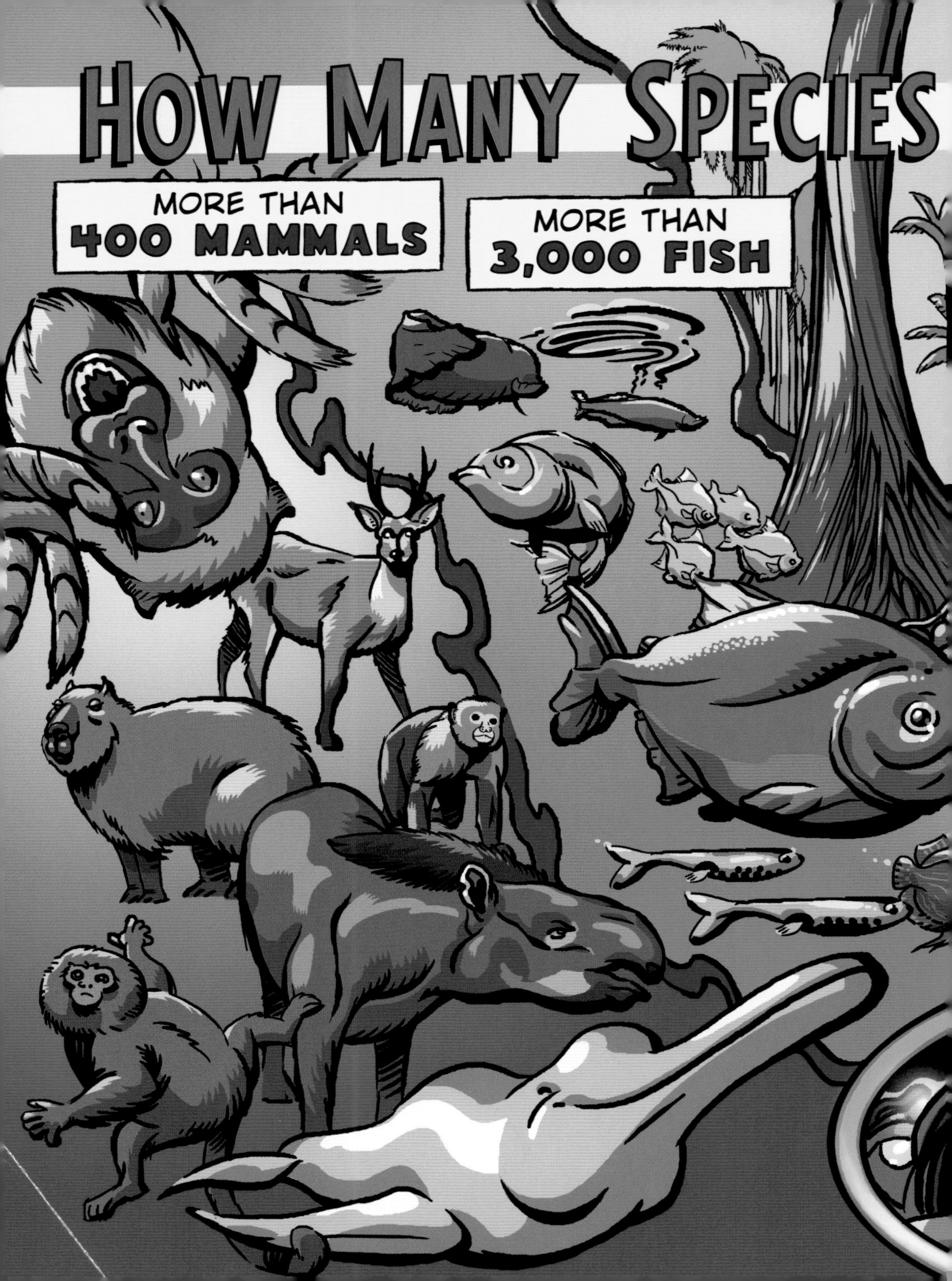
HOW MANY SPECIES
MORE THAN
400 MAMMALS
MORE THAN
3,000 FISH

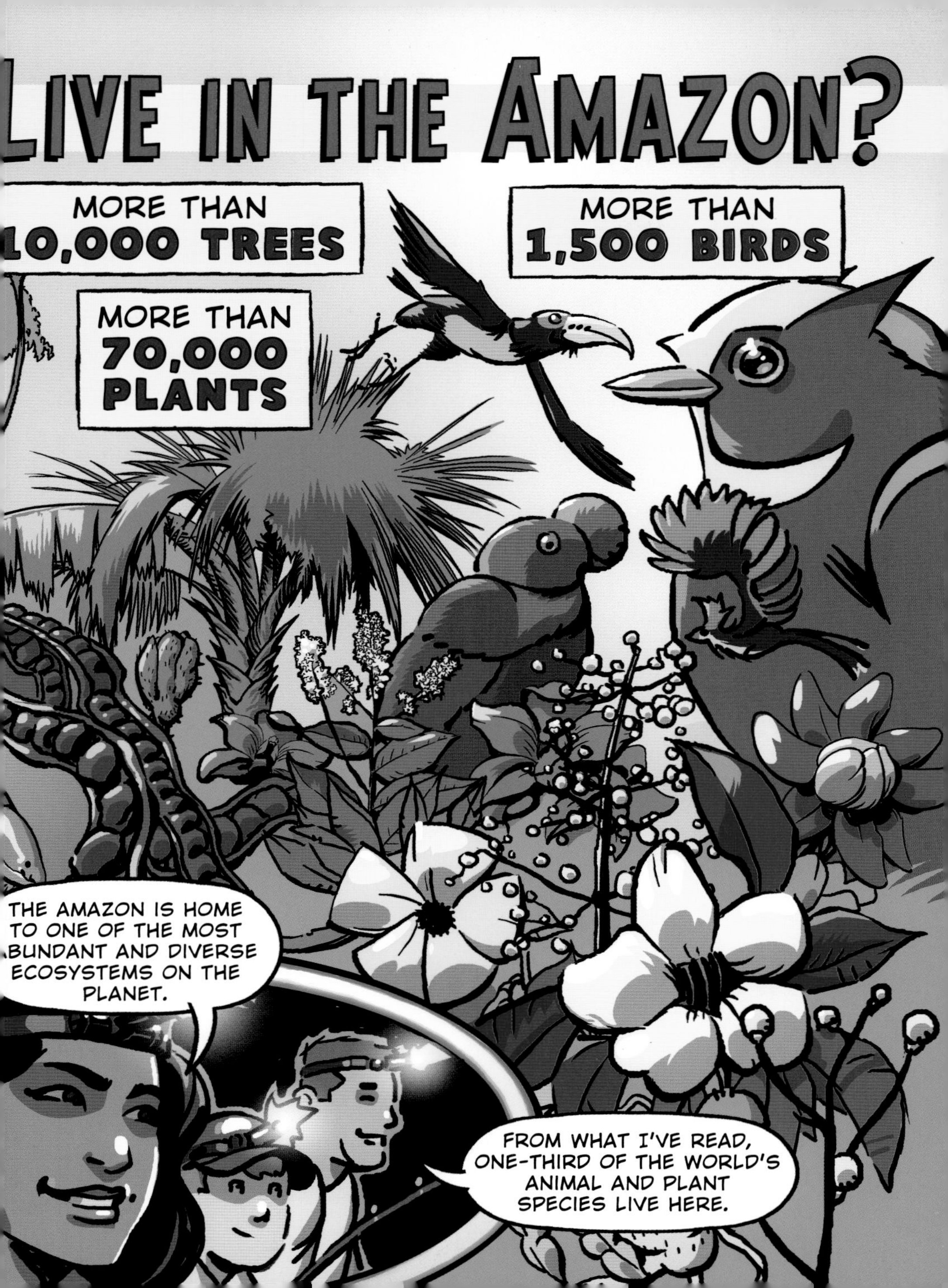
LIVE IN THE AMAZON?
MORE THAN 10,000 TREES
MORE THAN 70,000 PLANTS
MORE THAN 1,500 BIRDS
THE AMAZON IS HOME TO ONE OF THE MOST BUNDANT AND DIVERSE ECOSYSTEMS ON THE PLANET.
FROM WHAT I'VE READ, ONE-THIRD OF THE WORLD'S ANIMAL AND PLANT SPECIES LIVE HERE.

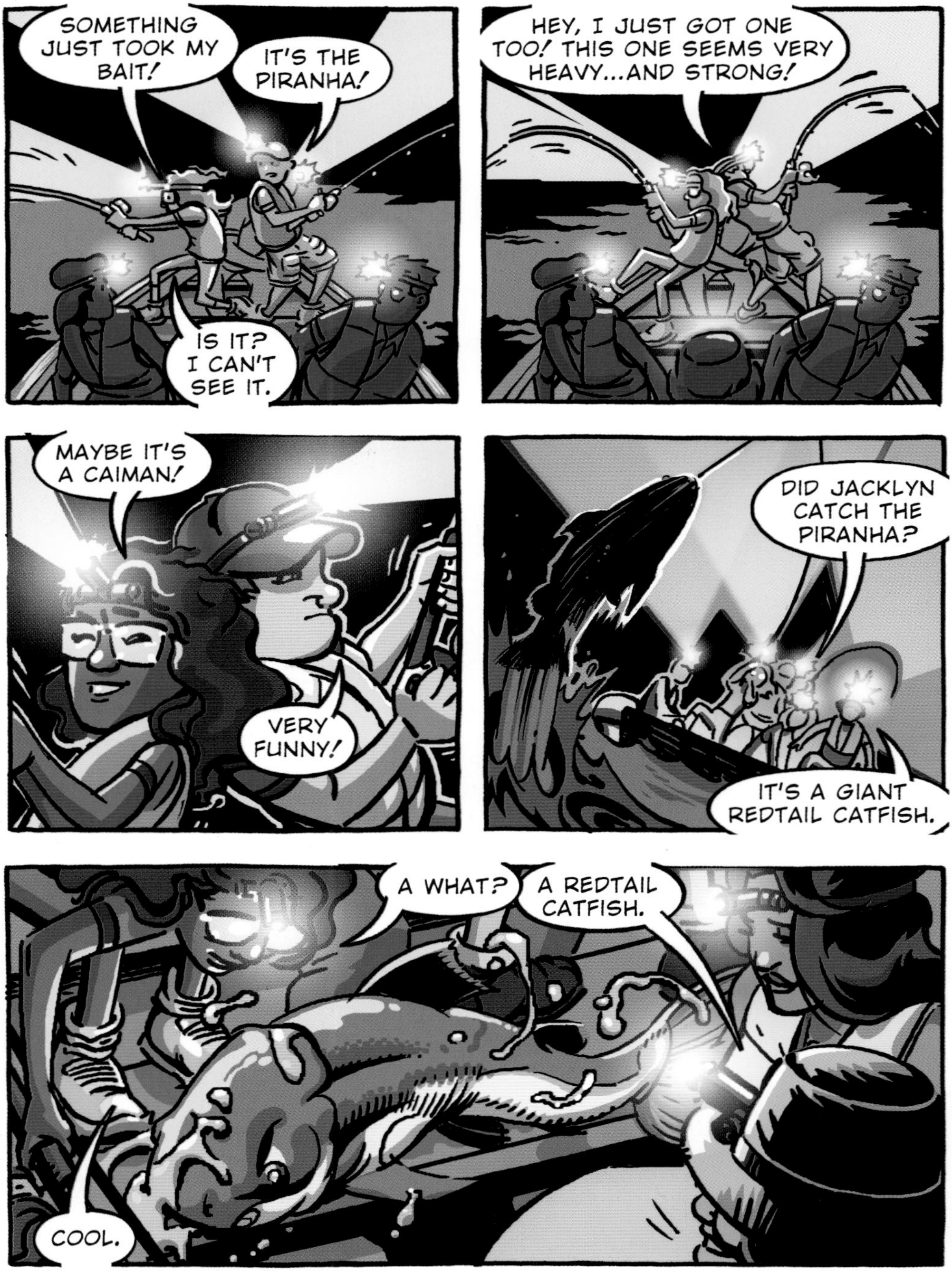
SOMETHING JUST TOOK MY BAIT!
IT'S THE PIRANHA!
IS IT? I CAN'T SEE IT.
HEY, I JUST GOT ONE TOO! THIS ONE SEEMS VERY HEAVY...AND STRONG!
MAYBE IT'S A CAIMAN!
VERY FUNNY!
DID JACKLYN CATCH THE PIRANHA?
IT'S A GIANT REDTAIL CATFISH.
A WHAT?
A REDTAIL CATFISH.
COOL.

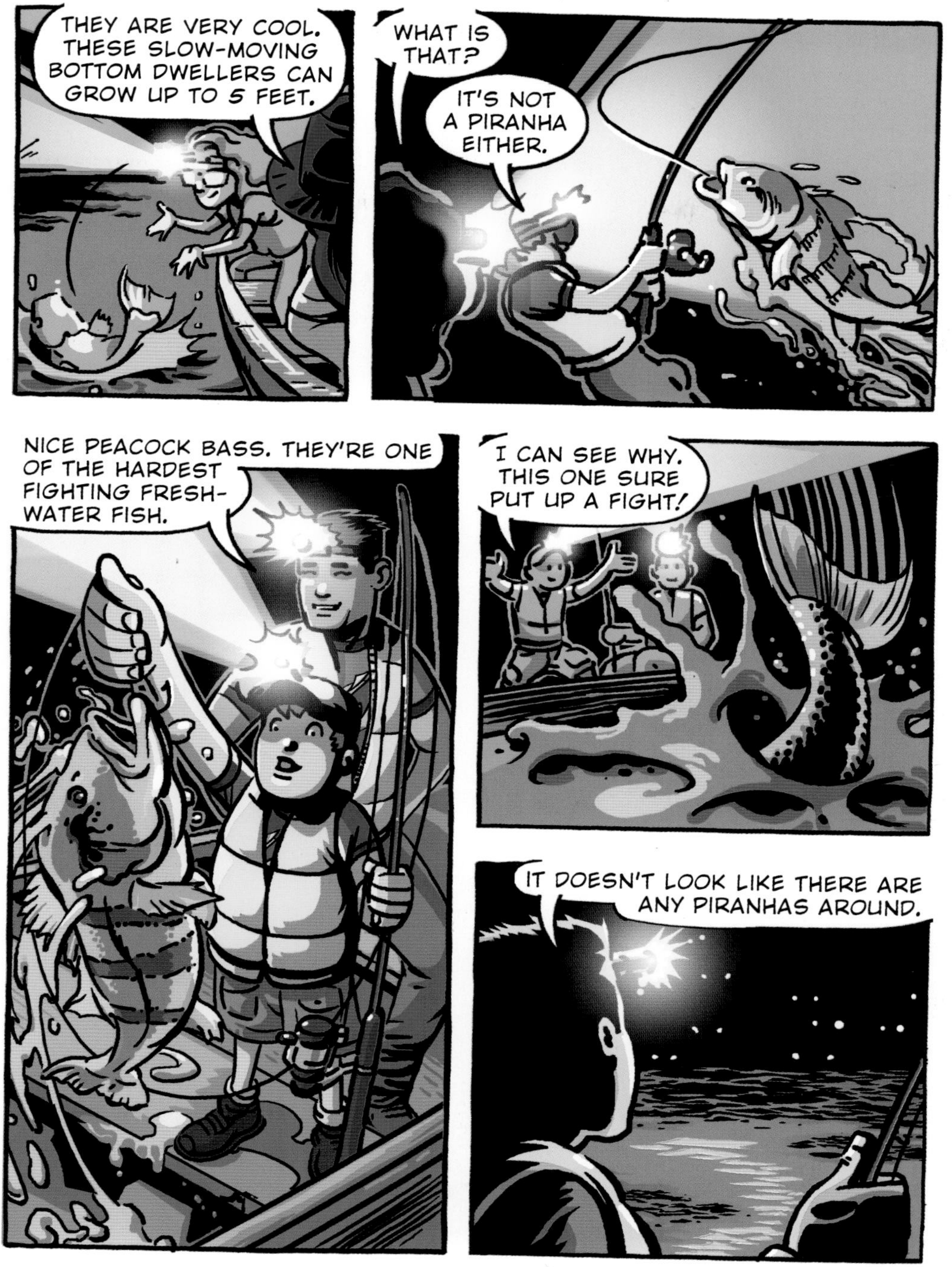
THEY ARE VERY COOL. THESE SLOW-MOVING BOTTOM DWELLERS CAN GROW UP TO 5 FEET.
WHAT IS THAT?
IT'S NOT A PIRANHA EITHER.
NICE PEACOCK BASS. THEY'RE ONE OF THE HARDEST FIGHTING FRESH-WATER FISH.
I CAN SEE WHY. THIS ONE SURE PUT UP A FIGHT!
IT DOESN'T LOOK LIKE THERE ARE ANY PIRANHAS AROUND.

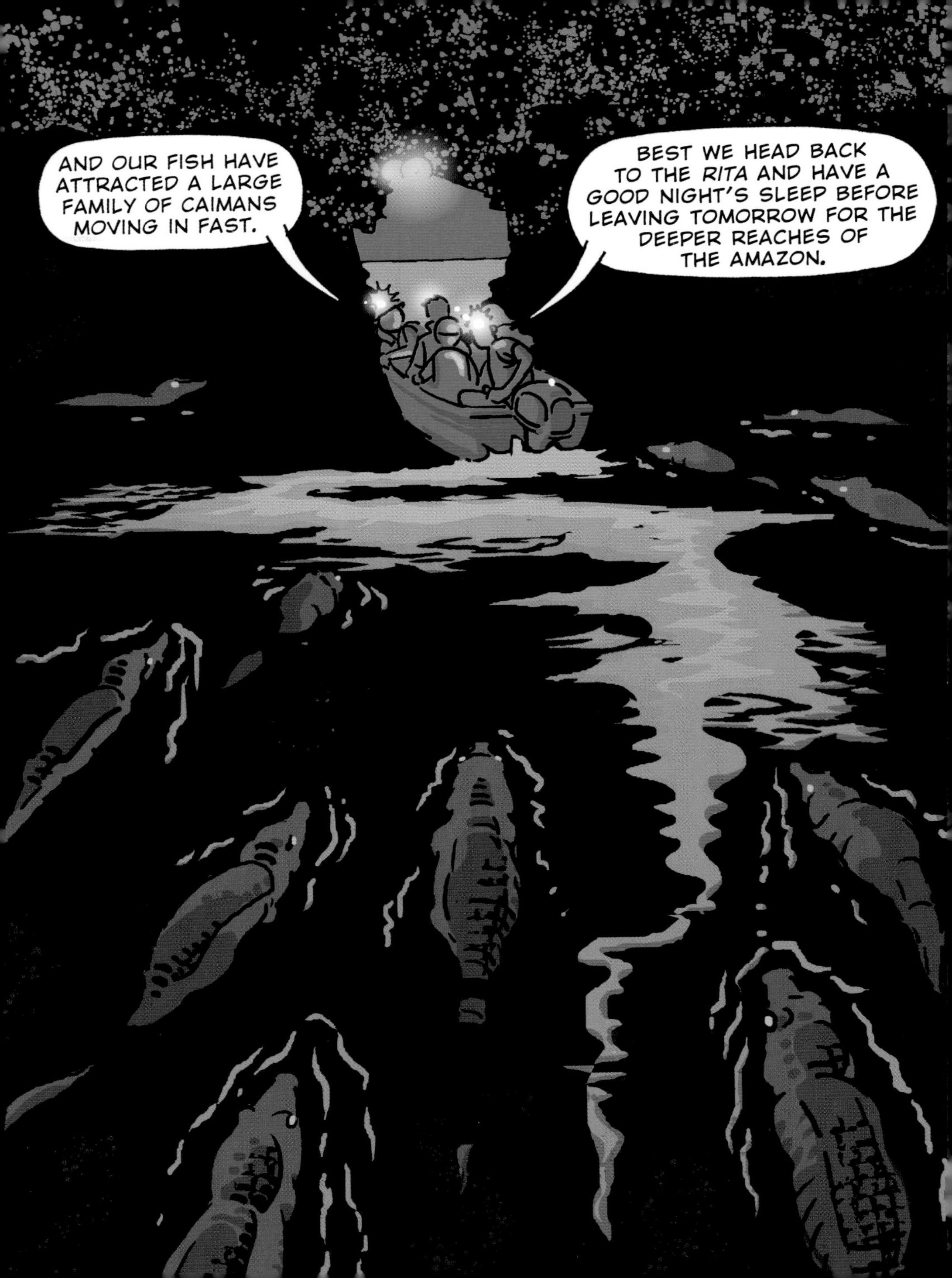
AND OUR FISH HAVE ATTRACTED A LARGE FAMILY OF CAIMANS MOVING IN FAST.
BEST WE HEAD BACK TO THE *RITA* AND HAVE A GOOD NIGHT'S SLEEP BEFORE LEAVING TOMORROW FOR THE DEEPER REACHES OF THE AMAZON.

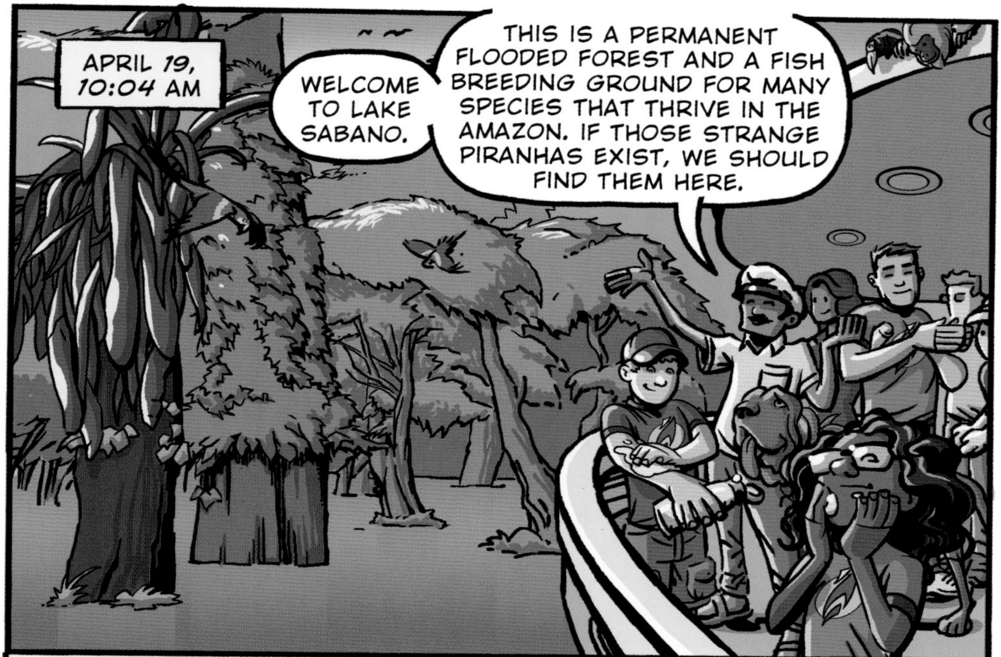
APRIL 19, 10:04 AM
WELCOME TO LAKE SABANO.
THIS IS A PERMANENT FLOODED FOREST AND A FISH BREEDING GROUND FOR MANY SPECIES THAT THRIVE IN THE AMAZON. IF THOSE STRANGE PIRANHAS EXIST, WE SHOULD FIND THEM HERE.

FLOODED FORESTS OCCUR DURING THE "WET" SEASON, WHEN SNOW FROM THE MOUNTAINS MELTS AND MAKES ITS WAY INTO THE RIVER SYSTEM. AS THE EXCESS WATER MOVES DOWNSTREAM IT BEGINS TO FILL THE LOWER ECOSYSTEMS OF THE AMAZON FOREST, EVENTUALLY CAUSING CERTAIN AREAS TO FLOOD.

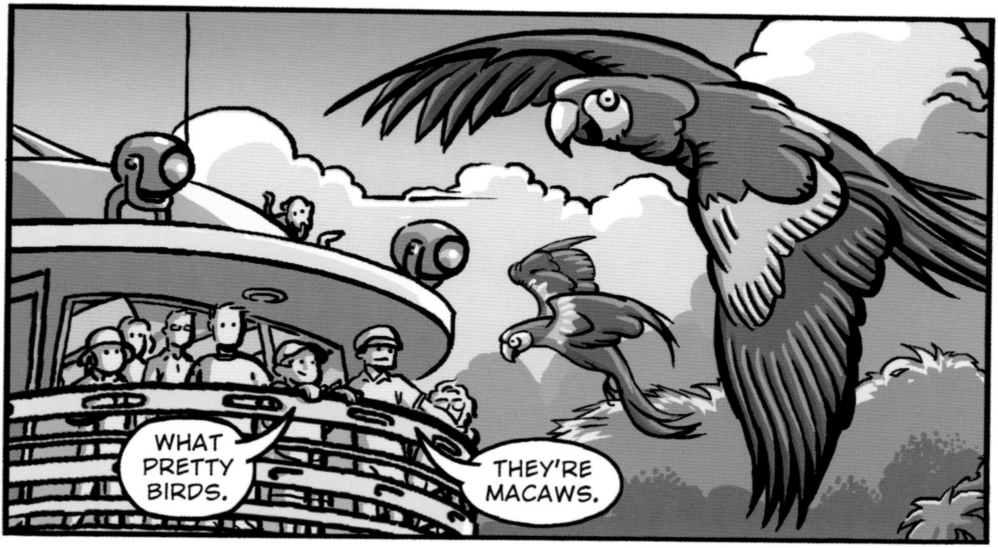
WHAT PRETTY BIRDS.
THEY'RE MACAWS.

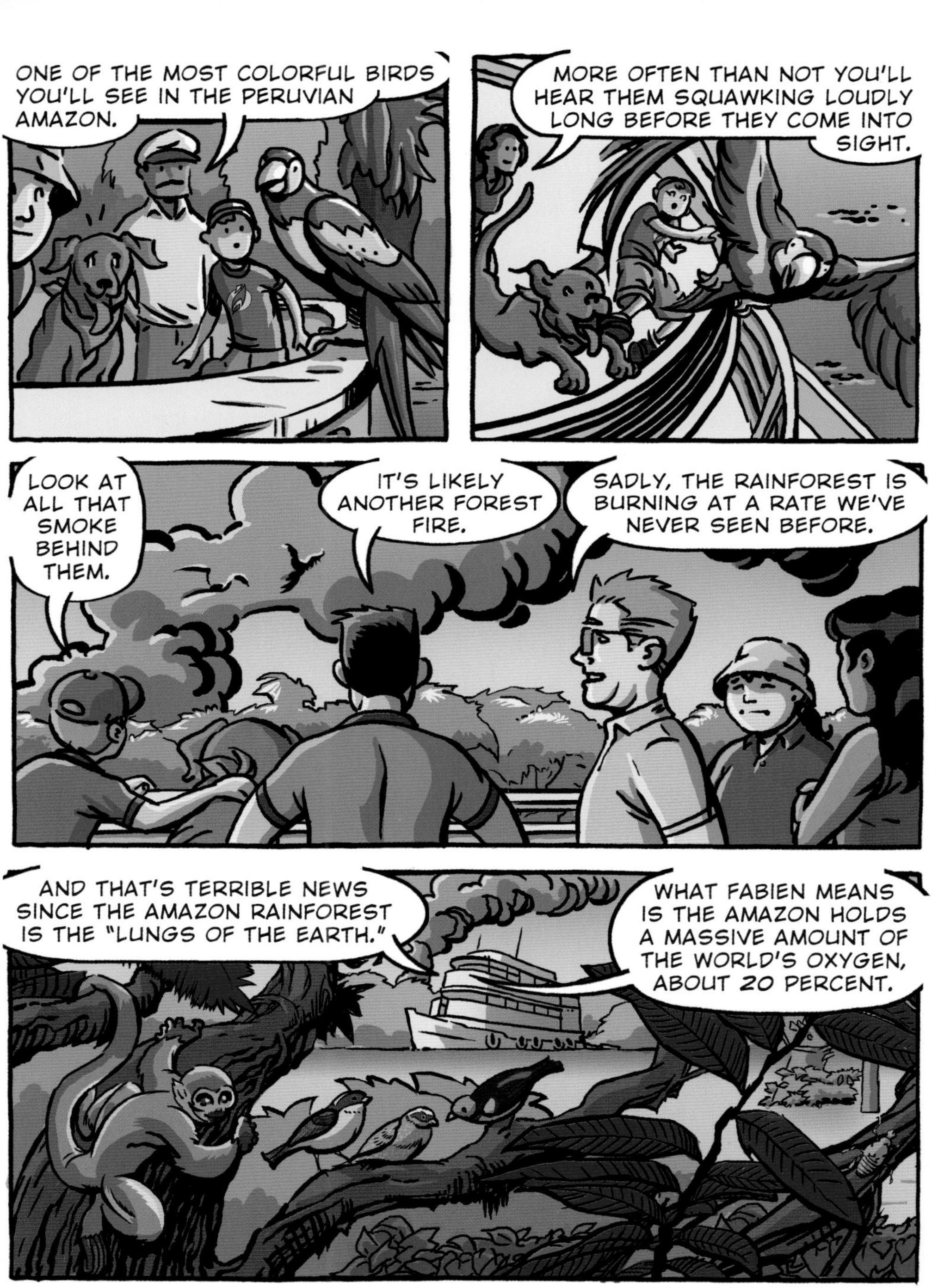

ONE OF THE MOST COLORFUL BIRDS YOU'LL SEE IN THE PERUVIAN AMAZON.
MORE OFTEN THAN NOT YOU'LL HEAR THEM SQUAWKING LOUDLY LONG BEFORE THEY COME INTO SIGHT.
LOOK AT ALL THAT SMOKE BEHIND THEM.
IT'S LIKELY ANOTHER FOREST FIRE.
SADLY, THE RAINFOREST IS BURNING AT A RATE WE'VE NEVER SEEN BEFORE.
AND THAT'S TERRIBLE NEWS SINCE THE AMAZON RAINFOREST IS THE "LUNGS OF THE EARTH."
WHAT FABIEN MEANS IS THE AMAZON HOLDS A MASSIVE AMOUNT OF THE WORLD'S OXYGEN, ABOUT 20 PERCENT.

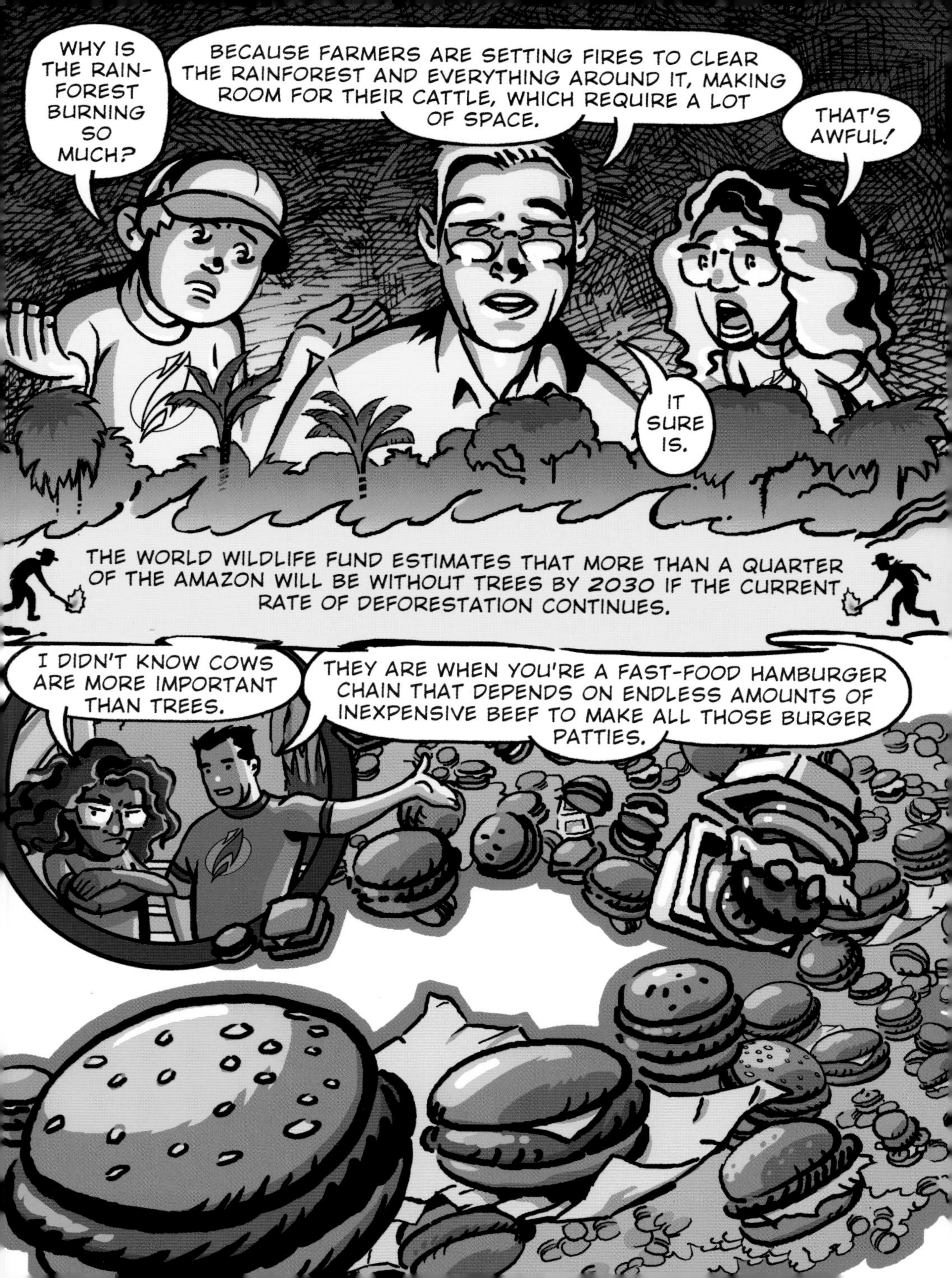
WHY IS THE RAIN-FOREST BURNING SO MUCH?
BECAUSE FARMERS ARE SETTING FIRES TO CLEAR THE RAINFOREST AND EVERYTHING AROUND IT, MAKING ROOM FOR THEIR CATTLE, WHICH REQUIRE A LOT OF SPACE.
THAT'S AWFUL!
IT SURE IS.
THE WORLD WILDLIFE FUND ESTIMATES THAT MORE THAN A QUARTER OF THE AMAZON WILL BE WITHOUT TREES BY 2030 IF THE CURRENT RATE OF DEFORESTATION CONTINUES.
I DIDN'T KNOW COWS ARE MORE IMPORTANT THAN TREES.
THEY ARE WHEN YOU'RE A FAST-FOOD HAMBURGER CHAIN THAT DEPENDS ON ENDLESS AMOUNTS OF INEXPENSIVE BEEF TO MAKE ALL THOSE BURGER PATTIES.

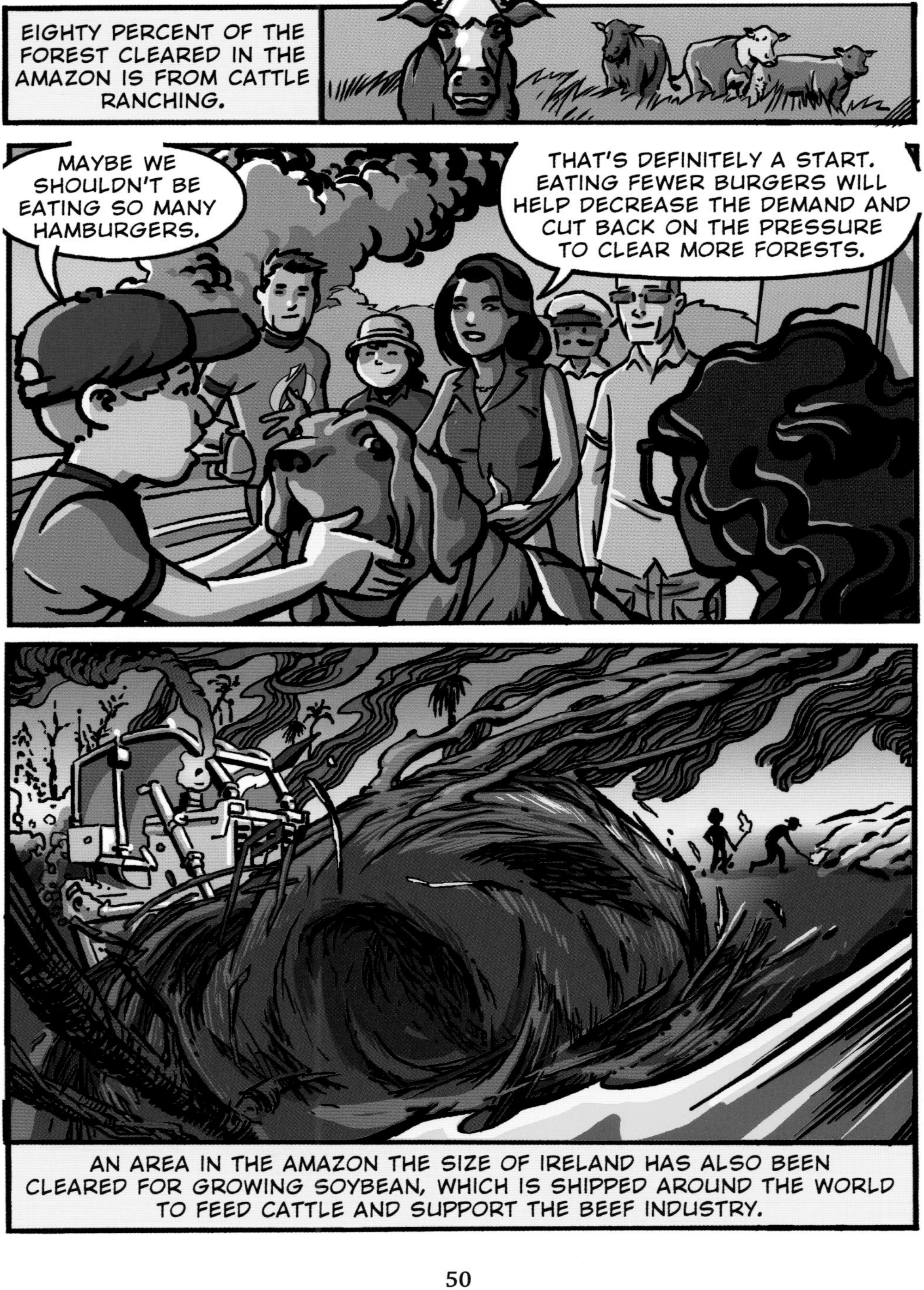
EIGHTY PERCENT OF THE FOREST CLEARED IN THE AMAZON IS FROM CATTLE RANCHING.
MAYBE WE SHOULDN'T BE EATING SO MANY HAMBURGERS.
THAT'S DEFINITELY A START. EATING FEWER BURGERS WILL HELP DECREASE THE DEMAND AND CUT BACK ON THE PRESSURE TO CLEAR MORE FORESTS.
AN AREA IN THE AMAZON THE SIZE OF IRELAND HAS ALSO BEEN CLEARED FOR GROWING SOYBEAN, WHICH IS SHIPPED AROUND THE WORLD TO FEED CATTLE AND SUPPORT THE BEEF INDUSTRY.

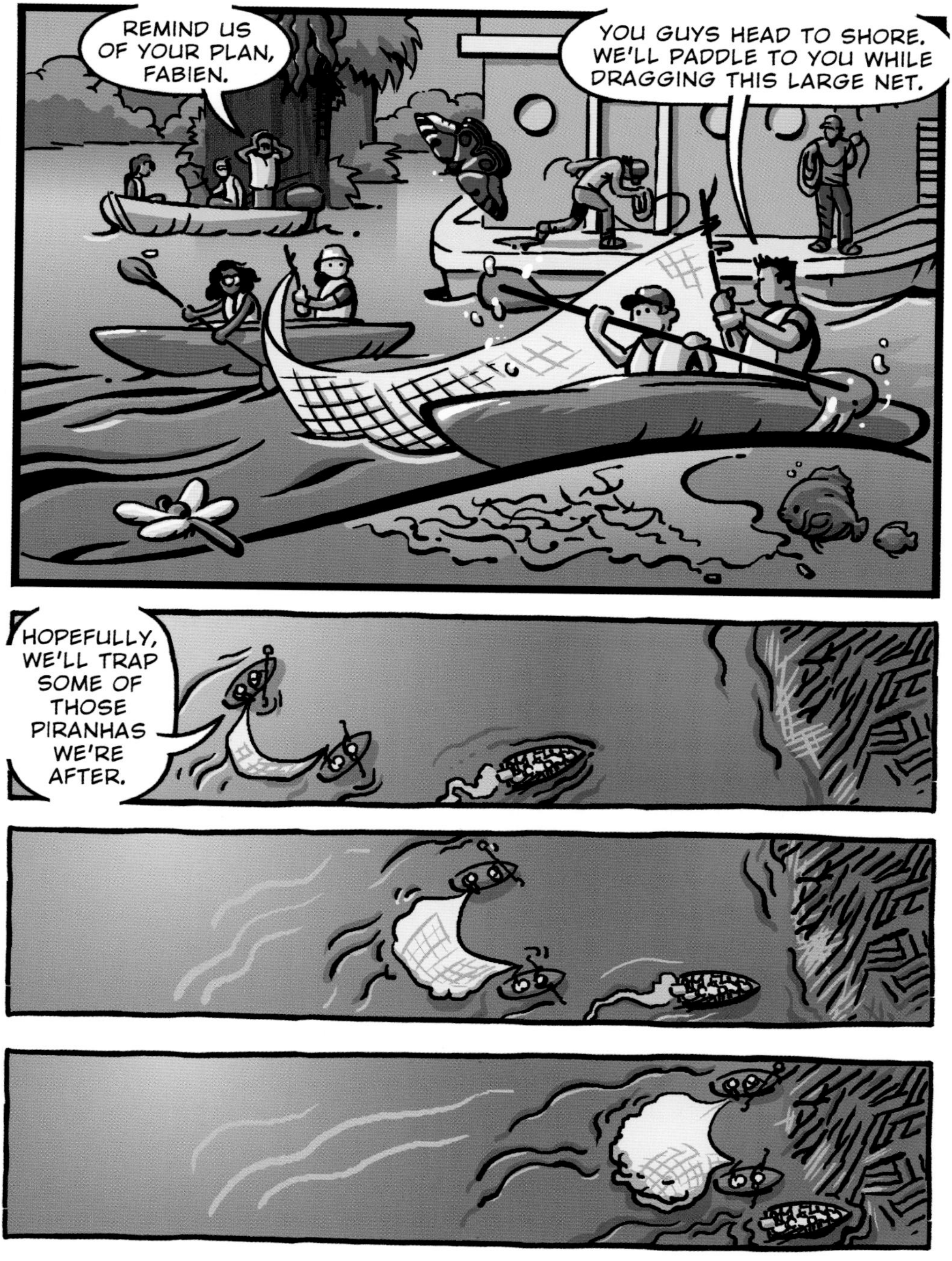
REMIND US OF YOUR PLAN, FABIEN.
YOU GUYS HEAD TO SHORE. WE'LL PADDLE TO YOU WHILE DRAGGING THIS LARGE NET.
HOPEFULLY, WE'LL TRAP SOME OF THOSE PIRANHAS WE'RE AFTER.

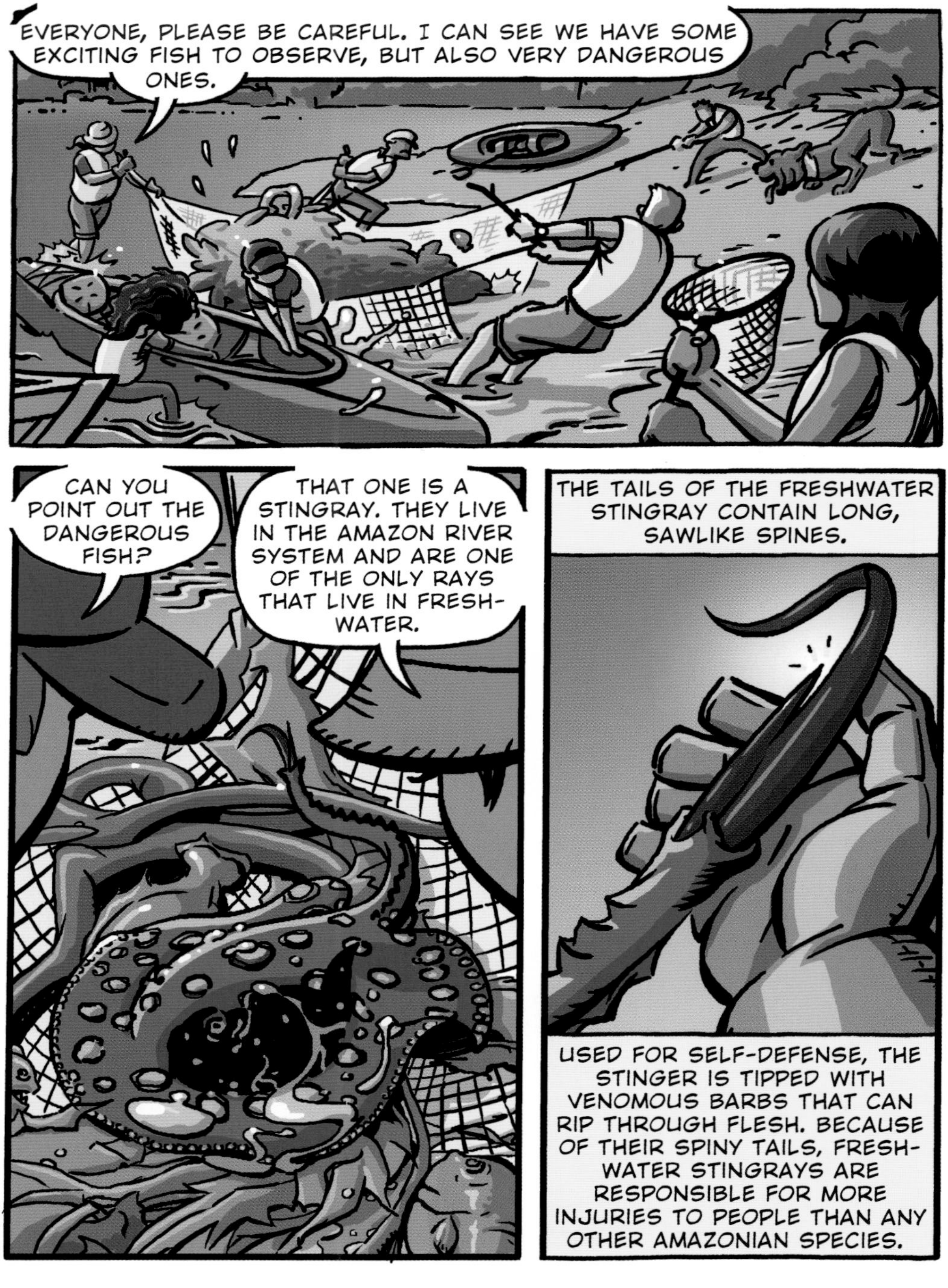
EVERYONE, PLEASE BE CAREFUL. I CAN SEE WE HAVE SOME EXCITING FISH TO OBSERVE, BUT ALSO VERY DANGEROUS ONES.
CAN YOU POINT OUT THE DANGEROUS FISH?
THAT ONE IS A STINGRAY. THEY LIVE IN THE AMAZON RIVER SYSTEM AND ARE ONE OF THE ONLY RAYS THAT LIVE IN FRESH-WATER.
THE TAILS OF THE FRESHWATER STINGRAY CONTAIN LONG, SAWLIKE SPINES.
USED FOR SELF-DEFENSE, THE STINGER IS TIPPED WITH VENOMOUS BARBS THAT CAN RIP THROUGH FLESH. BECAUSE OF THEIR SPINY TAILS, FRESH-WATER STINGRAYS ARE RESPONSIBLE FOR MORE INJURIES TO PEOPLE THAN ANY OTHER AMAZONIAN SPECIES.

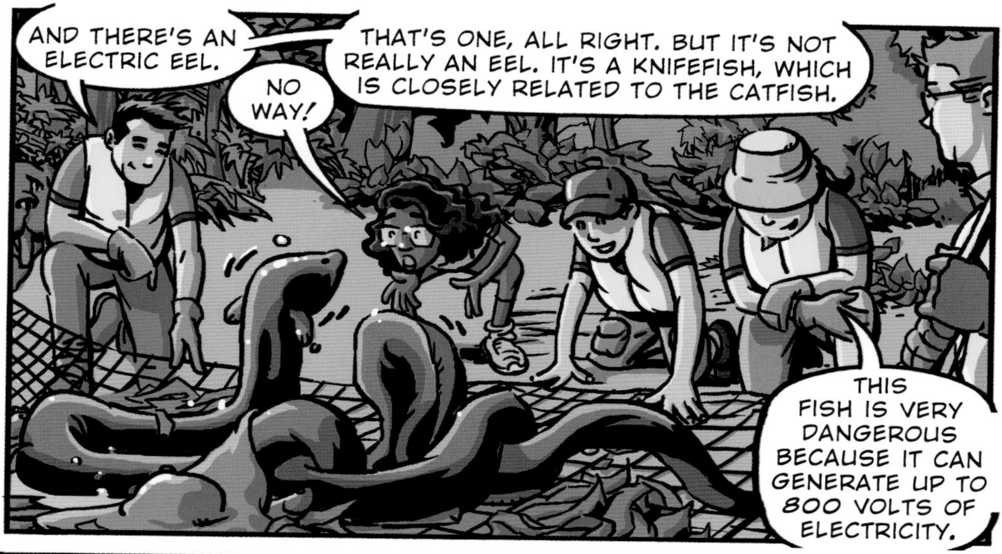
AND THERE'S AN ELECTRIC EEL.
NO WAY!
THAT'S ONE, ALL RIGHT. BUT IT'S NOT REALLY AN EEL. IT'S A KNIFEFISH, WHICH IS CLOSELY RELATED TO THE CATFISH.
THIS FISH IS VERY DANGEROUS BECAUSE IT CAN GENERATE UP TO 800 VOLTS OF ELECTRICITY.

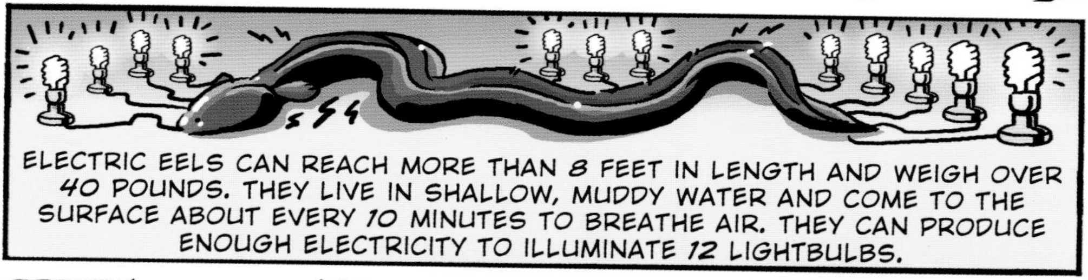
ELECTRIC EELS CAN REACH MORE THAN 8 FEET IN LENGTH AND WEIGH OVER 40 POUNDS. THEY LIVE IN SHALLOW, MUDDY WATER AND COME TO THE SURFACE ABOUT EVERY 10 MINUTES TO BREATHE AIR. THEY CAN PRODUCE ENOUGH ELECTRICITY TO ILLUMINATE 12 LIGHTBULBS.

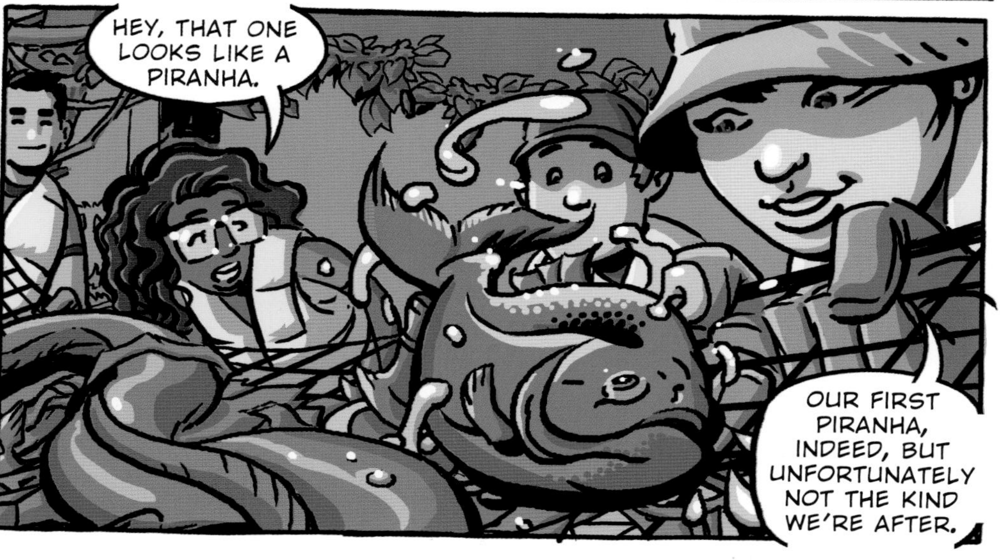
HEY, THAT ONE LOOKS LIKE A PIRANHA.
OUR FIRST PIRANHA, INDEED, BUT UNFORTUNATELY NOT THE KIND WE'RE AFTER.

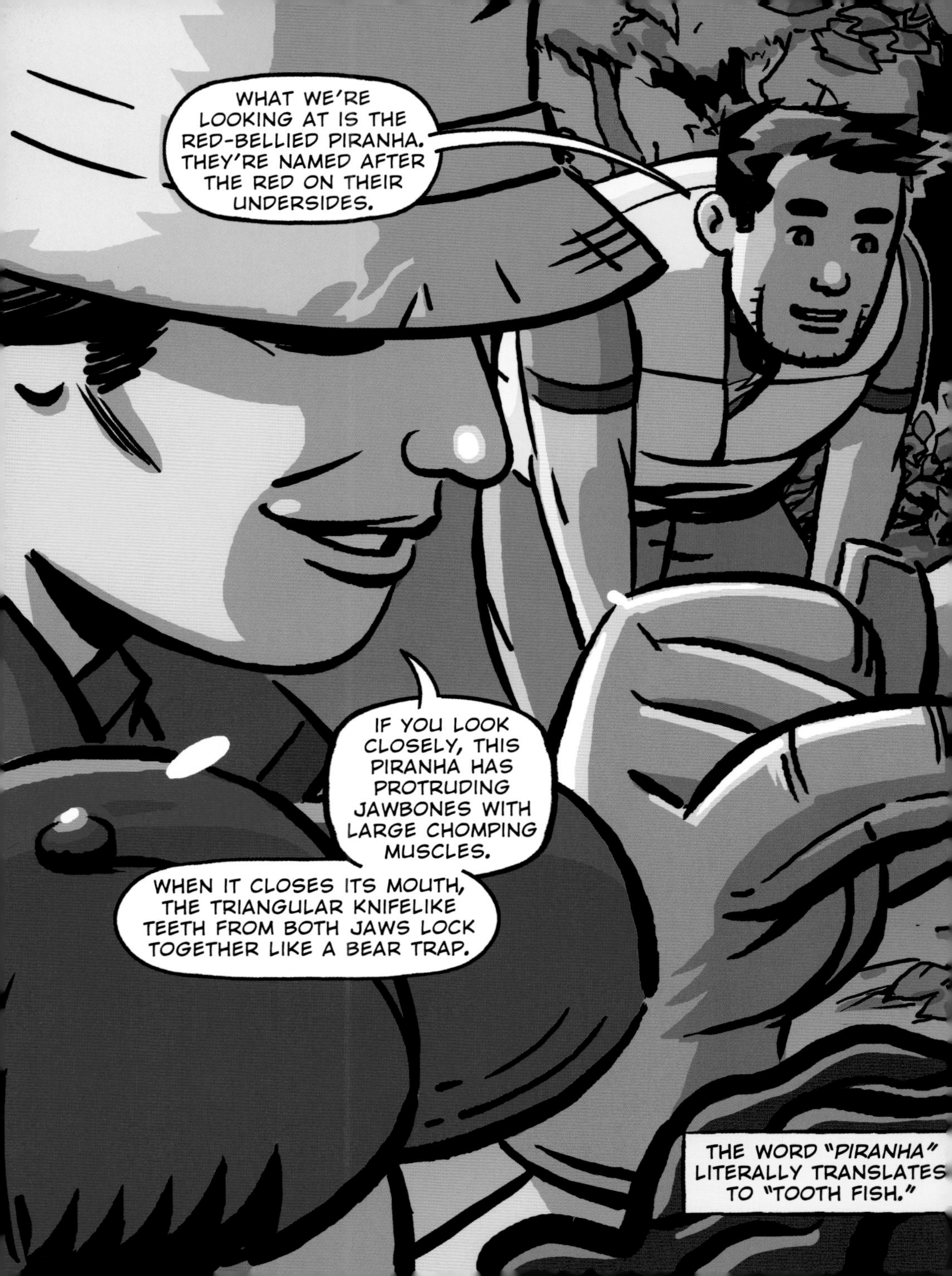
WHAT WE'RE LOOKING AT IS THE RED-BELLIED PIRANHA. THEY'RE NAMED AFTER THE RED ON THEIR UNDERSIDES.
IF YOU LOOK CLOSELY, THIS PIRANHA HAS PROTRUDING JAWBONES WITH LARGE CHOMPING MUSCLES.
WHEN IT CLOSES ITS MOUTH, THE TRIANGULAR KNIFELIKE TEETH FROM BOTH JAWS LOCK TOGETHER LIKE A BEAR TRAP.
THE WORD "*PIRANHA*" LITERALLY TRANSLATES TO "TOOTH FISH."

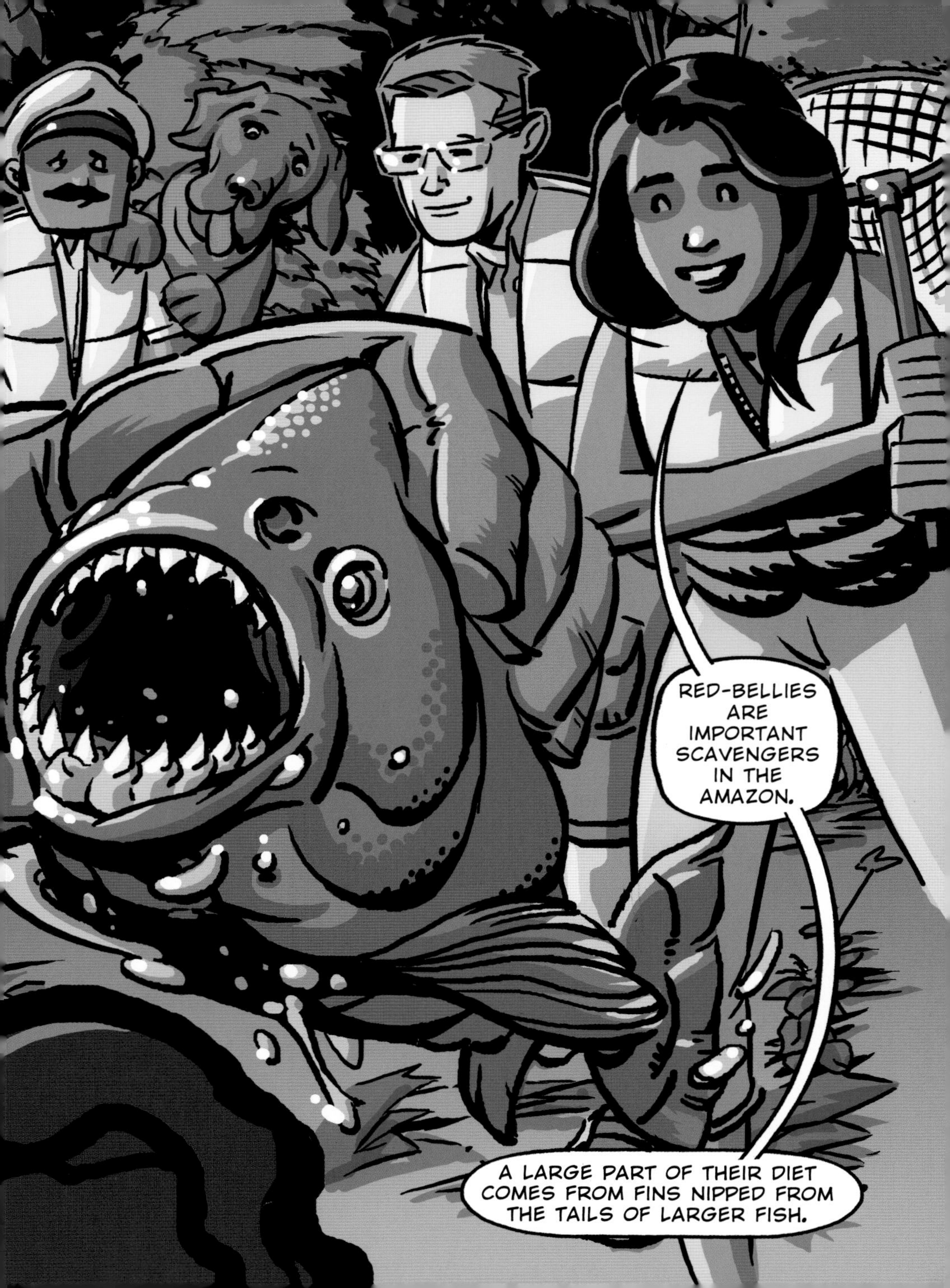
RED-BELLIES ARE IMPORTANT SCAVENGERS IN THE AMAZON.
A LARGE PART OF THEIR DIET COMES FROM FINS NIPPED FROM THE TAILS OF LARGER FISH.

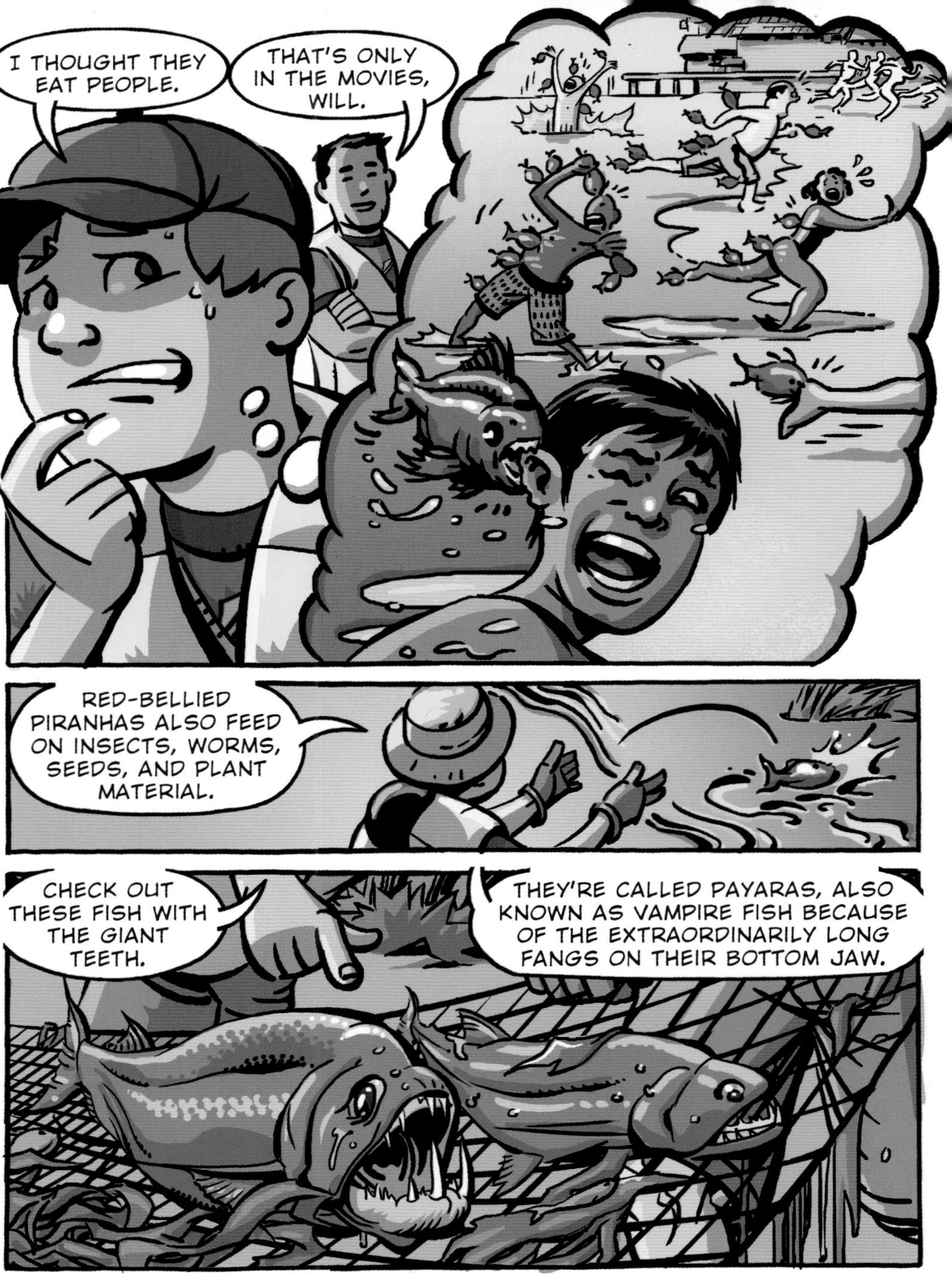
I THOUGHT THEY EAT PEOPLE.
THAT'S ONLY IN THE MOVIES, WILL.
RED-BELLIED PIRANHAS ALSO FEED ON INSECTS, WORMS, SEEDS, AND PLANT MATERIAL.
CHECK OUT THESE FISH WITH THE GIANT TEETH.
THEY'RE CALLED PAYARAS, ALSO KNOWN AS VAMPIRE FISH BECAUSE OF THE EXTRAORDINARILY LONG FANGS ON THEIR BOTTOM JAW.

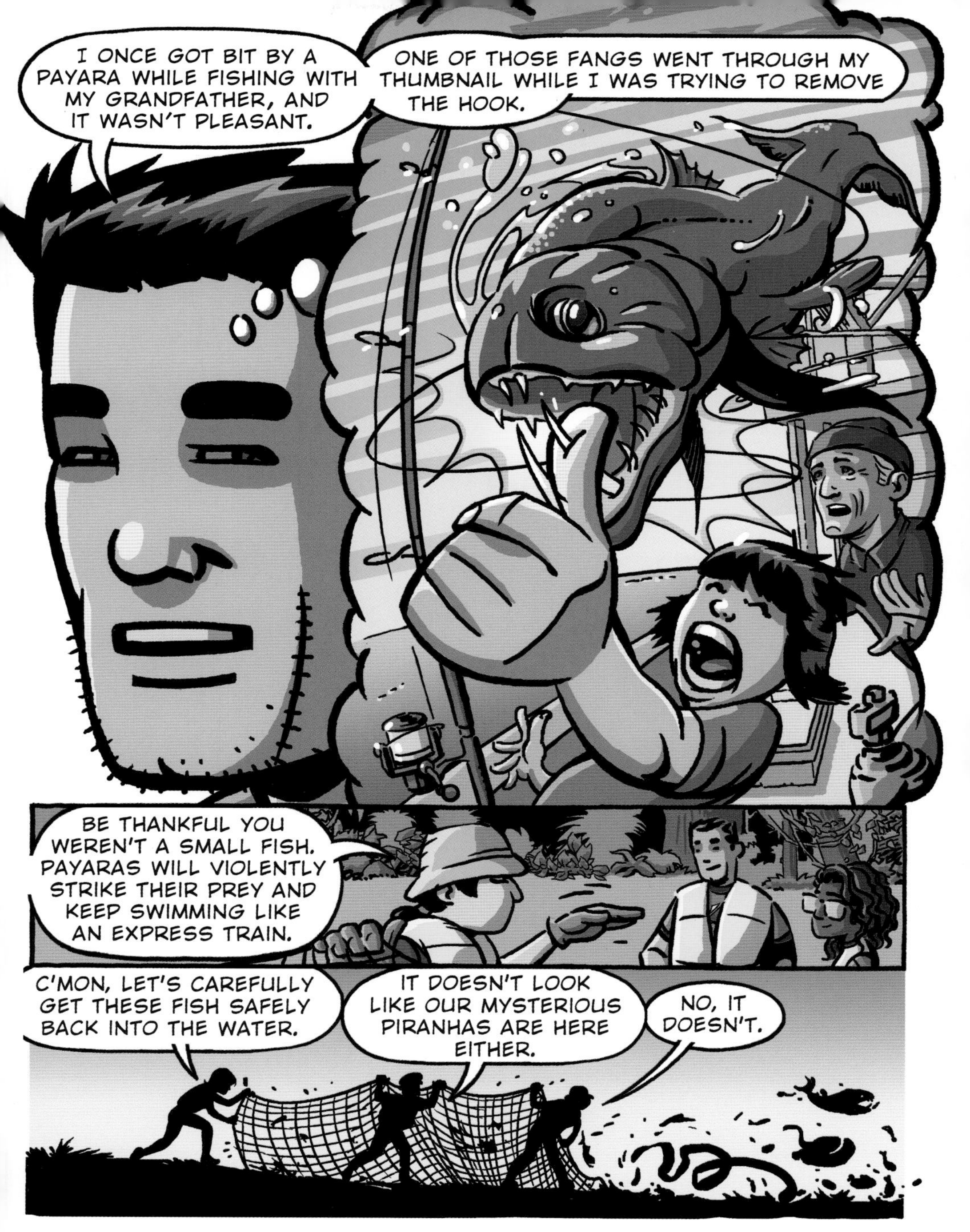
I ONCE GOT BIT BY A PAYARA WHILE FISHING WITH MY GRANDFATHER, AND IT WASN'T PLEASANT.
ONE OF THOSE FANGS WENT THROUGH MY THUMBNAIL WHILE I WAS TRYING TO REMOVE THE HOOK.
BE THANKFUL YOU WEREN'T A SMALL FISH. PAYARAS WILL VIOLENTLY STRIKE THEIR PREY AND KEEP SWIMMING LIKE AN EXPRESS TRAIN.
C'MON, LET'S CAREFULLY GET THESE FISH SAFELY BACK INTO THE WATER.
IT DOESN'T LOOK LIKE OUR MYSTERIOUS PIRANHAS ARE HERE EITHER.
NO, IT DOESN'T.

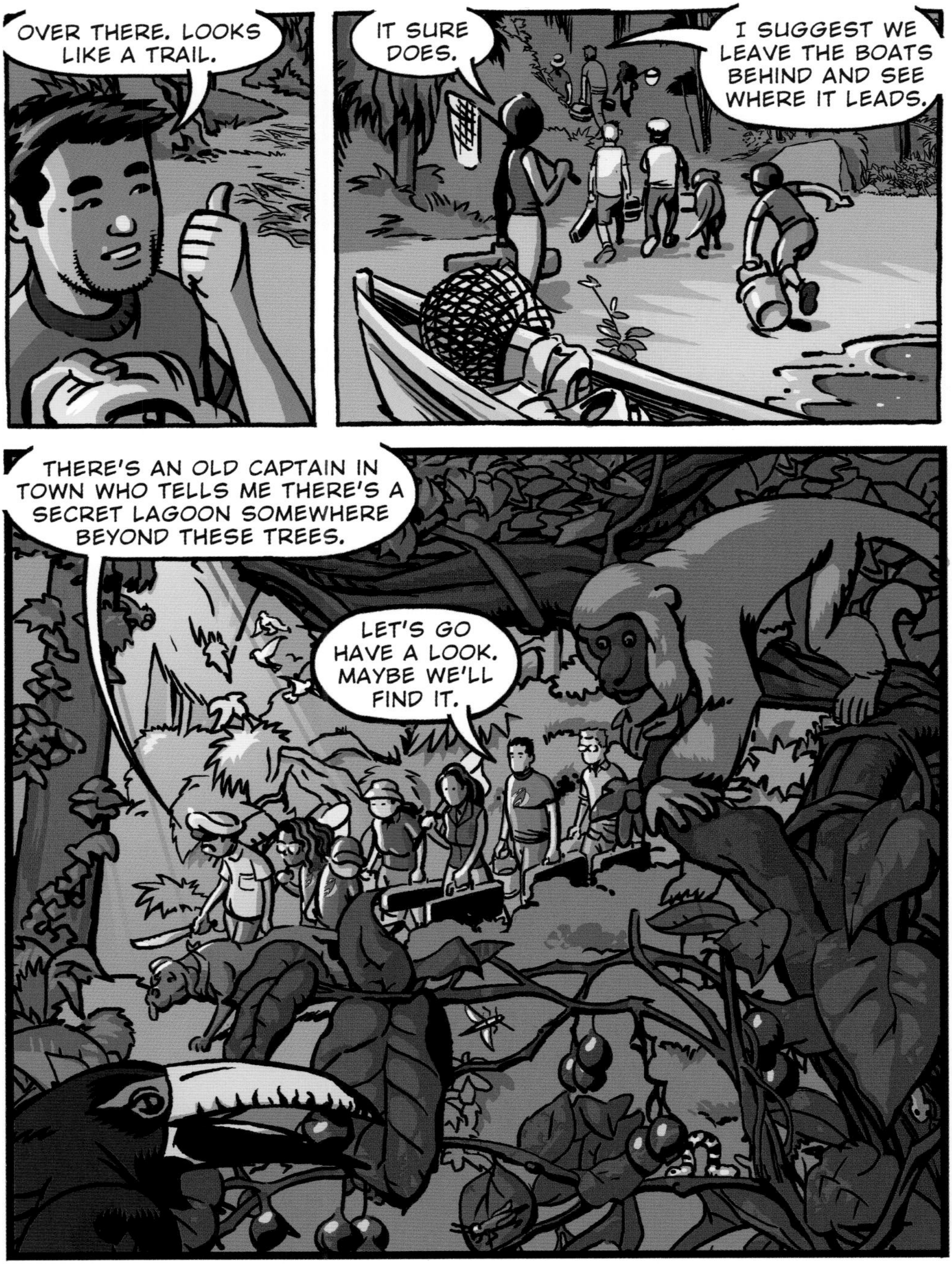
OVER THERE. LOOKS LIKE A TRAIL.
IT SURE DOES.
I SUGGEST WE LEAVE THE BOATS BEHIND AND SEE WHERE IT LEADS.
THERE'S AN OLD CAPTAIN IN TOWN WHO TELLS ME THERE'S A SECRET LAGOON SOMEWHERE BEYOND THESE TREES.
LET'S GO HAVE A LOOK. MAYBE WE'LL FIND IT.

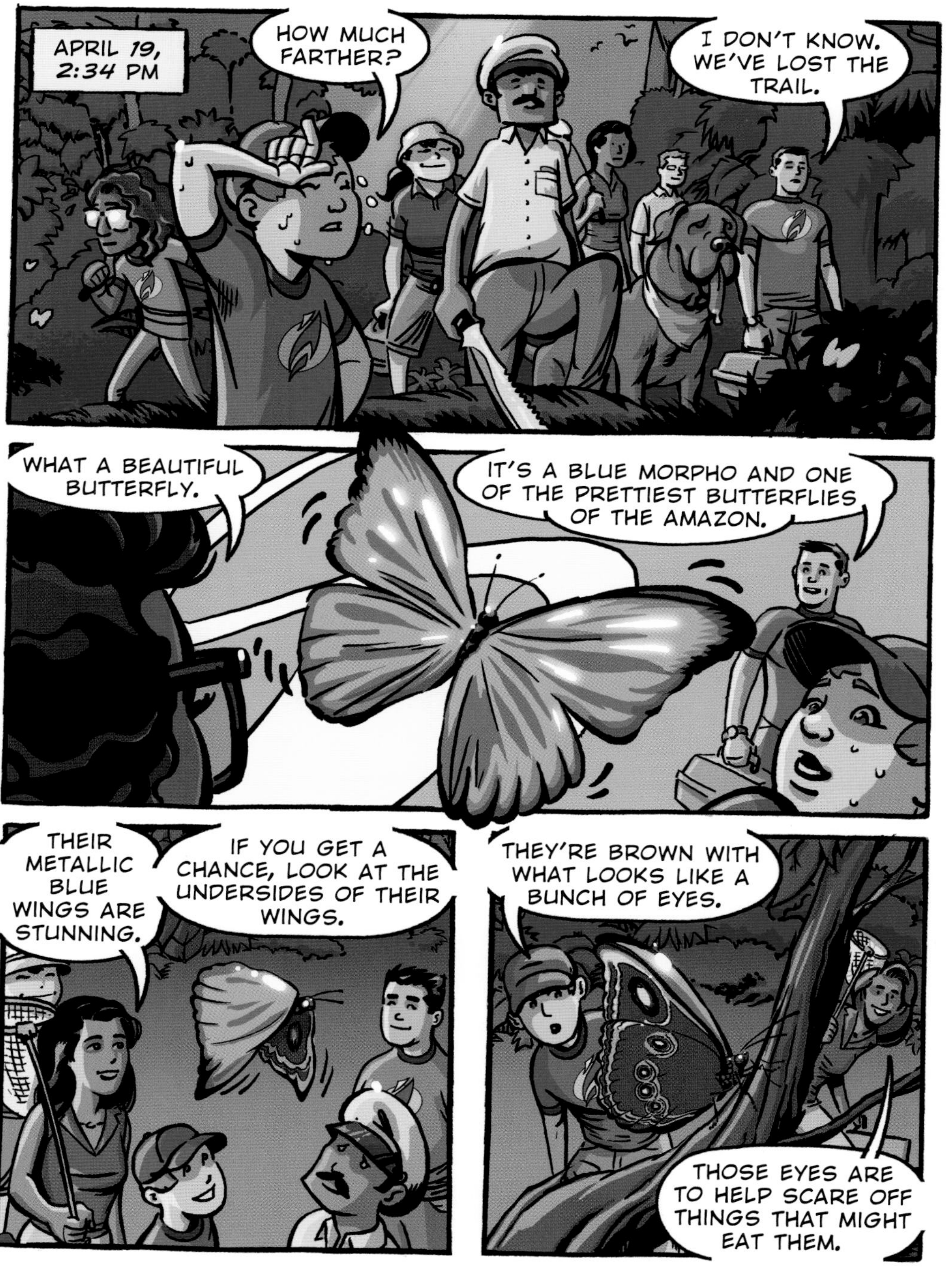
APRIL 19, 2:34 PM
HOW MUCH FARTHER?
I DON'T KNOW. WE'VE LOST THE TRAIL.
WHAT A BEAUTIFUL BUTTERFLY.
IT'S A BLUE MORPHO AND ONE OF THE PRETTIEST BUTTERFLIES OF THE AMAZON.
THEIR METALLIC BLUE WINGS ARE STUNNING.
IF YOU GET A CHANCE, LOOK AT THE UNDERSIDES OF THEIR WINGS.
THEY'RE BROWN WITH WHAT LOOKS LIKE A BUNCH OF EYES.
THOSE EYES ARE TO HELP SCARE OFF THINGS THAT MIGHT EAT THEM.

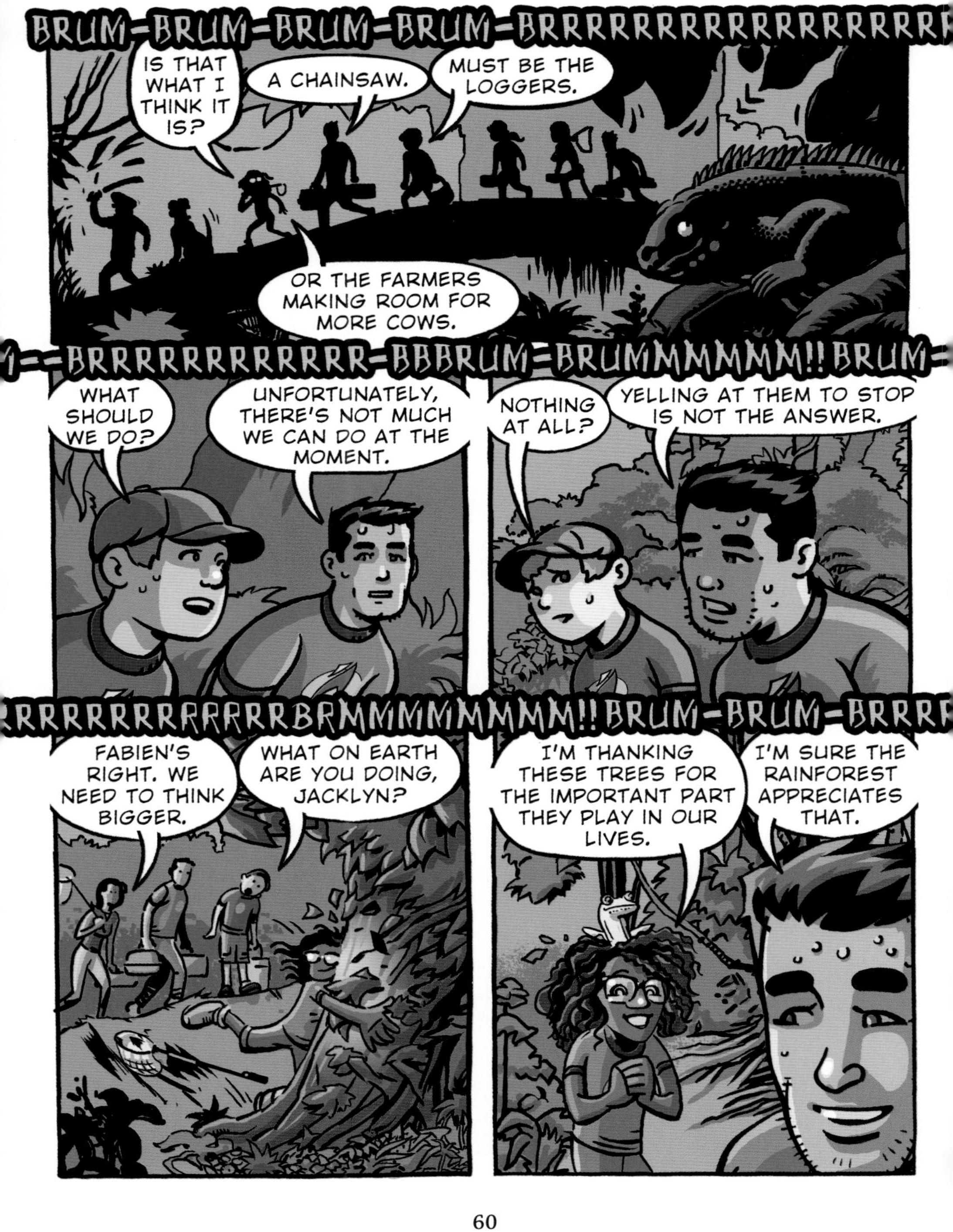
BRUM-BRUM-BRUM-BRUM-BRRRRRRRRRRRRRRRRRRRRR
IS THAT WHAT I THINK IT IS?
A CHAINSAW.
MUST BE THE LOGGERS.
OR THE FARMERS MAKING ROOM FOR MORE COWS.
BRRRRRRRRRRRRRR-BBBRUM-BRUMMMMMM!! BRUM
WHAT SHOULD WE DO?
UNFORTUNATELY, THERE'S NOT MUCH WE CAN DO AT THE MOMENT.
NOTHING AT ALL?
YELLING AT THEM TO STOP IS NOT THE ANSWER.
RRRRRRRRRRRRRBRMMMMMMMMMM!! BRUM-BRUM-BRRRR
FABIEN'S RIGHT. WE NEED TO THINK BIGGER.
WHAT ON EARTH ARE YOU DOING, JACKLYN?
I'M THANKING THESE TREES FOR THE IMPORTANT PART THEY PLAY IN OUR LIVES.
I'M SURE THE RAINFOREST APPRECIATES THAT.

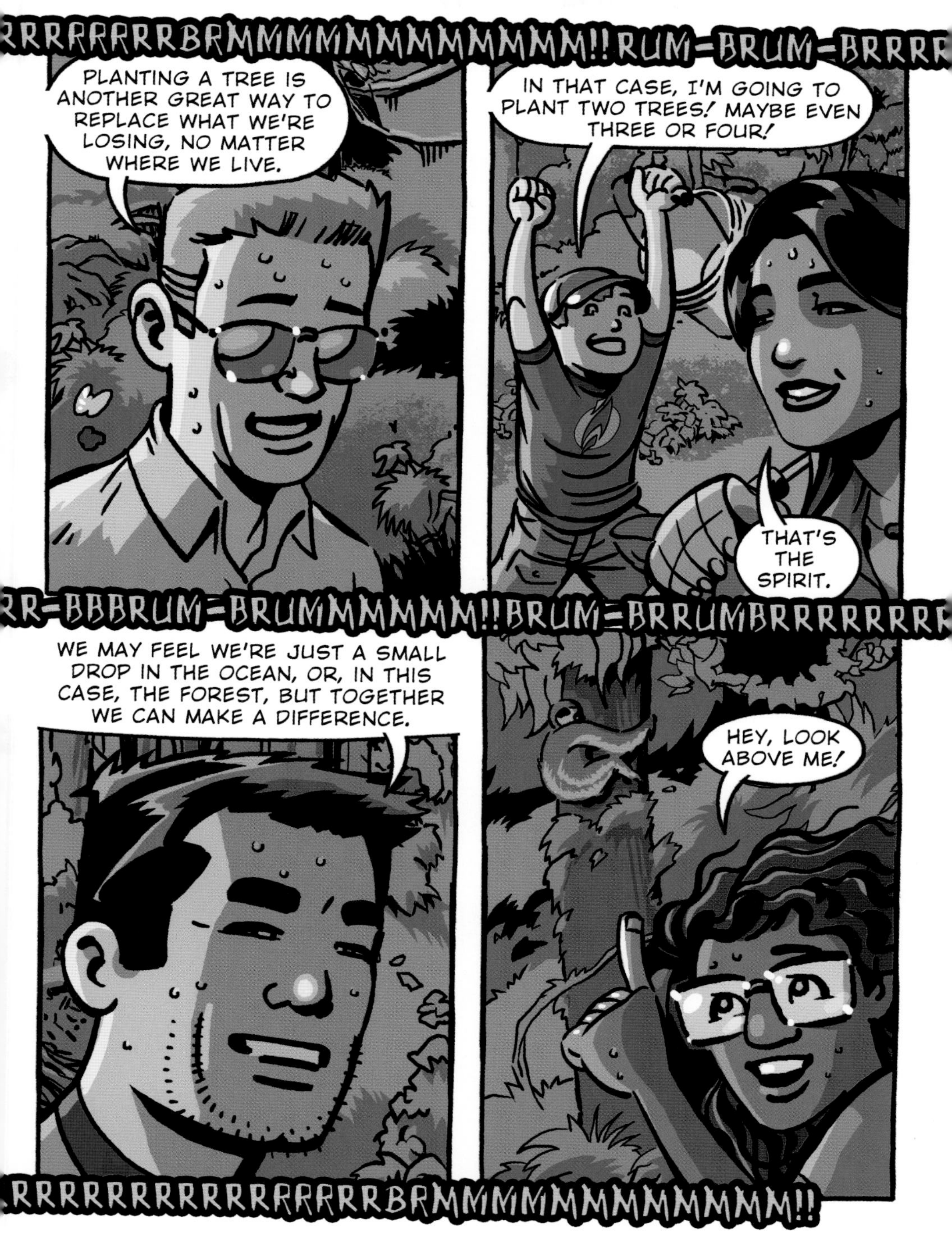
RRRRRRRRBRMMMMMMMMMMMMM!! RUM-BRUM-BRRRR
PLANTING A TREE IS ANOTHER GREAT WAY TO REPLACE WHAT WE'RE LOSING, NO MATTER WHERE WE LIVE.
IN THAT CASE, I'M GOING TO PLANT TWO TREES! MAYBE EVEN THREE OR FOUR!
THAT'S THE SPIRIT.
RR-BBBRUM-BRUMMMMMMM!! BRUM-BRRUMBRRRRRRRR
WE MAY FEEL WE'RE JUST A SMALL DROP IN THE OCEAN, OR, IN THIS CASE, THE FOREST, BUT TOGETHER WE CAN MAKE A DIFFERENCE.
HEY, LOOK ABOVE ME!
RRRRRRRRRRRRRRRRRRRBRMMMMMMMMMMMMMMM!!

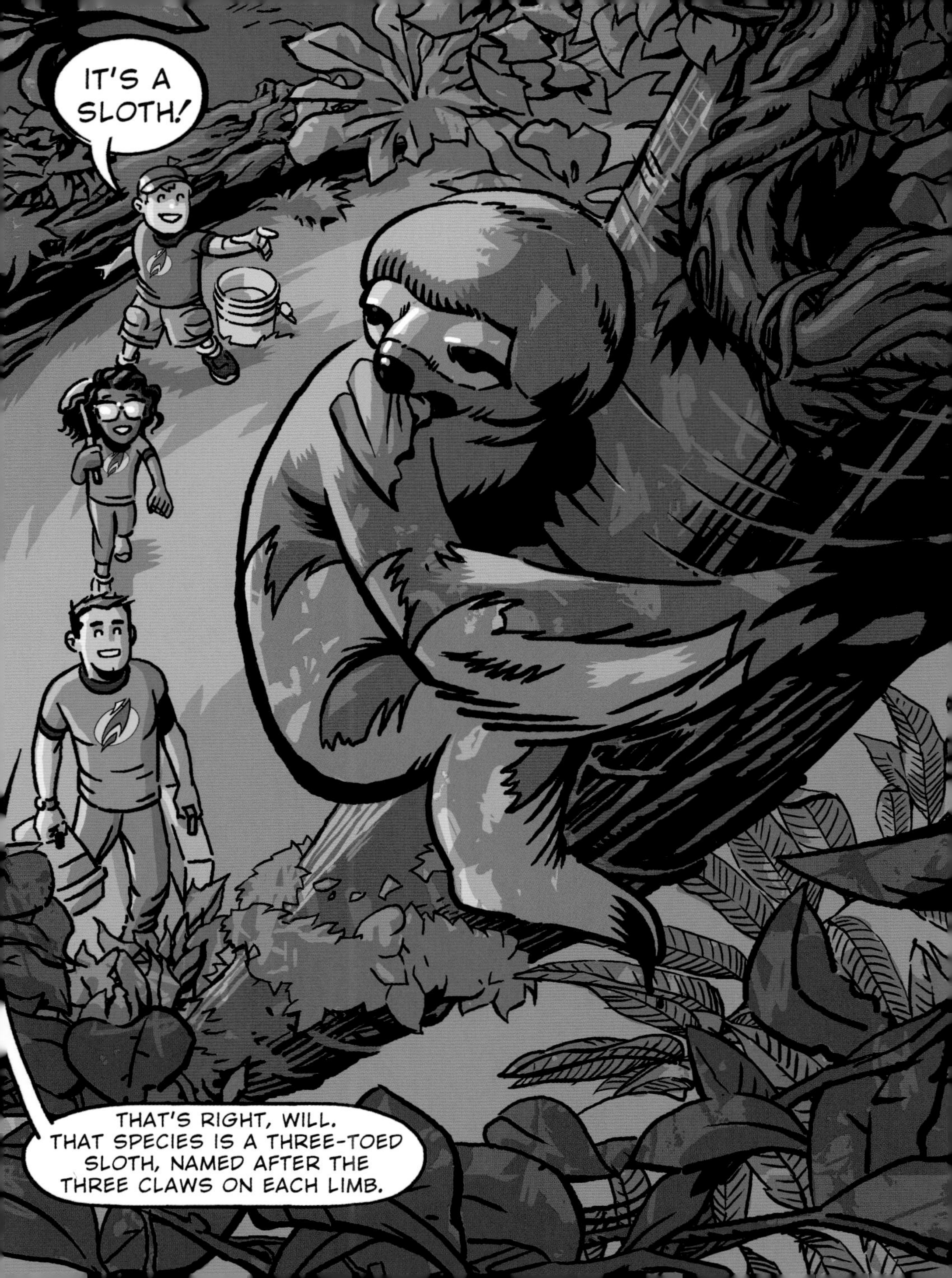
IT'S A SLOTH!
THAT'S RIGHT, WILL. THAT SPECIES IS A THREE-TOED SLOTH, NAMED AFTER THE THREE CLAWS ON EACH LIMB.

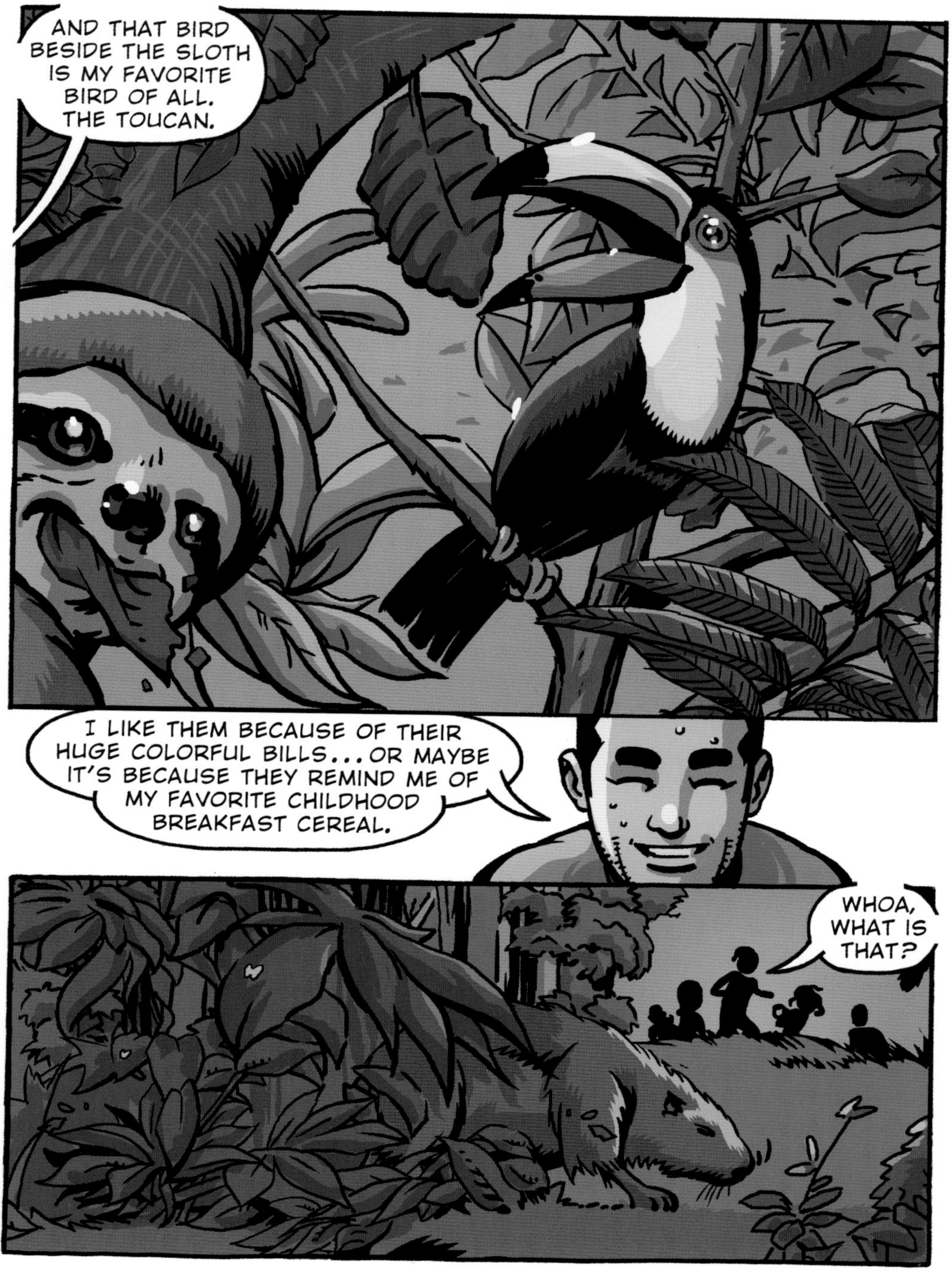
AND THAT BIRD BESIDE THE SLOTH IS MY FAVORITE BIRD OF ALL. THE TOUCAN.
I LIKE THEM BECAUSE OF THEIR HUGE COLORFUL BILLS...OR MAYBE IT'S BECAUSE THEY REMIND ME OF MY FAVORITE CHILDHOOD BREAKFAST CEREAL.
WHOA, WHAT IS THAT?

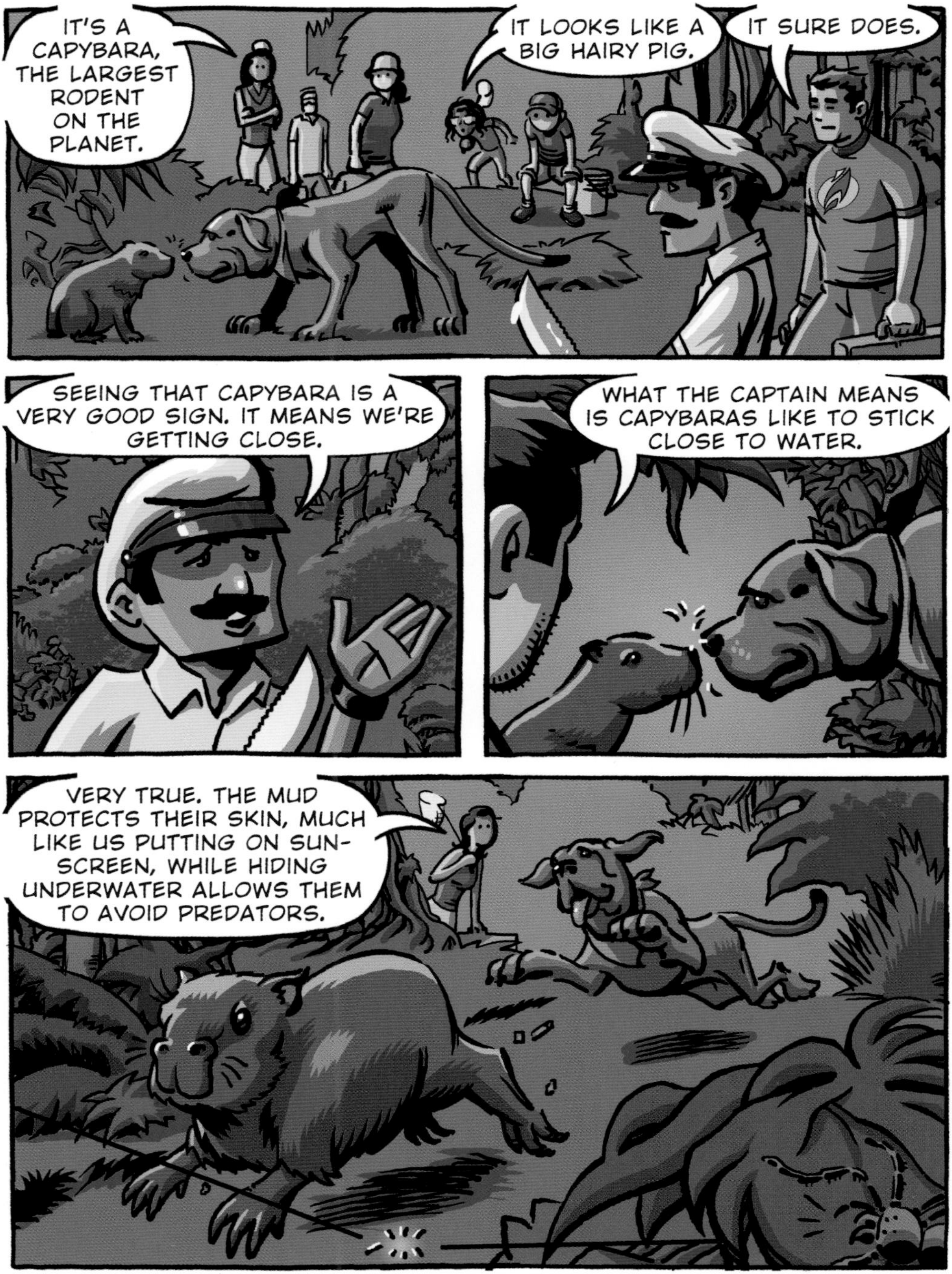
IT'S A CAPYBARA, THE LARGEST RODENT ON THE PLANET.
IT LOOKS LIKE A BIG HAIRY PIG.
IT SURE DOES.
SEEING THAT CAPYBARA IS A VERY GOOD SIGN. IT MEANS WE'RE GETTING CLOSE.
WHAT THE CAPTAIN MEANS IS CAPYBARAS LIKE TO STICK CLOSE TO WATER.
VERY TRUE. THE MUD PROTECTS THEIR SKIN, MUCH LIKE US PUTTING ON SUN-SCREEN, WHILE HIDING UNDERWATER ALLOWS THEM TO AVOID PREDATORS.

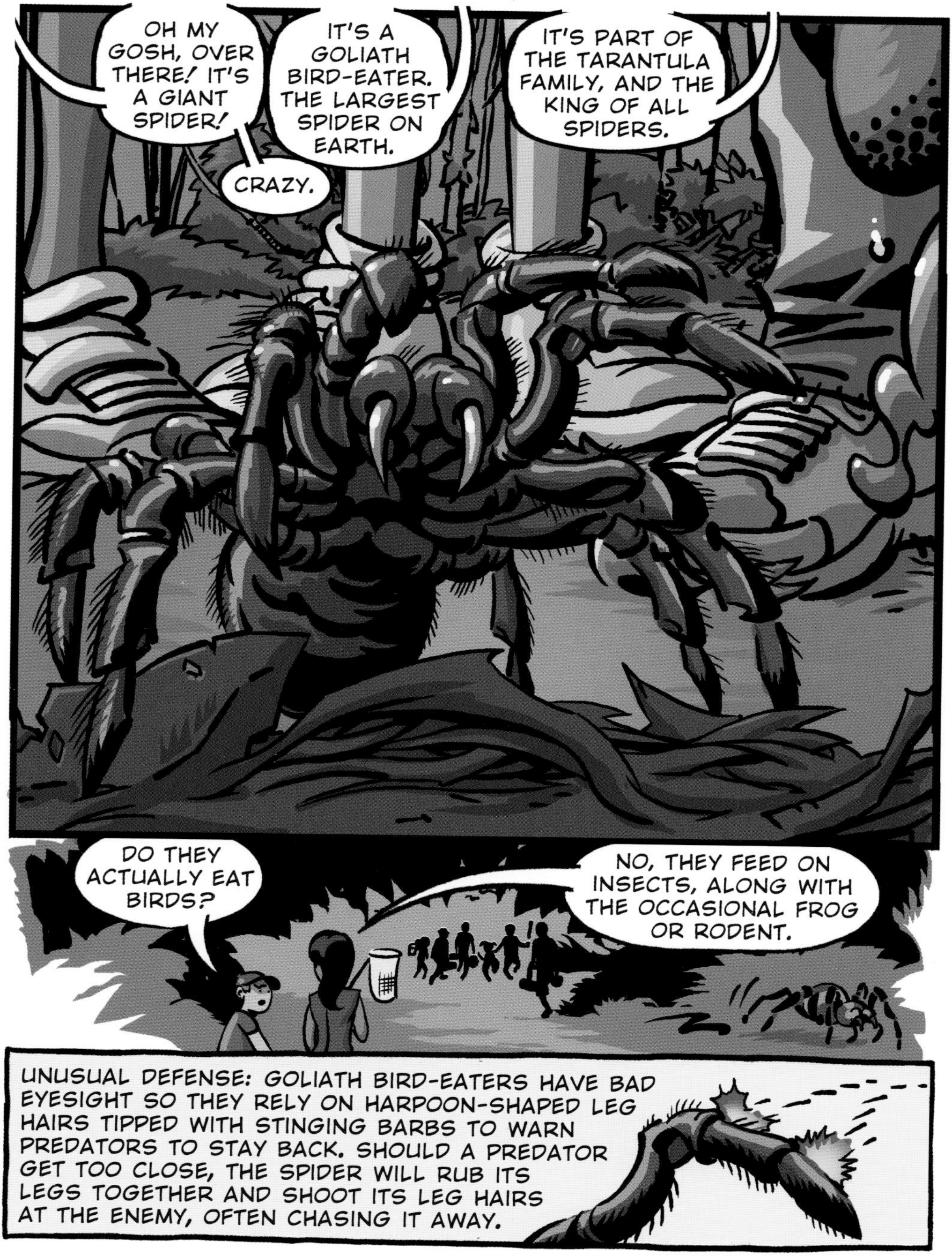
OH MY GOSH, OVER THERE! IT'S A GIANT SPIDER!
IT'S A GOLIATH BIRD-EATER. THE LARGEST SPIDER ON EARTH.
CRAZY.
IT'S PART OF THE TARANTULA FAMILY, AND THE KING OF ALL SPIDERS.
DO THEY ACTUALLY EAT BIRDS?
NO, THEY FEED ON INSECTS, ALONG WITH THE OCCASIONAL FROG OR RODENT.
UNUSUAL DEFENSE: GOLIATH BIRD-EATERS HAVE BAD EYESIGHT SO THEY RELY ON HARPOON-SHAPED LEG HAIRS TIPPED WITH STINGING BARBS TO WARN PREDATORS TO STAY BACK. SHOULD A PREDATOR GET TOO CLOSE, THE SPIDER WILL RUB ITS LEGS TOGETHER AND SHOOT ITS LEG HAIRS AT THE ENEMY, OFTEN CHASING IT AWAY.

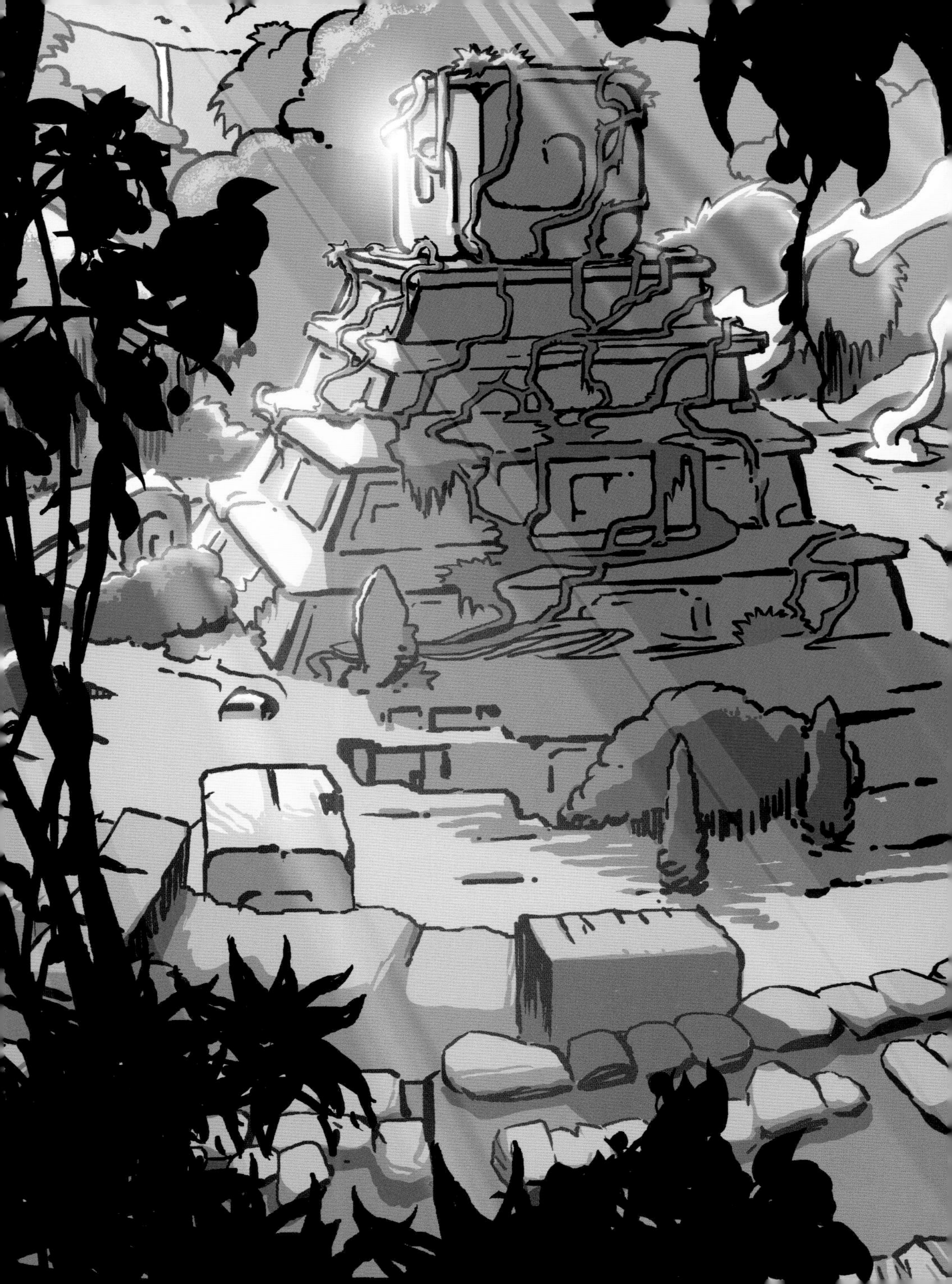

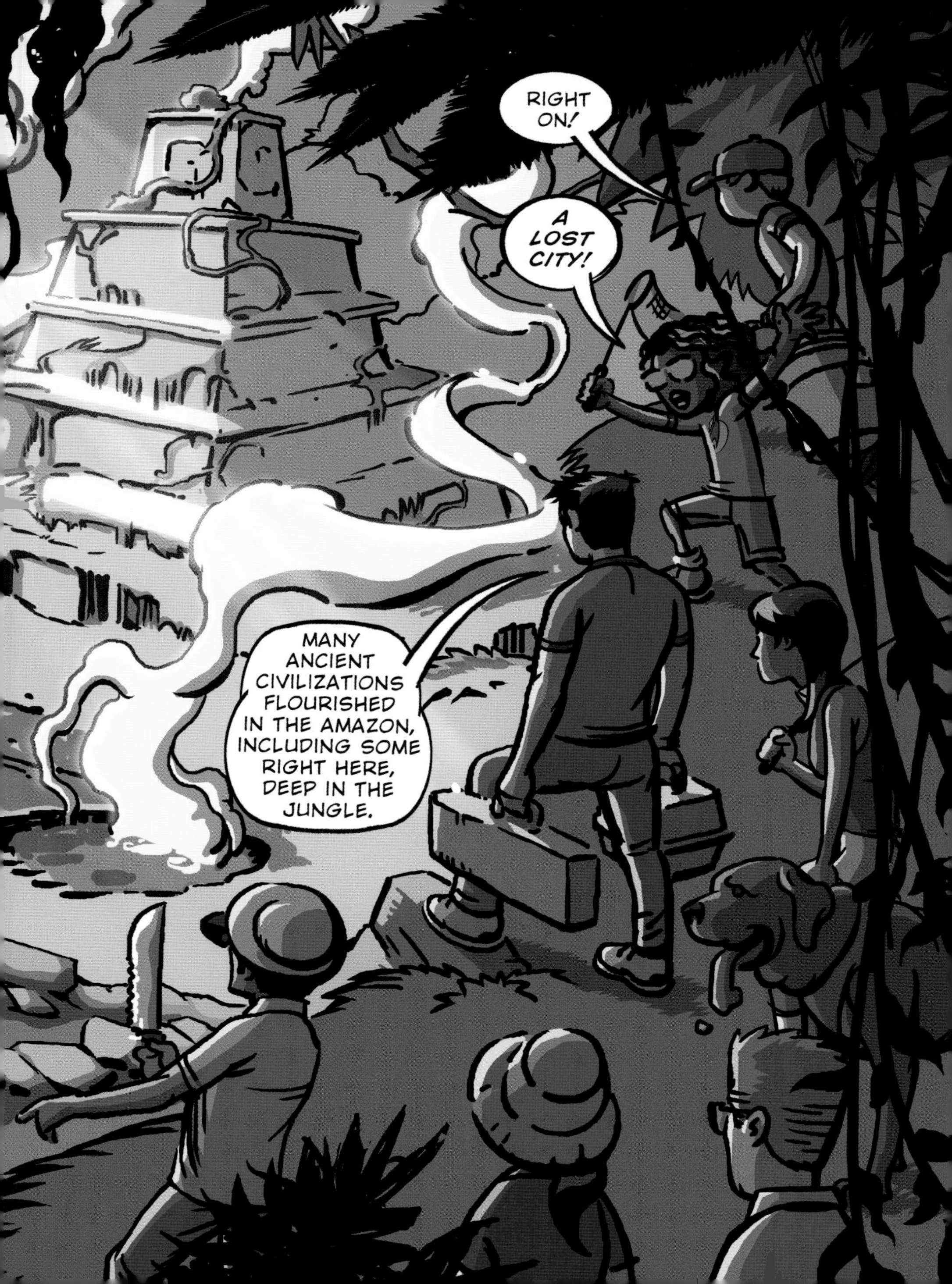
RIGHT ON!
A LOST CITY!
MANY ANCIENT CIVILIZATIONS FLOURISHED IN THE AMAZON, INCLUDING SOME RIGHT HERE, DEEP IN THE JUNGLE.

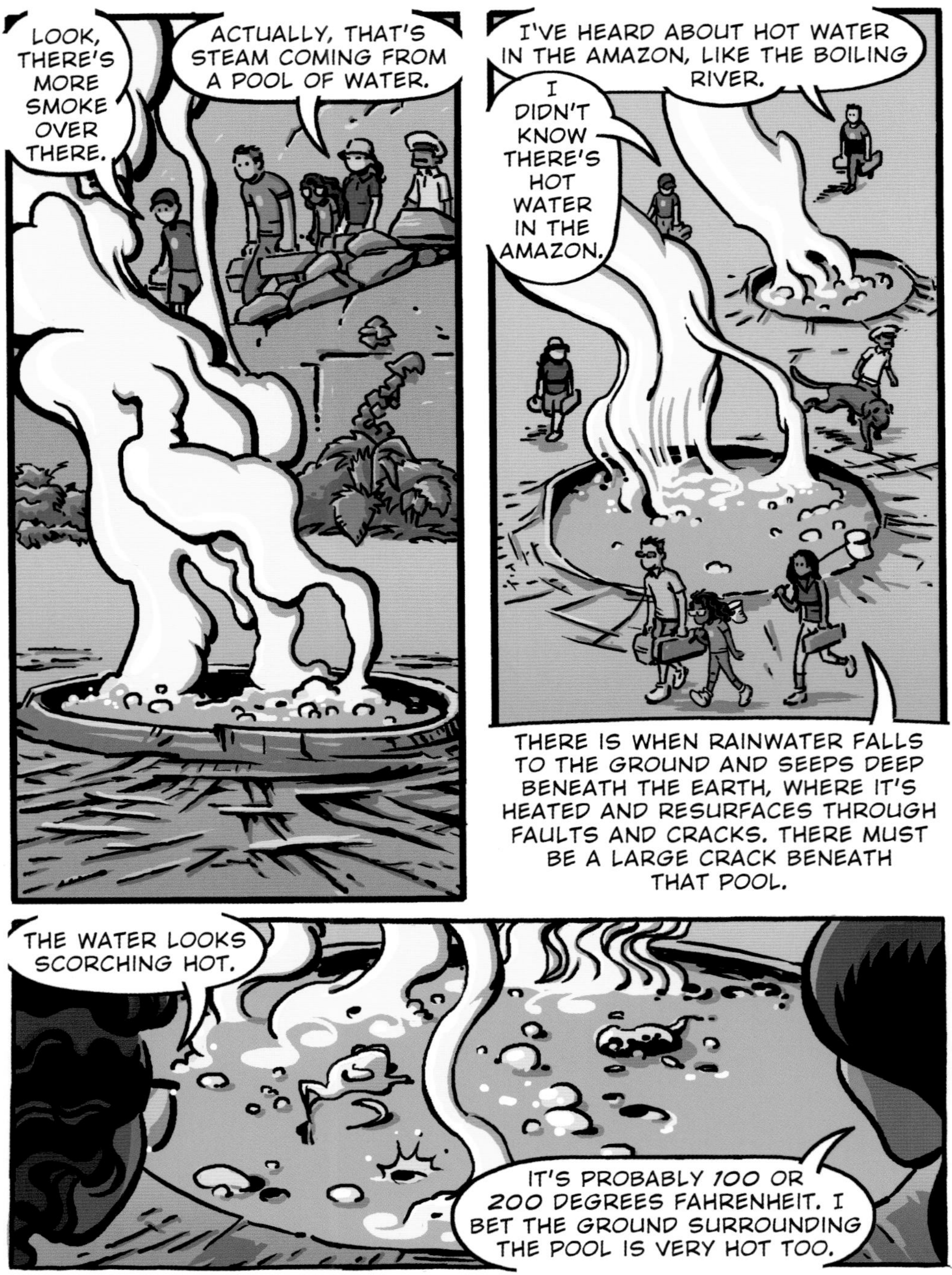
LOOK, THERE'S MORE SMOKE OVER THERE.
ACTUALLY, THAT'S STEAM COMING FROM A POOL OF WATER.
I'VE HEARD ABOUT HOT WATER IN THE AMAZON, LIKE THE BOILING RIVER.
I DIDN'T KNOW THERE'S HOT WATER IN THE AMAZON.
THERE IS WHEN RAINWATER FALLS TO THE GROUND AND SEEPS DEEP BENEATH THE EARTH, WHERE IT'S HEATED AND RESURFACES THROUGH FAULTS AND CRACKS. THERE MUST BE A LARGE CRACK BENEATH THAT POOL.
THE WATER LOOKS SCORCHING HOT.
IT'S PROBABLY *100* OR *200* DEGREES FAHRENHEIT. I BET THE GROUND SURROUNDING THE POOL IS VERY HOT TOO.

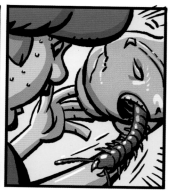

EEEGGGHH!

LOOKS LIKE YOU FOUND A GIANT CENTIPEDE.

IT'S HUGE!

LIKE MANY OF THE CREATURES IN THE JUNGLE, THE AMAZONIAN GIANT CENTIPEDE WON'T ATTACK UNLESS IT'S TRYING TO DEFEND ITSELF.

AND IF THAT HAPPENS, YOU CAN BET IT WILL BE AN EXPERIENCE YOU'LL NEVER FORGET. THAT GROUCHY CRITTER CARRIES A VENOM THAT CAUSES SEVERE PAIN.

CHECK OUT THESE FROGS.

ONE IS BRIGHT BLUE, THE OTHER SHINY GREEN.

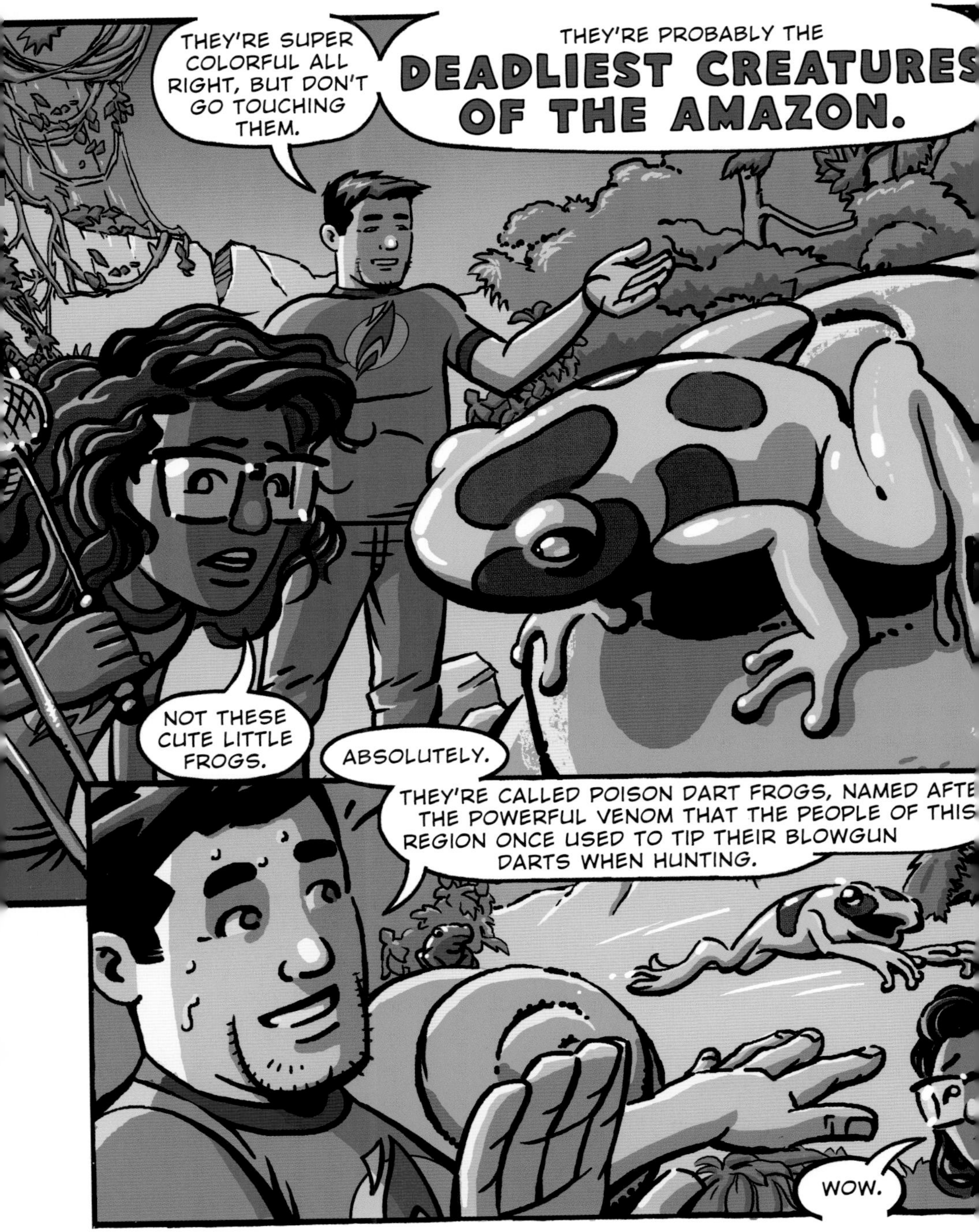
THEY'RE SUPER COLORFUL ALL RIGHT, BUT DON'T GO TOUCHING THEM.
THEY'RE PROBABLY THE DEADLIEST CREATURES OF THE AMAZON.
NOT THESE CUTE LITTLE FROGS.
ABSOLUTELY.
THEY'RE CALLED POISON DART FROGS, NAMED AFTE THE POWERFUL VENOM THAT THE PEOPLE OF THIS REGION ONCE USED TO TIP THEIR BLOWGUN DARTS WHEN HUNTING.
WOW.

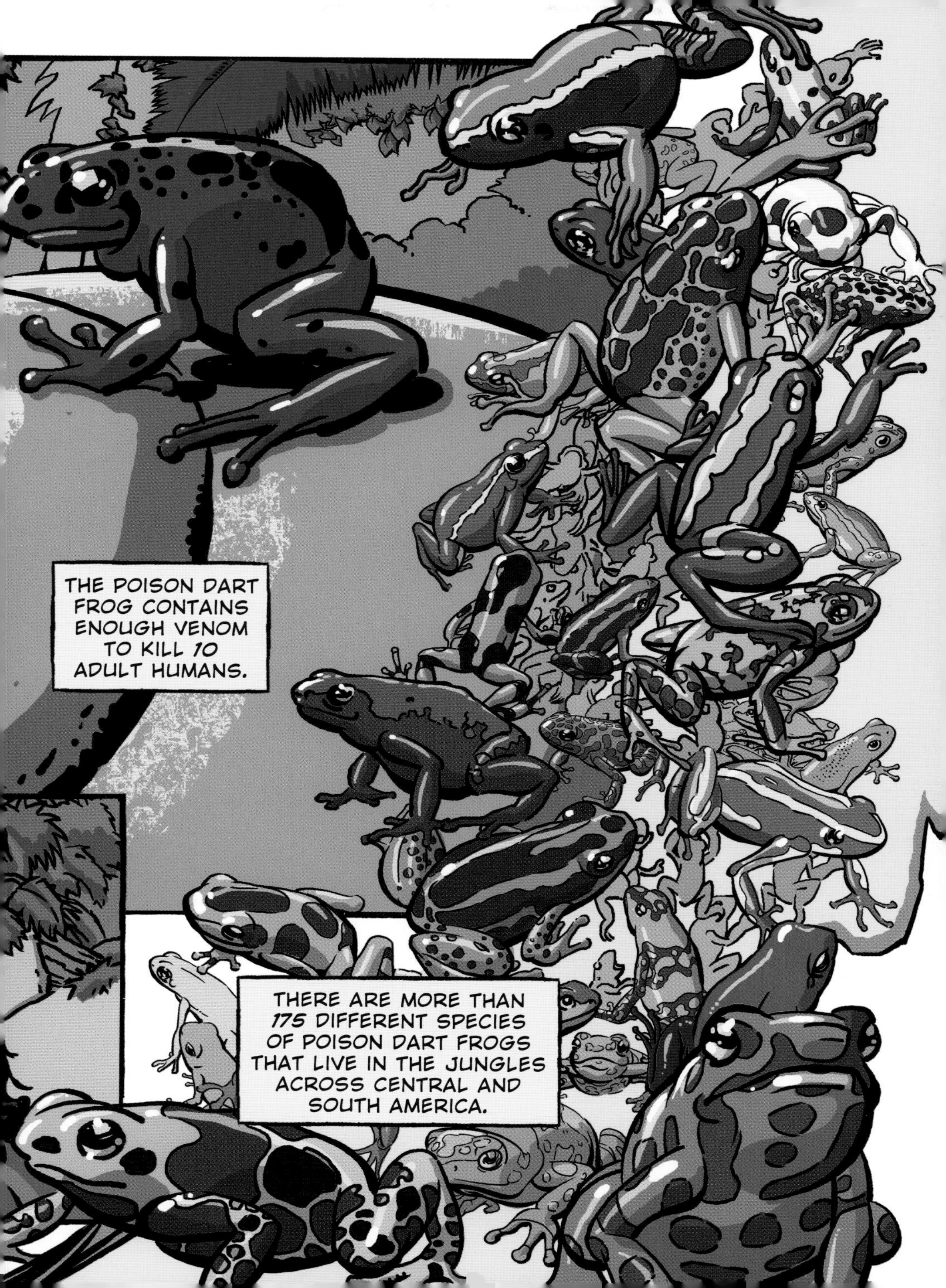
THE POISON DART FROG CONTAINS ENOUGH VENOM TO KILL 10 ADULT HUMANS.
THERE ARE MORE THAN 175 DIFFERENT SPECIES OF POISON DART FROGS THAT LIVE IN THE JUNGLES ACROSS CENTRAL AND SOUTH AMERICA.

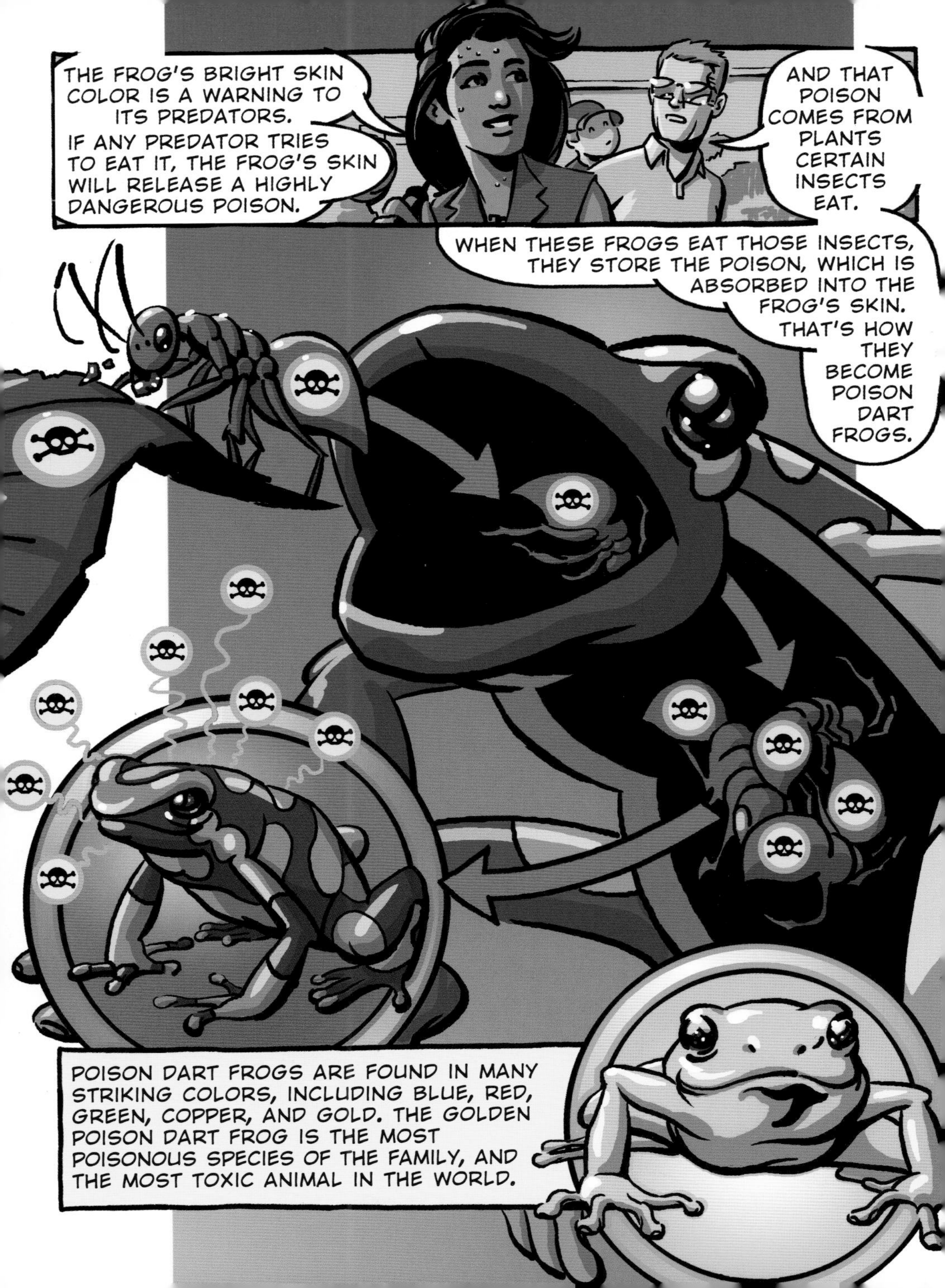
THE FROG'S BRIGHT SKIN COLOR IS A WARNING TO ITS PREDATORS.
IF ANY PREDATOR TRIES TO EAT IT, THE FROG'S SKIN WILL RELEASE A HIGHLY DANGEROUS POISON.
AND THAT POISON COMES FROM PLANTS CERTAIN INSECTS EAT.
WHEN THESE FROGS EAT THOSE INSECTS, THEY STORE THE POISON, WHICH IS ABSORBED INTO THE FROG'S SKIN.
THAT'S HOW THEY BECOME POISON DART FROGS.
POISON DART FROGS ARE FOUND IN MANY STRIKING COLORS, INCLUDING BLUE, RED, GREEN, COPPER, AND GOLD. THE GOLDEN POISON DART FROG IS THE MOST POISONOUS SPECIES OF THE FAMILY, AND THE MOST TOXIC ANIMAL IN THE WORLD.

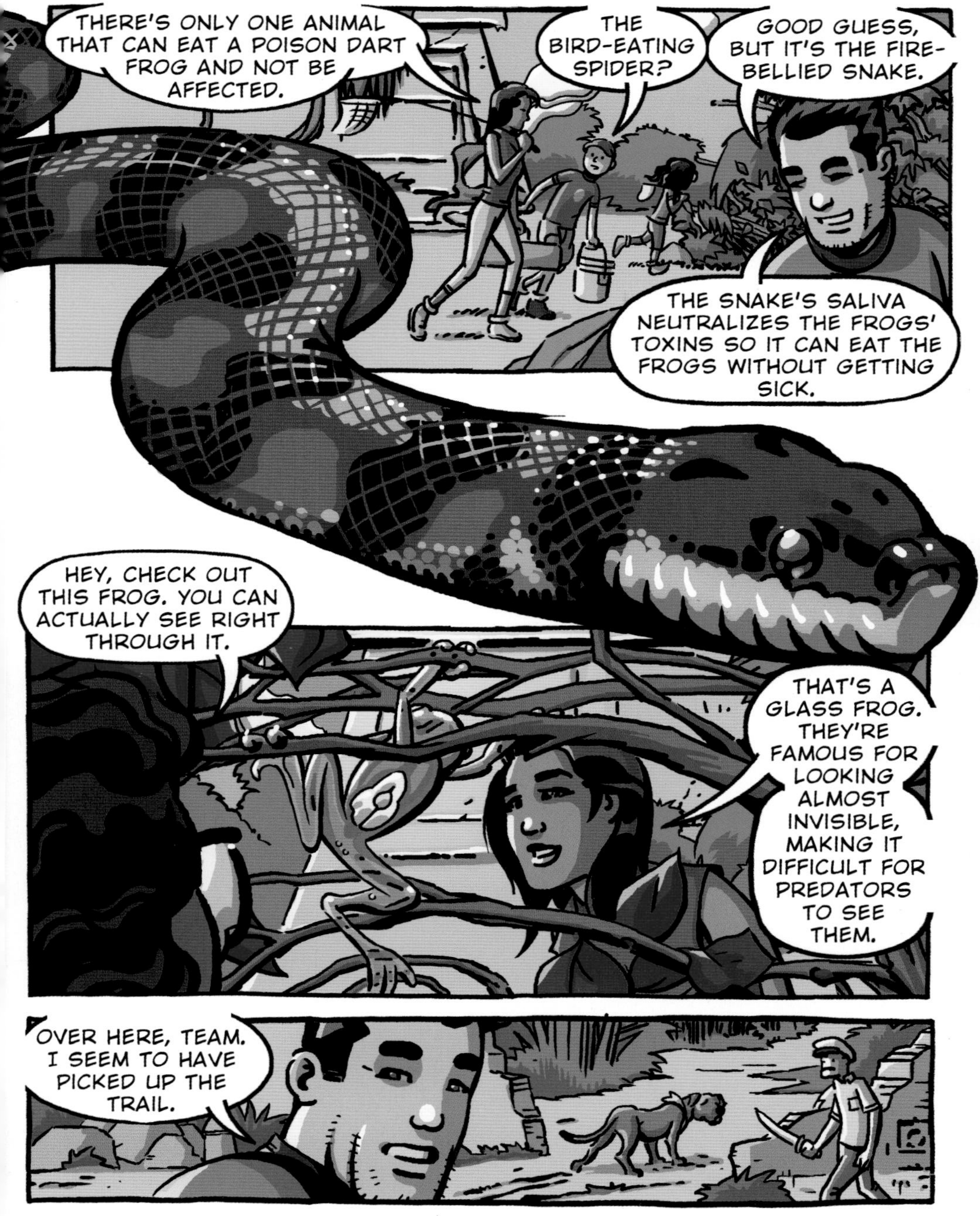

THERE'S ONLY ONE ANIMAL THAT CAN EAT A POISON DART FROG AND NOT BE AFFECTED.
THE BIRD-EATING SPIDER?
GOOD GUESS, BUT IT'S THE FIRE-BELLIED SNAKE.
THE SNAKE'S SALIVA NEUTRALIZES THE FROGS' TOXINS SO IT CAN EAT THE FROGS WITHOUT GETTING SICK.
HEY, CHECK OUT THIS FROG. YOU CAN ACTUALLY SEE RIGHT THROUGH IT.
THAT'S A GLASS FROG. THEY'RE FAMOUS FOR LOOKING ALMOST INVISIBLE, MAKING IT DIFFICULT FOR PREDATORS TO SEE THEM.
OVER HERE, TEAM. I SEEM TO HAVE PICKED UP THE TRAIL.

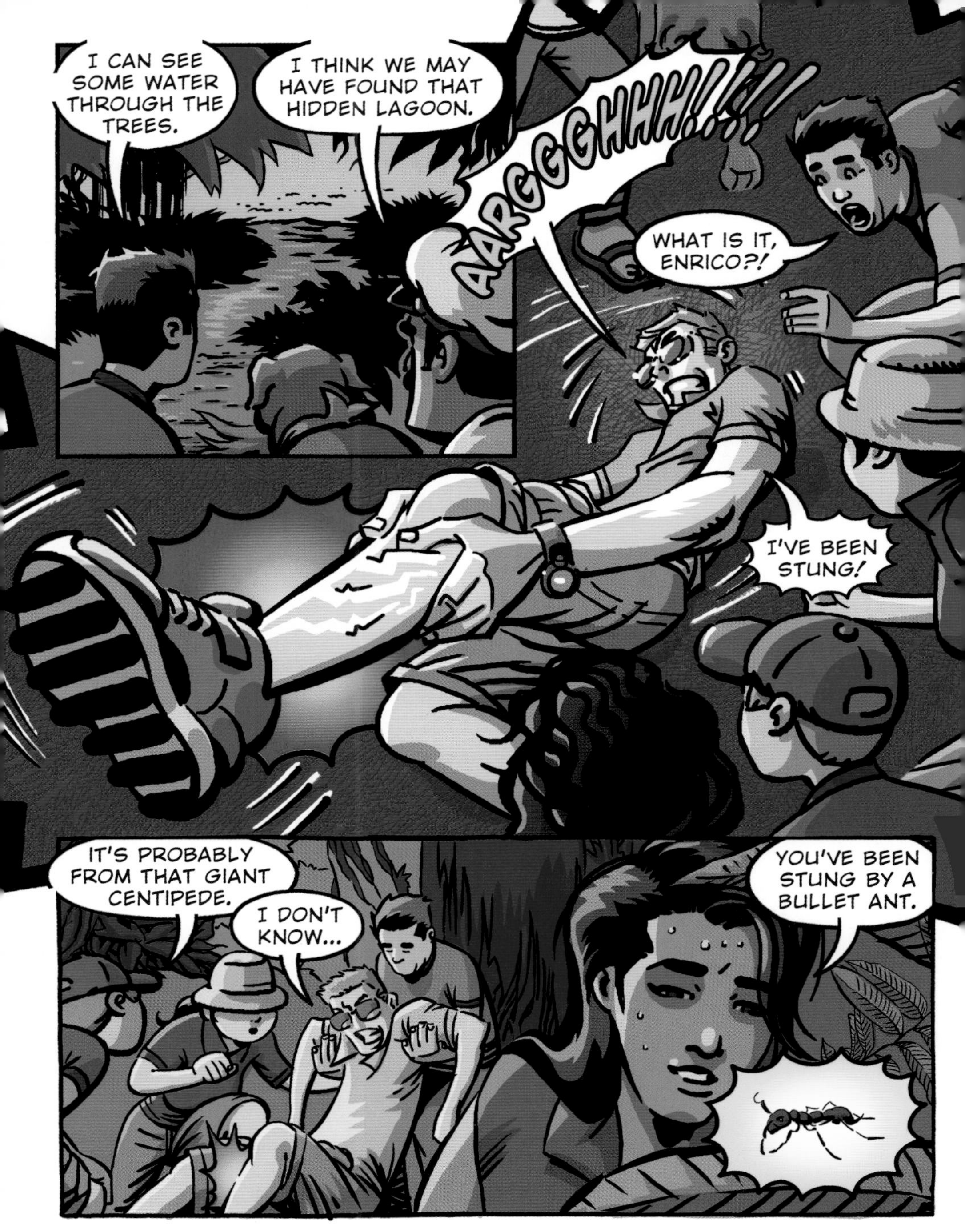
I CAN SEE SOME WATER THROUGH THE TREES.
I THINK WE MAY HAVE FOUND THAT HIDDEN LAGOON.
AARGGGHHH!!!!!
WHAT IS IT, ENRICO?!
I'VE BEEN STUNG!
IT'S PROBABLY FROM THAT GIANT CENTIPEDE.
I DON'T KNOW...
YOU'VE BEEN STUNG BY A BULLET ANT.

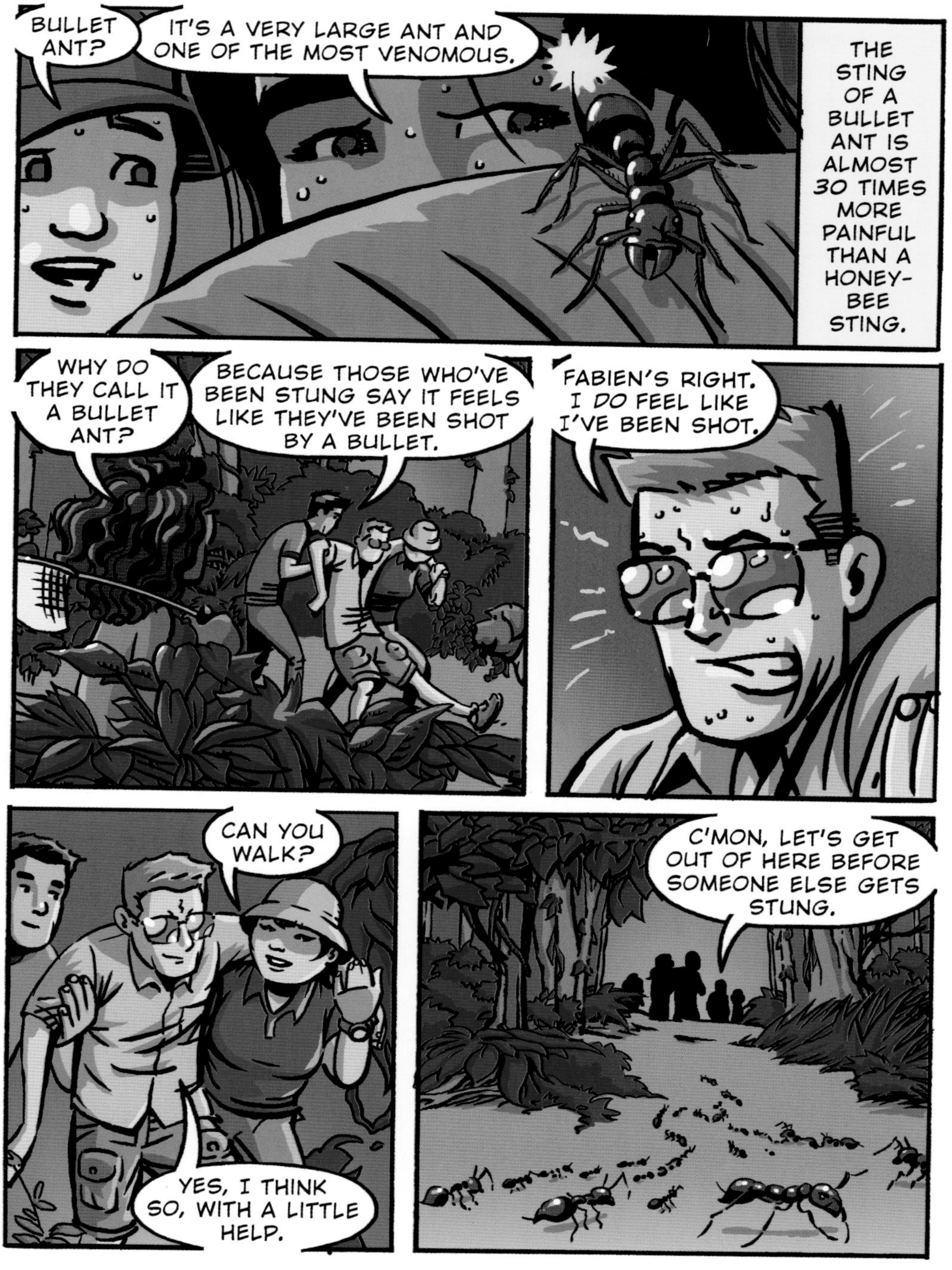
BULLET ANT?
IT'S A VERY LARGE ANT AND ONE OF THE MOST VENOMOUS.
THE STING OF A BULLET ANT IS ALMOST 30 TIMES MORE PAINFUL THAN A HONEY-BEE STING.
WHY DO THEY CALL IT A BULLET ANT?
BECAUSE THOSE WHO'VE BEEN STUNG SAY IT FEELS LIKE THEY'VE BEEN SHOT BY A BULLET.
FABIEN'S RIGHT. I DO FEEL LIKE I'VE BEEN SHOT.
CAN YOU WALK?
YES, I THINK SO, WITH A LITTLE HELP.
C'MON, LET'S GET OUT OF HERE BEFORE SOMEONE ELSE GETS STUNG.

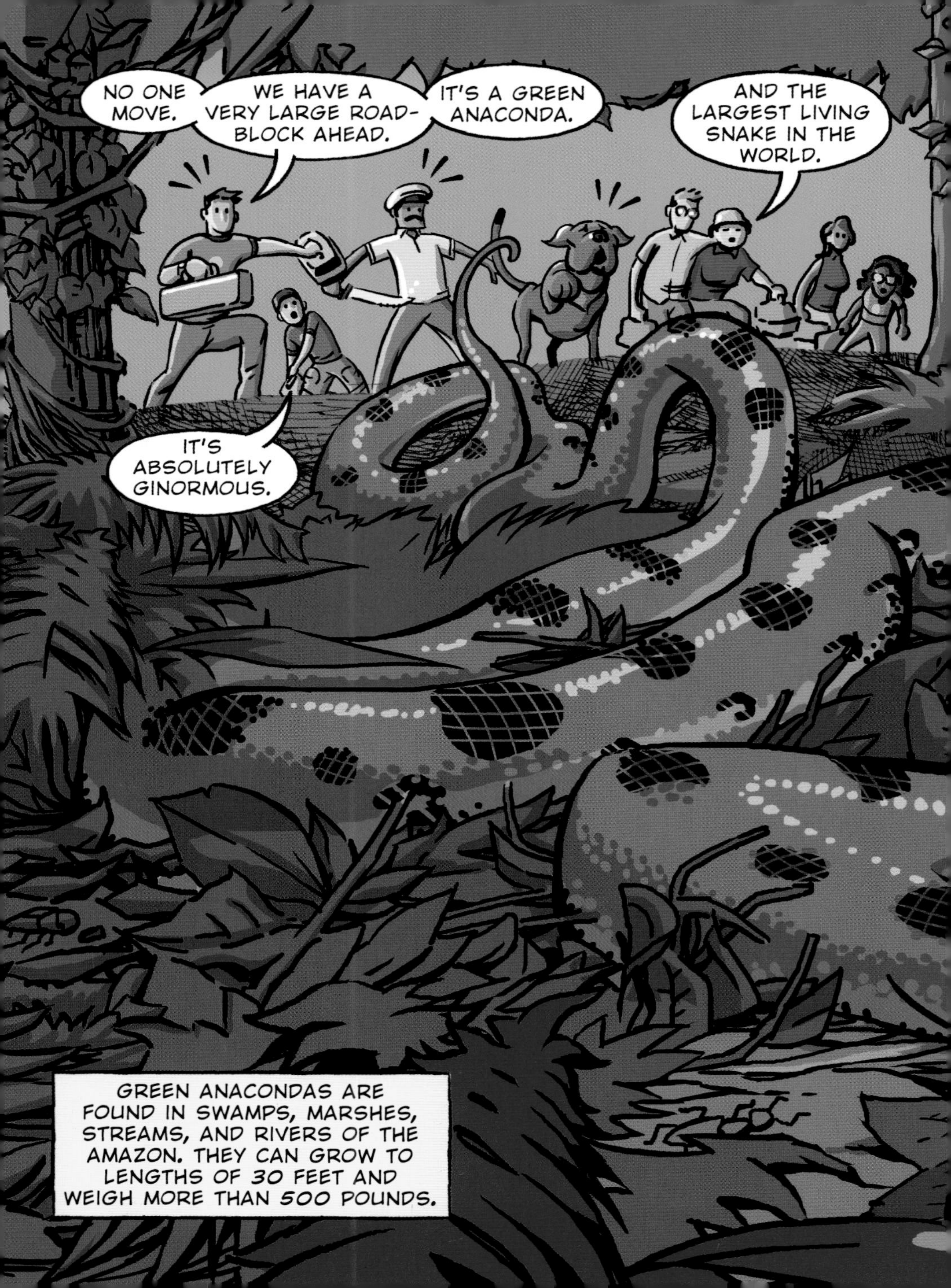
NO ONE MOVE.
WE HAVE A VERY LARGE ROAD-BLOCK AHEAD.
IT'S A GREEN ANACONDA.
AND THE LARGEST LIVING SNAKE IN THE WORLD.
IT'S ABSOLUTELY GINORMOUS.
GREEN ANACONDAS ARE FOUND IN SWAMPS, MARSHES, STREAMS, AND RIVERS OF THE AMAZON. THEY CAN GROW TO LENGTHS OF 30 FEET AND WEIGH MORE THAN 500 POUNDS.

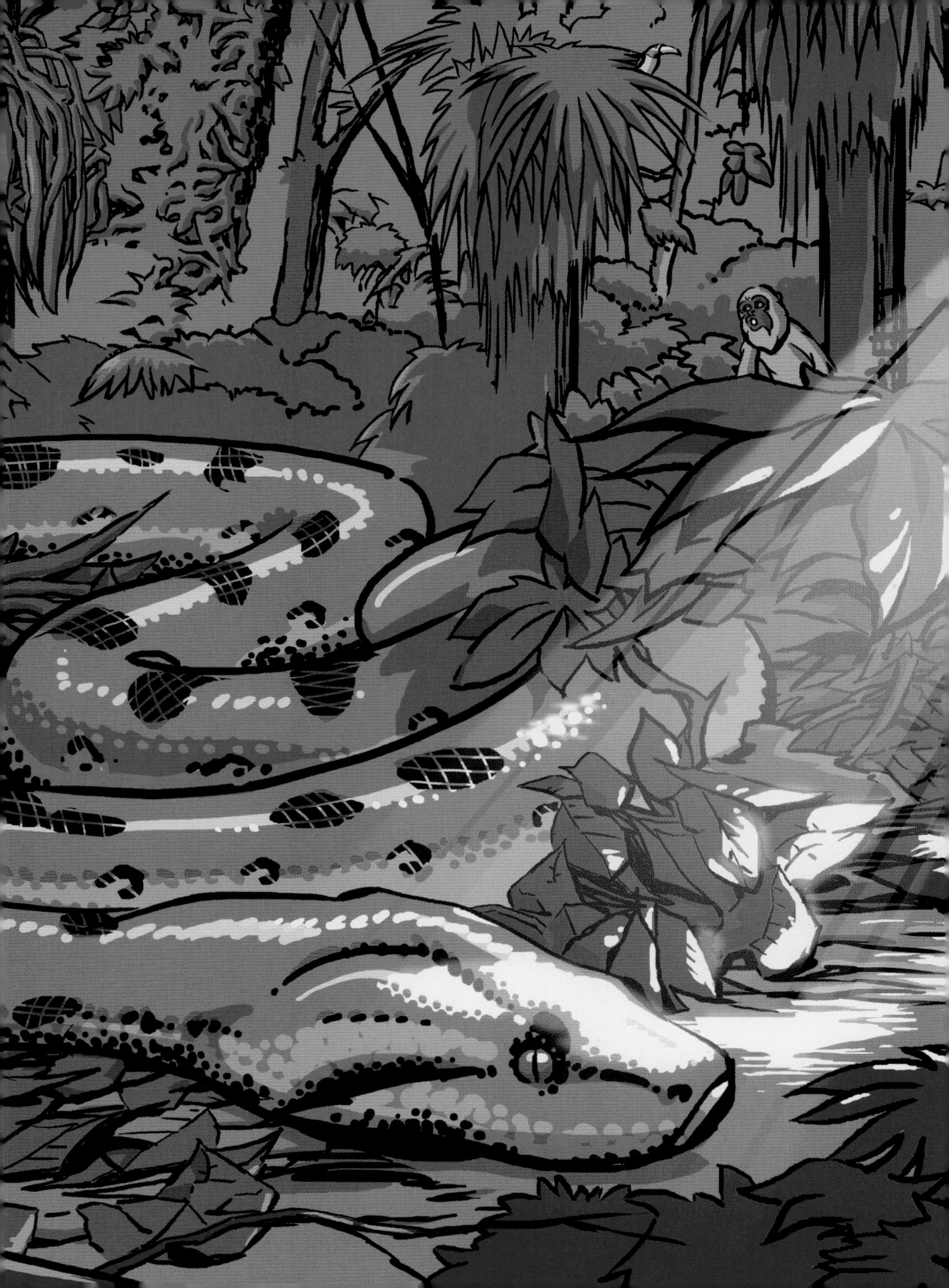

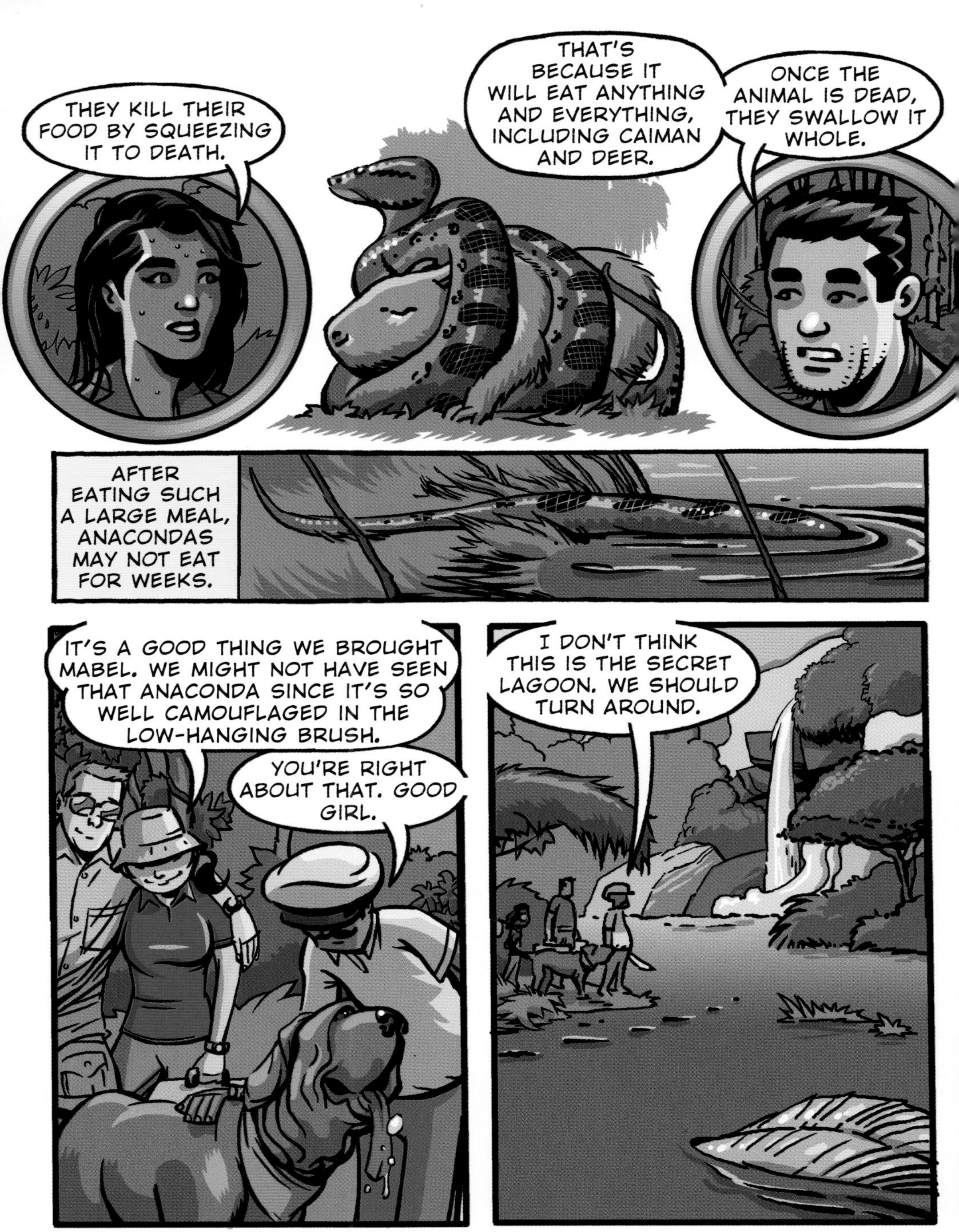
THEY KILL THEIR FOOD BY SQUEEZING IT TO DEATH.
THAT'S BECAUSE IT WILL EAT ANYTHING AND EVERYTHING, INCLUDING CAIMAN AND DEER.
ONCE THE ANIMAL IS DEAD, THEY SWALLOW IT WHOLE.
AFTER EATING SUCH A LARGE MEAL, ANACONDAS MAY NOT EAT FOR WEEKS.
IT'S A GOOD THING WE BROUGHT MABEL. WE MIGHT NOT HAVE SEEN THAT ANACONDA SINCE IT'S SO WELL CAMOUFLAGED IN THE LOW-HANGING BRUSH.
YOU'RE RIGHT ABOUT THAT. GOOD GIRL.
I DON'T THINK THIS IS THE SECRET LAGOON. WE SHOULD TURN AROUND.

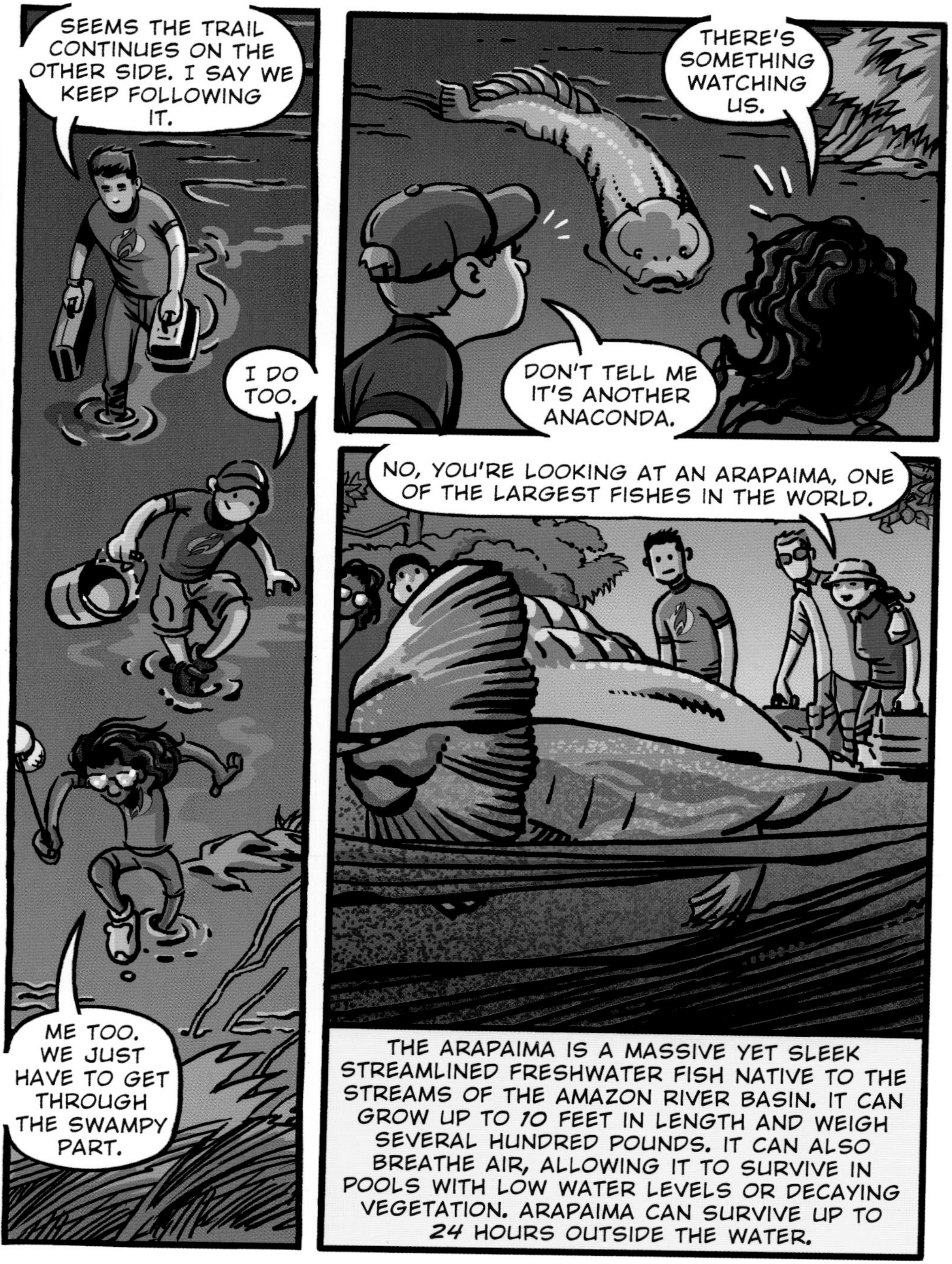
SEEMS THE TRAIL CONTINUES ON THE OTHER SIDE. I SAY WE KEEP FOLLOWING IT.
I DO TOO.
ME TOO. WE JUST HAVE TO GET THROUGH THE SWAMPY PART.
THERE'S SOMETHING WATCHING US.
DON'T TELL ME IT'S ANOTHER ANACONDA.
NO, YOU'RE LOOKING AT AN ARAPAIMA, ONE OF THE LARGEST FISHES IN THE WORLD.
THE ARAPAIMA IS A MASSIVE YET SLEEK STREAMLINED FRESHWATER FISH NATIVE TO THE STREAMS OF THE AMAZON RIVER BASIN. IT CAN GROW UP TO 10 FEET IN LENGTH AND WEIGH SEVERAL HUNDRED POUNDS. IT CAN ALSO BREATHE AIR, ALLOWING IT TO SURVIVE IN POOLS WITH LOW WATER LEVELS OR DECAYING VEGETATION. ARAPAIMA CAN SURVIVE UP TO 24 HOURS OUTSIDE THE WATER.

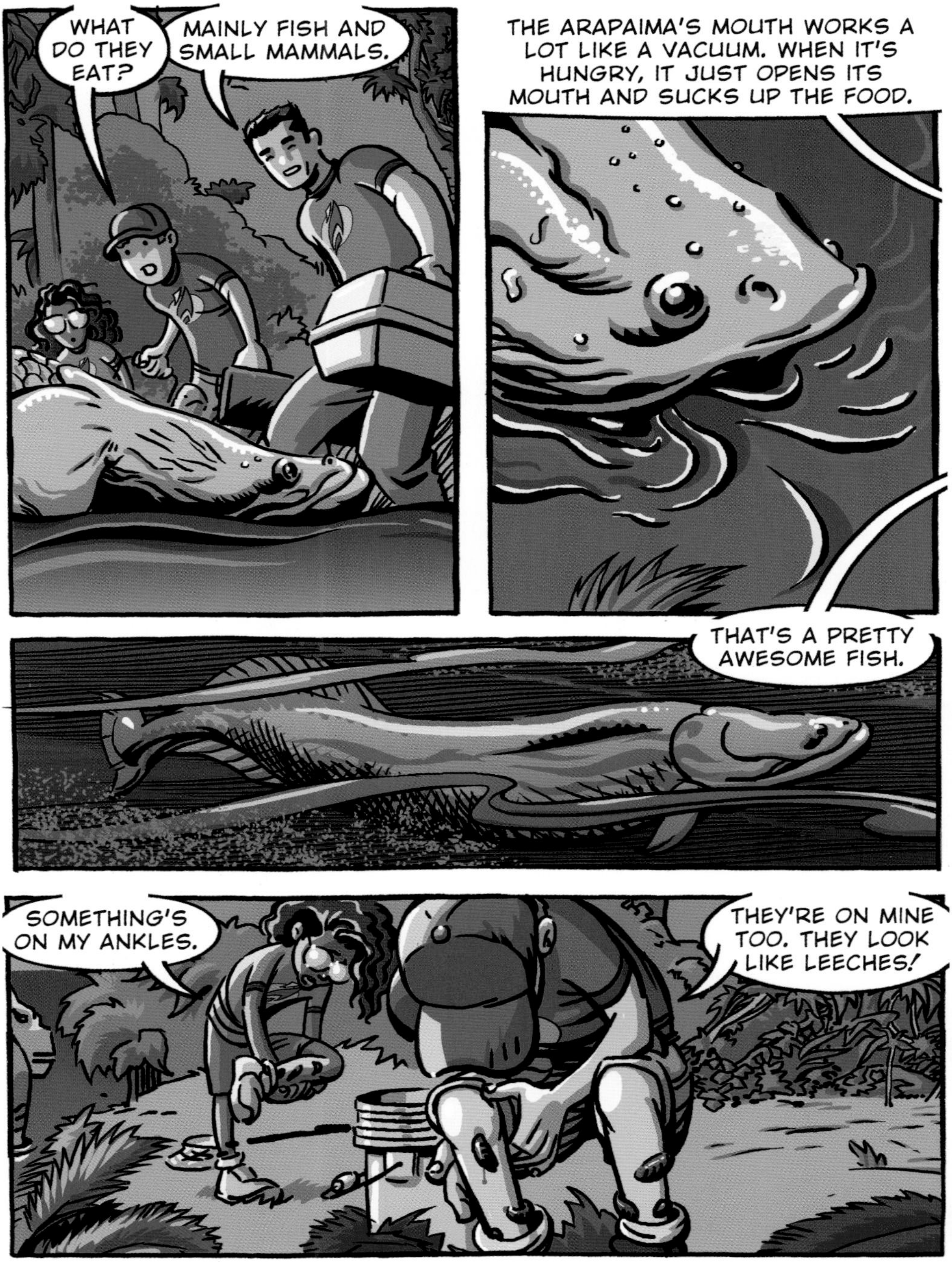
WHAT DO THEY EAT?
MAINLY FISH AND SMALL MAMMALS.
THE ARAPAIMA'S MOUTH WORKS A LOT LIKE A VACUUM. WHEN IT'S HUNGRY, IT JUST OPENS ITS MOUTH AND SUCKS UP THE FOOD.
THAT'S A PRETTY AWESOME FISH.
SOMETHING'S ON MY ANKLES.
THEY'RE ON MINE TOO. THEY LOOK LIKE LEECHES!

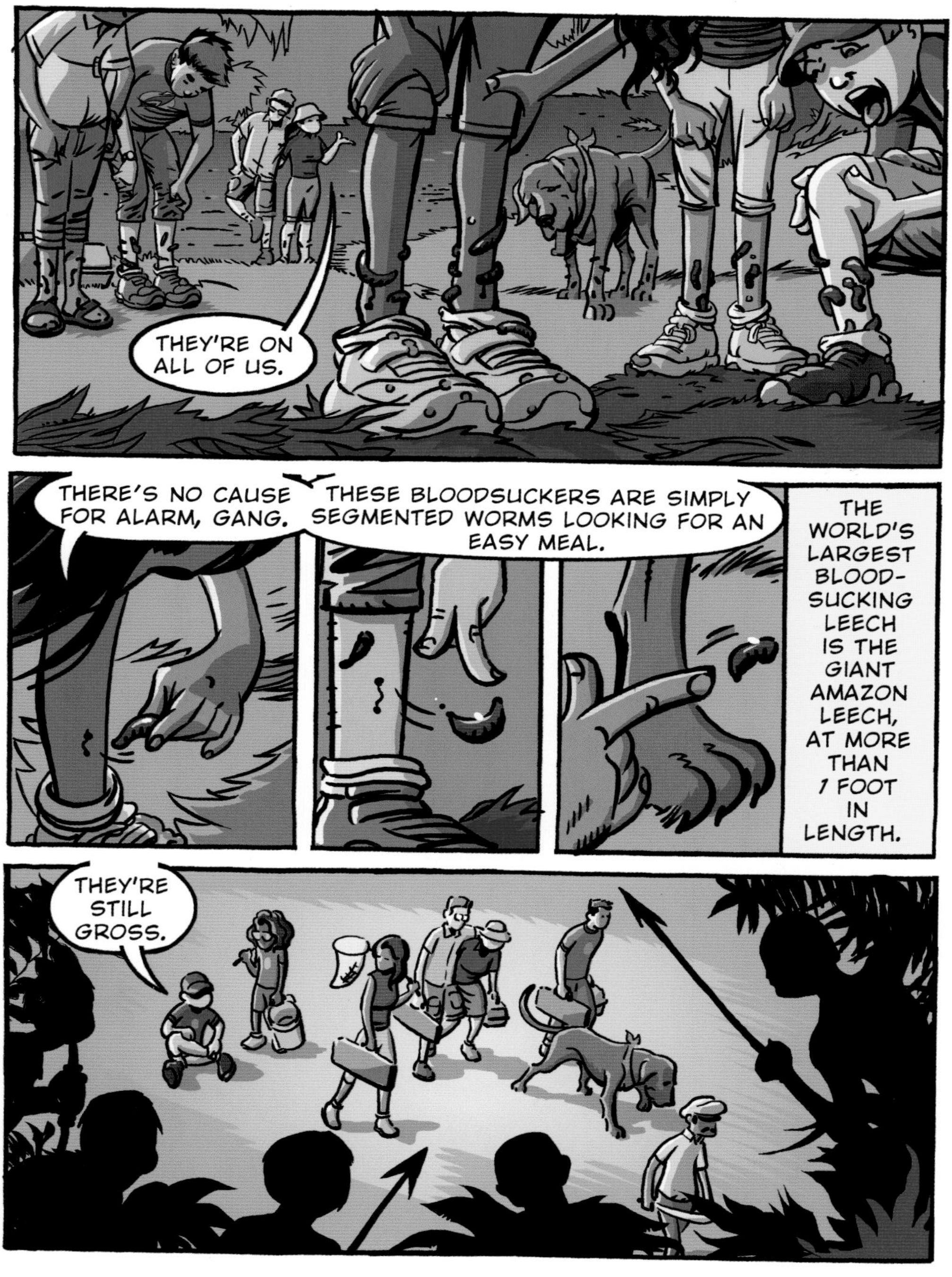
THEY'RE ON ALL OF US.
THERE'S NO CAUSE FOR ALARM, GANG.
THESE BLOODSUCKERS ARE SIMPLY SEGMENTED WORMS LOOKING FOR AN EASY MEAL.
THE WORLD'S LARGEST BLOOD-SUCKING LEECH IS THE GIANT AMAZON LEECH, AT MORE THAN 1 FOOT IN LENGTH.
THEY'RE STILL GROSS.

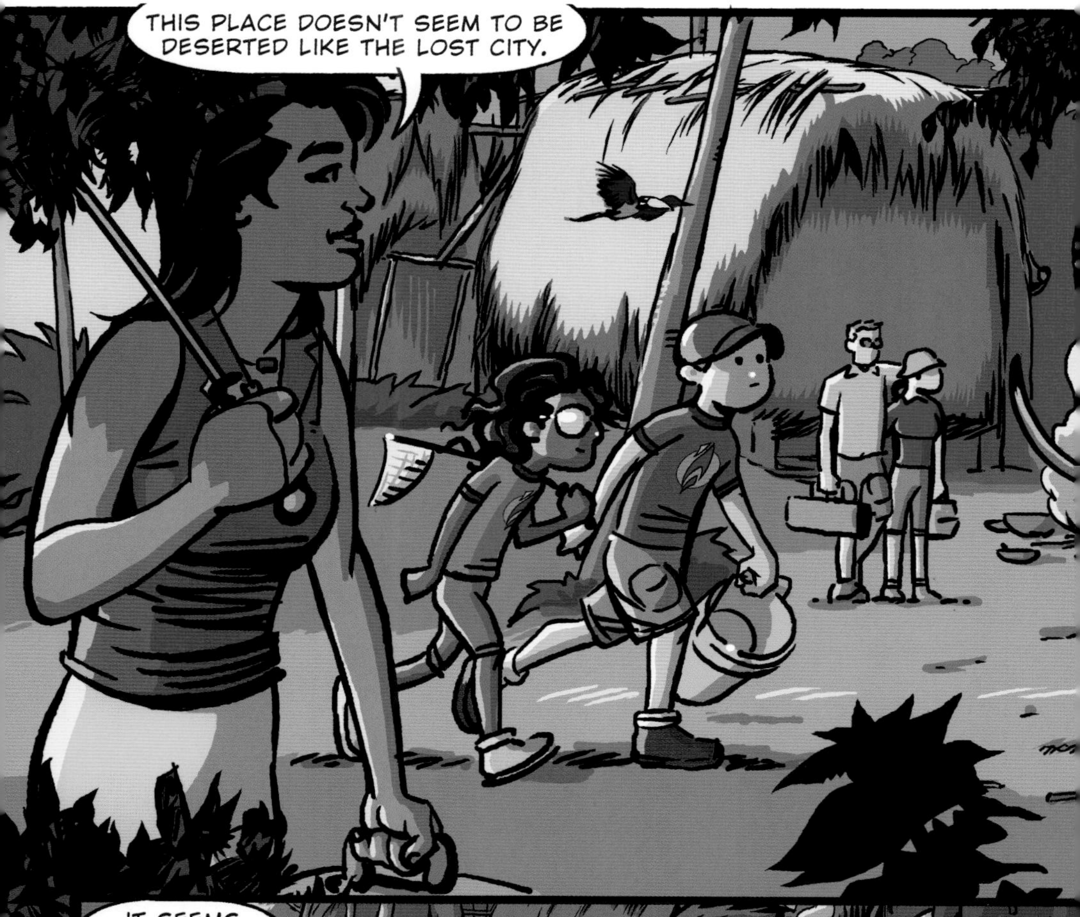
THIS PLACE DOESN'T SEEM TO BE DESERTED LIKE THE LOST CITY.

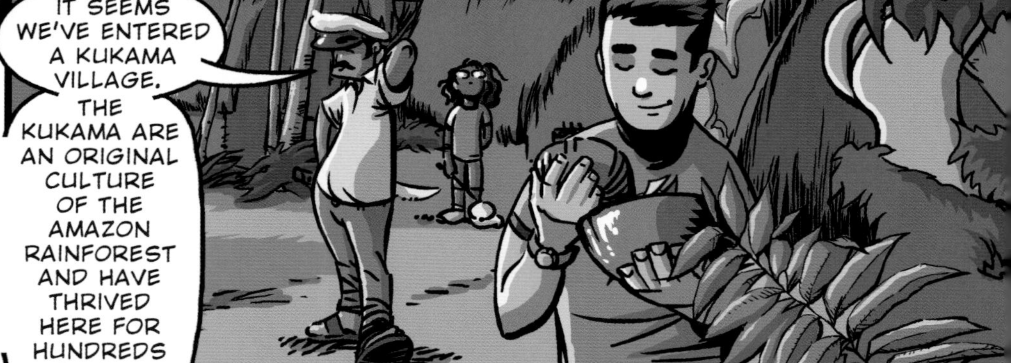
IT SEEMS WE'VE ENTERED A KUKAMA VILLAGE.
THE KUKAMA ARE AN ORIGINAL CULTURE OF THE AMAZON RAINFOREST AND HAVE THRIVED HERE FOR HUNDREDS OF YEARS.

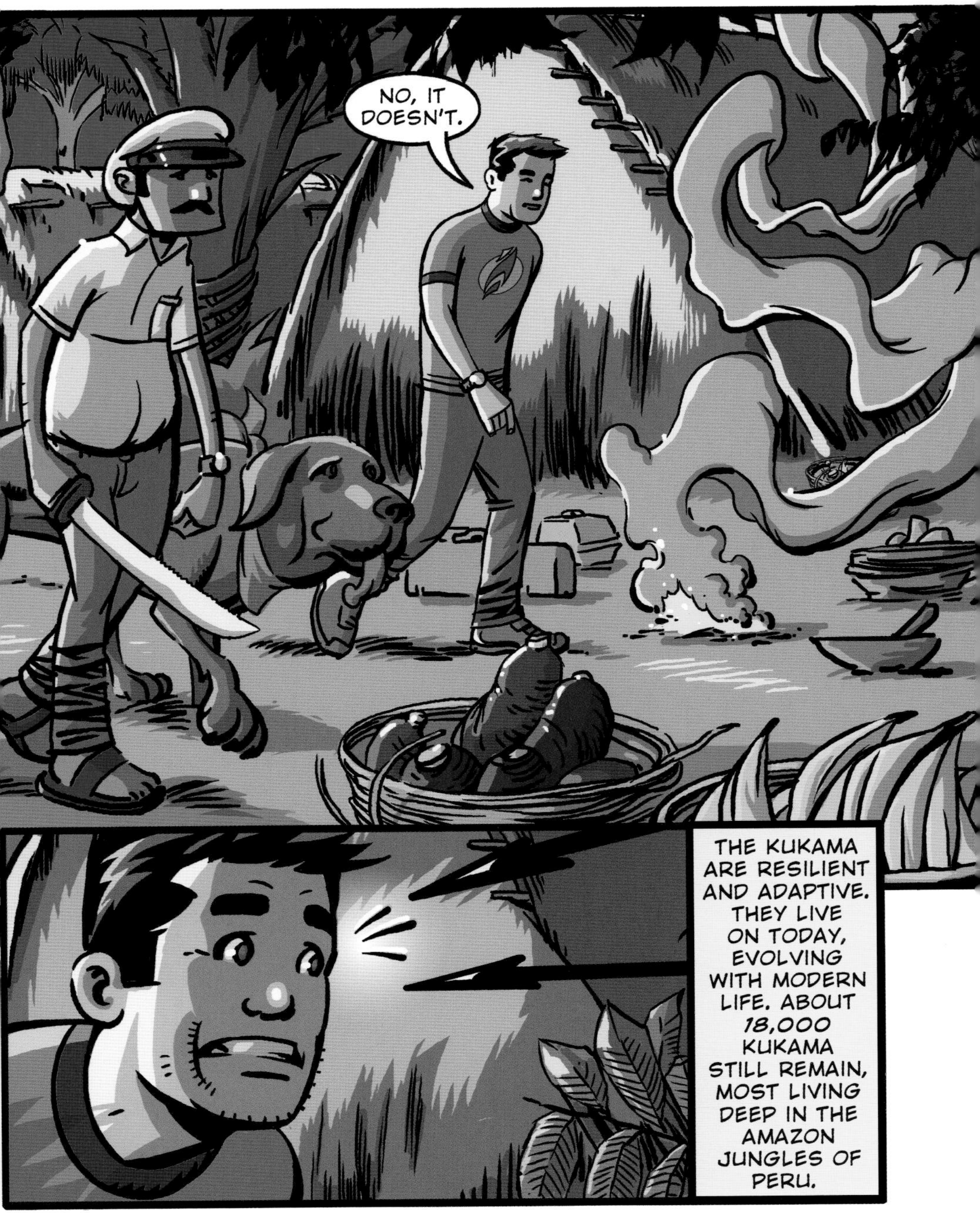
NO, IT DOESN'T.
THE KUKAMA ARE RESILIENT AND ADAPTIVE. THEY LIVE ON TODAY, EVOLVING WITH MODERN LIFE. ABOUT *18,000* KUKAMA STILL REMAIN, MOST LIVING DEEP IN THE AMAZON JUNGLES OF PERU.

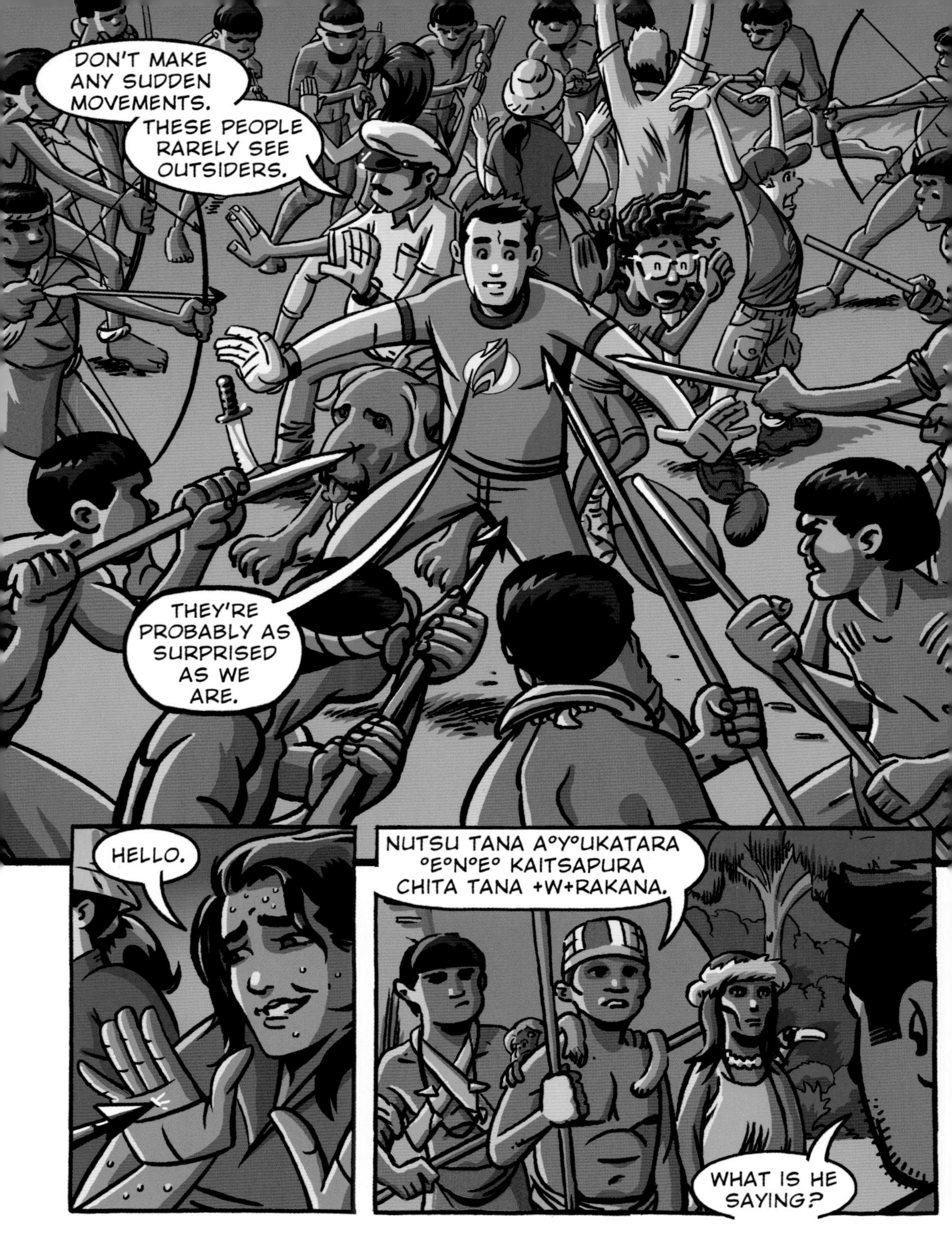
DON'T MAKE ANY SUDDEN MOVEMENTS.
THESE PEOPLE RARELY SEE OUTSIDERS.
THEY'RE PROBABLY AS SURPRISED AS WE ARE.
HELLO.
NUTSU TANA A°Y°UKATARA °E°N°E° KAITSAPURA CHITA TANA +W+RAKANA.
WHAT IS HE SAYING?

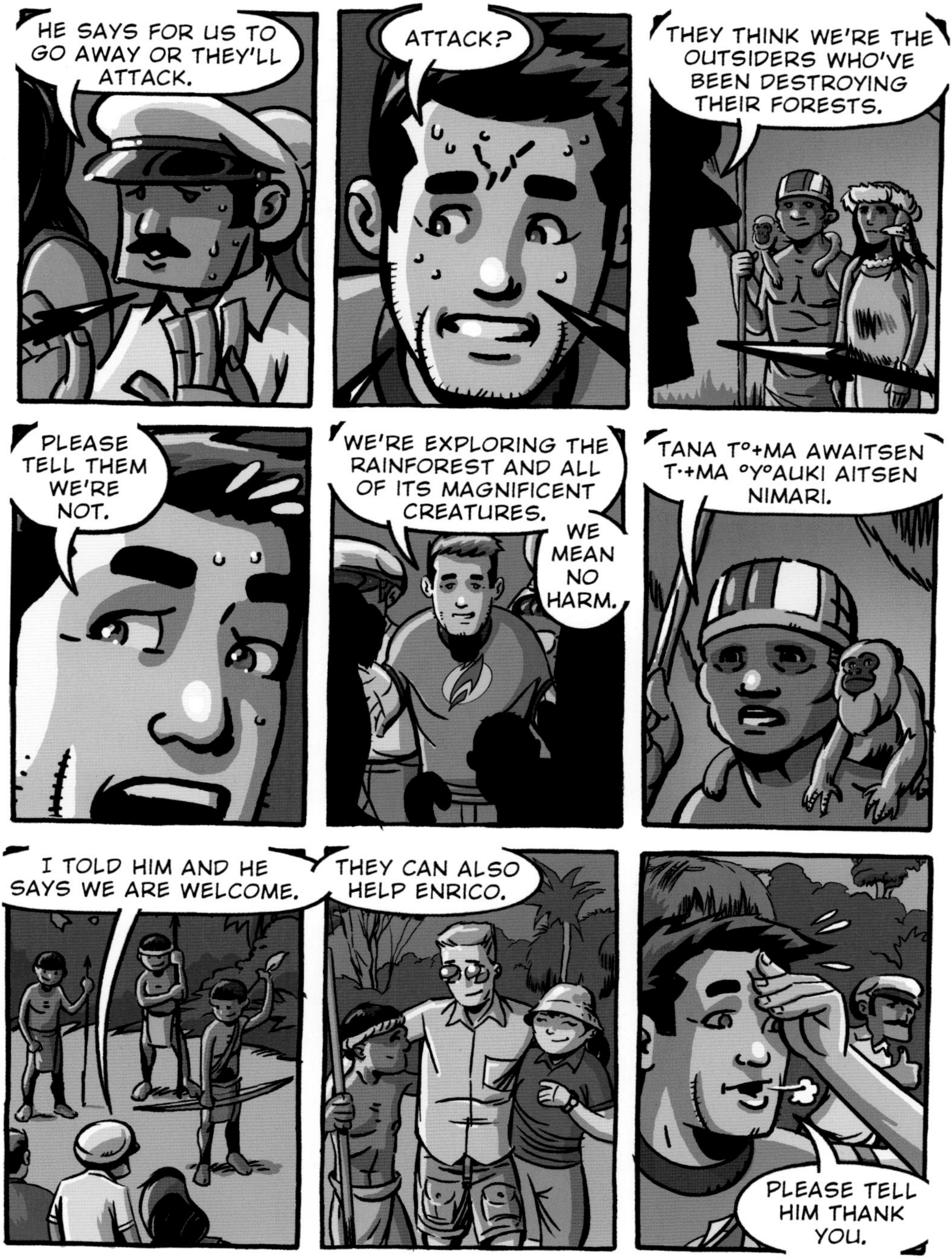
HE SAYS FOR US TO GO AWAY OR THEY'LL ATTACK.
ATTACK?
THEY THINK WE'RE THE OUTSIDERS WHO'VE BEEN DESTROYING THEIR FORESTS.
PLEASE TELL THEM WE'RE NOT.
WE'RE EXPLORING THE RAINFOREST AND ALL OF ITS MAGNIFICENT CREATURES.
WE MEAN NO HARM.
TANA T°+MA AWAITSEN T·+MA °Y°AUKI AITSEN NIMARI.
I TOLD HIM AND HE SAYS WE ARE WELCOME.
THEY CAN ALSO HELP ENRICO.
PLEASE TELL HIM THANK YOU.

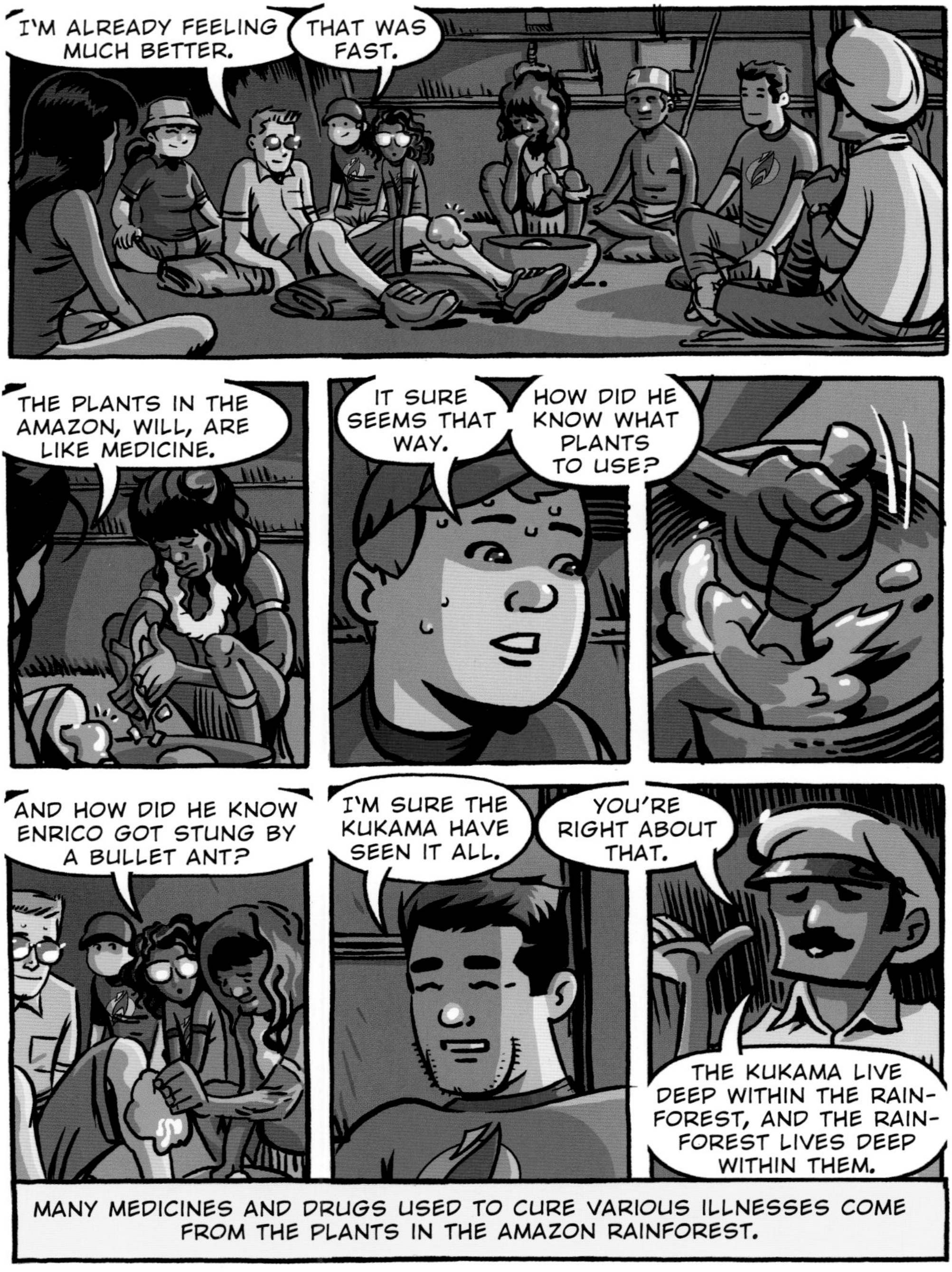
I'M ALREADY FEELING MUCH BETTER.
THAT WAS FAST.
THE PLANTS IN THE AMAZON, WILL, ARE LIKE MEDICINE.
IT SURE SEEMS THAT WAY.
HOW DID HE KNOW WHAT PLANTS TO USE?
AND HOW DID HE KNOW ENRICO GOT STUNG BY A BULLET ANT?
I'M SURE THE KUKAMA HAVE SEEN IT ALL.
YOU'RE RIGHT ABOUT THAT.
THE KUKAMA LIVE DEEP WITHIN THE RAIN-FOREST, AND THE RAIN-FOREST LIVES DEEP WITHIN THEM.
MANY MEDICINES AND DRUGS USED TO CURE VARIOUS ILLNESSES COME FROM THE PLANTS IN THE AMAZON RAINFOREST.

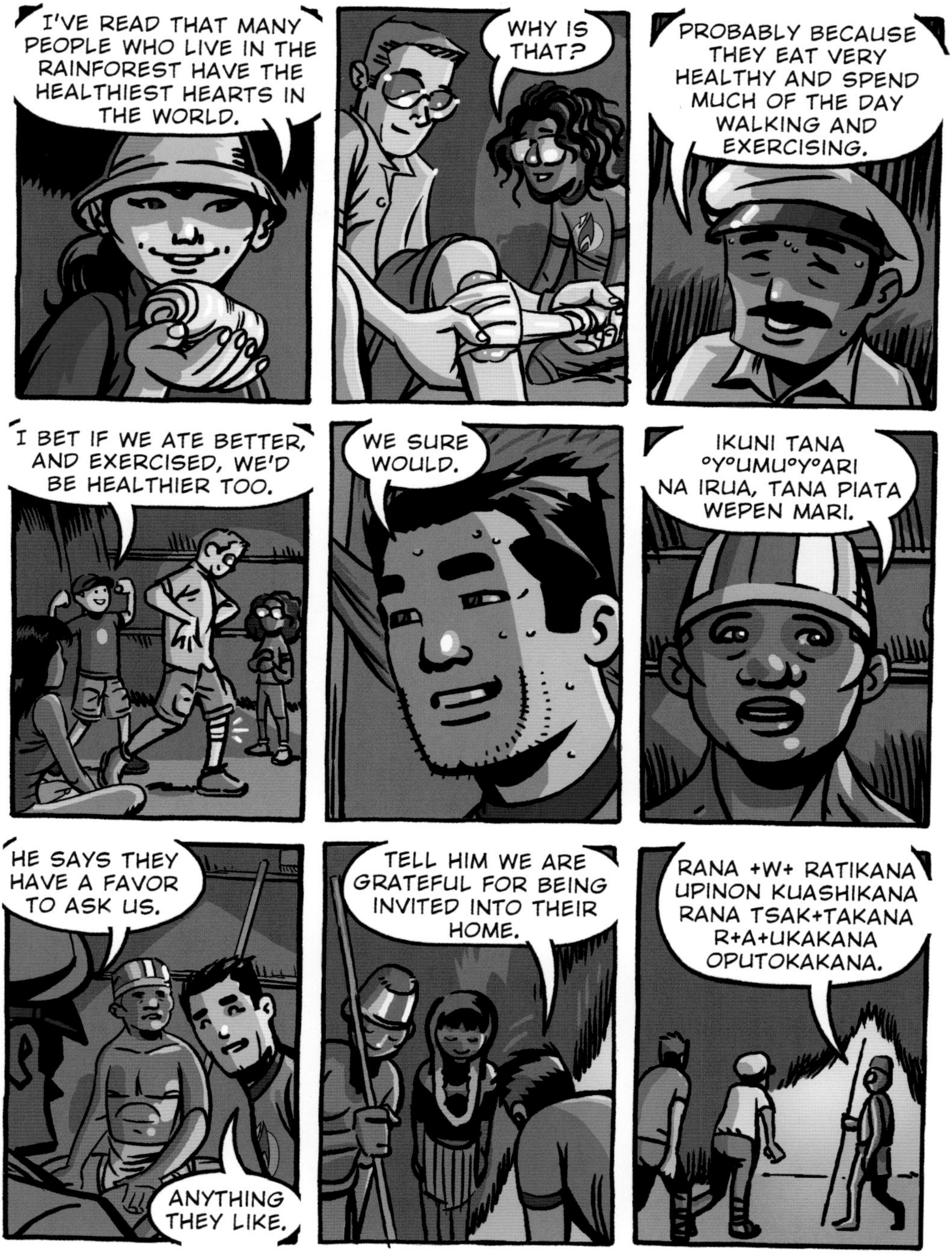
I'VE READ THAT MANY PEOPLE WHO LIVE IN THE RAINFOREST HAVE THE HEALTHIEST HEARTS IN THE WORLD.
WHY IS THAT?
PROBABLY BECAUSE THEY EAT VERY HEALTHY AND SPEND MUCH OF THE DAY WALKING AND EXERCISING.
I BET IF WE ATE BETTER, AND EXERCISED, WE'D BE HEALTHIER TOO.
WE SURE WOULD.
IKUNI TANA °Y°UMU°Y°ARI NA IRUA, TANA PIATA WEPEN MARI.
HE SAYS THEY HAVE A FAVOR TO ASK US.
ANYTHING THEY LIKE.
TELL HIM WE ARE GRATEFUL FOR BEING INVITED INTO THEIR HOME.
RANA +W+ RATIKANA UPINON KUASHIKANA RANA TSAK+TAKANA R+A+UKAKANA OPUTOKAKANA.

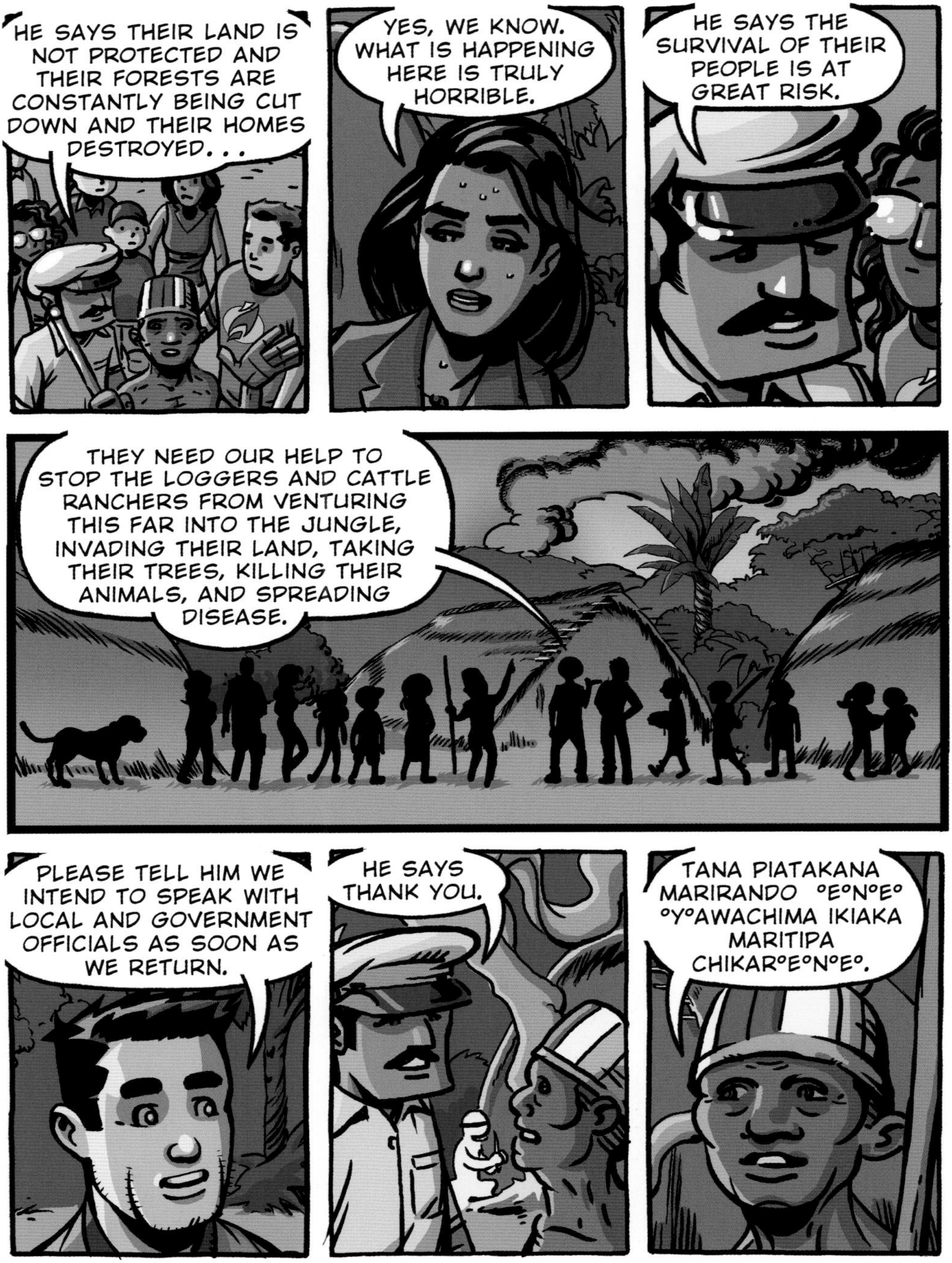
HE SAYS THEIR LAND IS NOT PROTECTED AND THEIR FORESTS ARE CONSTANTLY BEING CUT DOWN AND THEIR HOMES DESTROYED. . .
YES, WE KNOW. WHAT IS HAPPENING HERE IS TRULY HORRIBLE.
HE SAYS THE SURVIVAL OF THEIR PEOPLE IS AT GREAT RISK.
THEY NEED OUR HELP TO STOP THE LOGGERS AND CATTLE RANCHERS FROM VENTURING THIS FAR INTO THE JUNGLE, INVADING THEIR LAND, TAKING THEIR TREES, KILLING THEIR ANIMALS, AND SPREADING DISEASE.
PLEASE TELL HIM WE INTEND TO SPEAK WITH LOCAL AND GOVERNMENT OFFICIALS AS SOON AS WE RETURN.
HE SAYS THANK YOU.
TANA PIATAKANA MARIRANDO °E°N°E° °Y°AWACHIMA IKIAKA MARITIPA CHIKAR°E°N°E°.

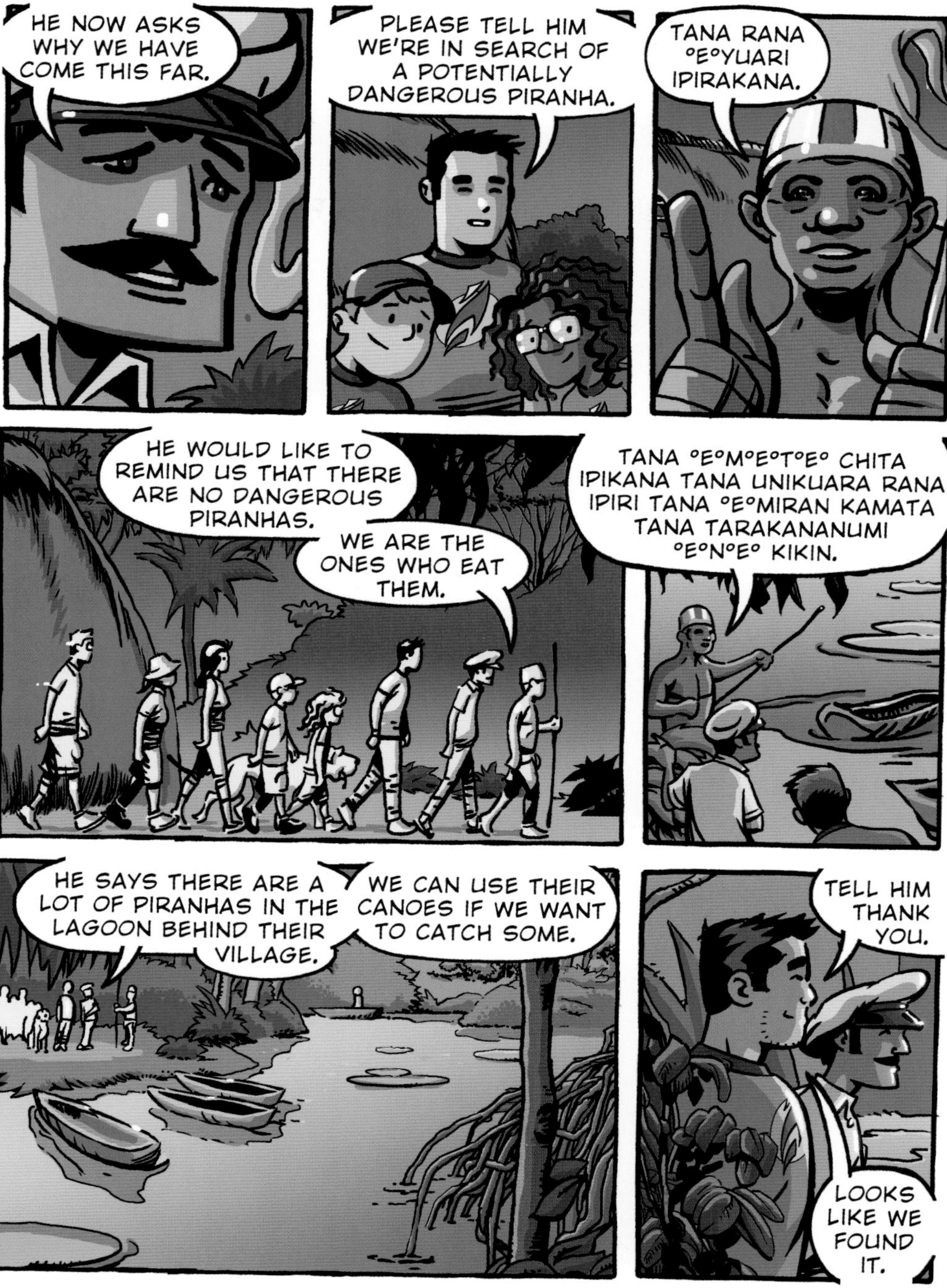
HE NOW ASKS WHY WE HAVE COME THIS FAR.
PLEASE TELL HIM WE'RE IN SEARCH OF A POTENTIALLY DANGEROUS PIRANHA.
TANA RANA °E°YUARI IPIRAKANA.
HE WOULD LIKE TO REMIND US THAT THERE ARE NO DANGEROUS PIRANHAS.
WE ARE THE ONES WHO EAT THEM.
TANA °E°M°E°T°E° CHITA IPIKANA TANA UNIKUARA RANA IPIRI TANA °E°MIRAN KAMATA TANA TARAKANANUMI °E°N°E° KIKIN.
HE SAYS THERE ARE A LOT OF PIRANHAS IN THE LAGOON BEHIND THEIR VILLAGE.
WE CAN USE THEIR CANOES IF WE WANT TO CATCH SOME.
TELL HIM THANK YOU.
LOOKS LIKE WE FOUND IT.

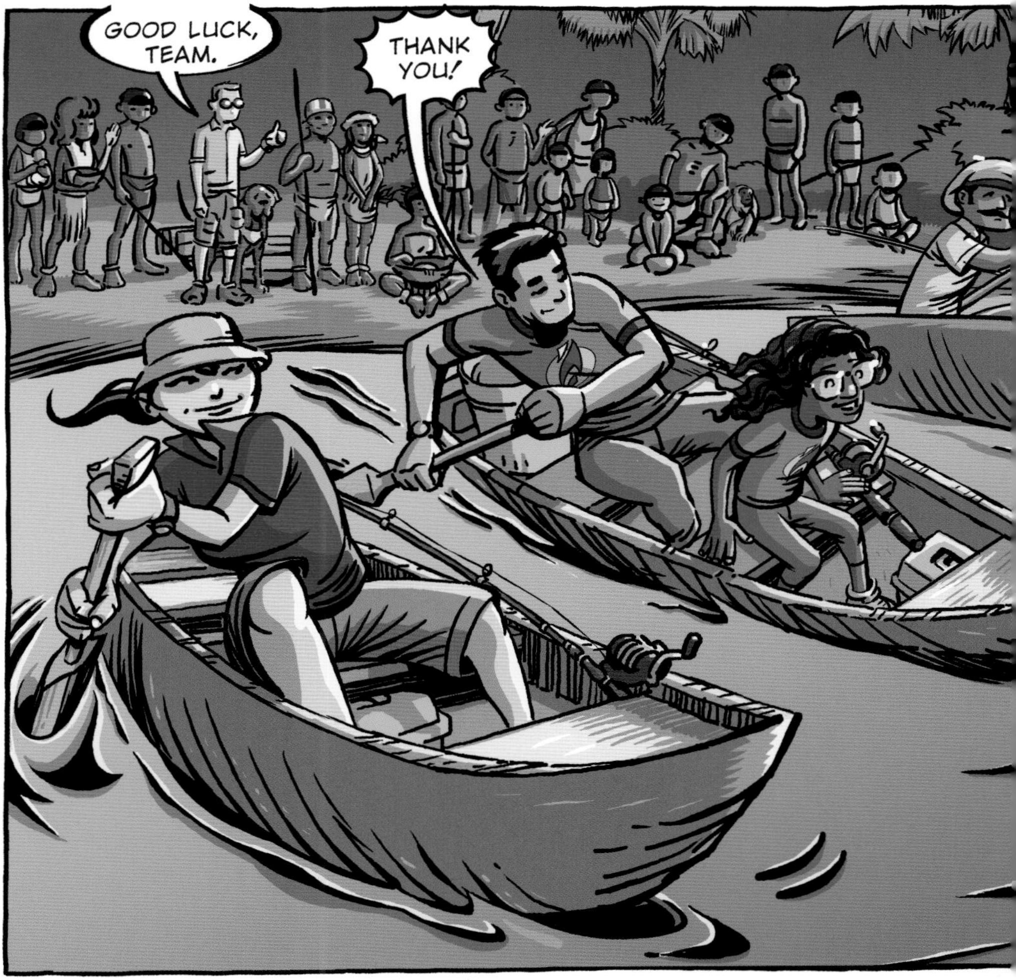
GOOD LUCK, TEAM.
THANK YOU!

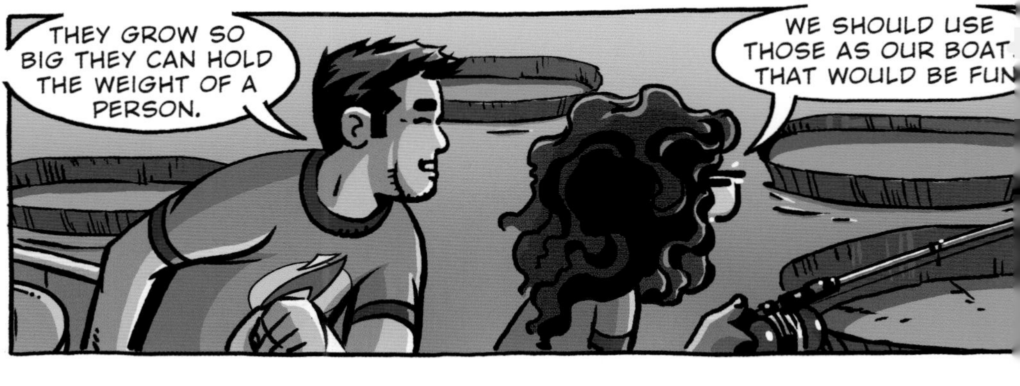
THEY GROW SO BIG THEY CAN HOLD THE WEIGHT OF A PERSON.
WE SHOULD USE THOSE AS OUR BOAT. THAT WOULD BE FUN

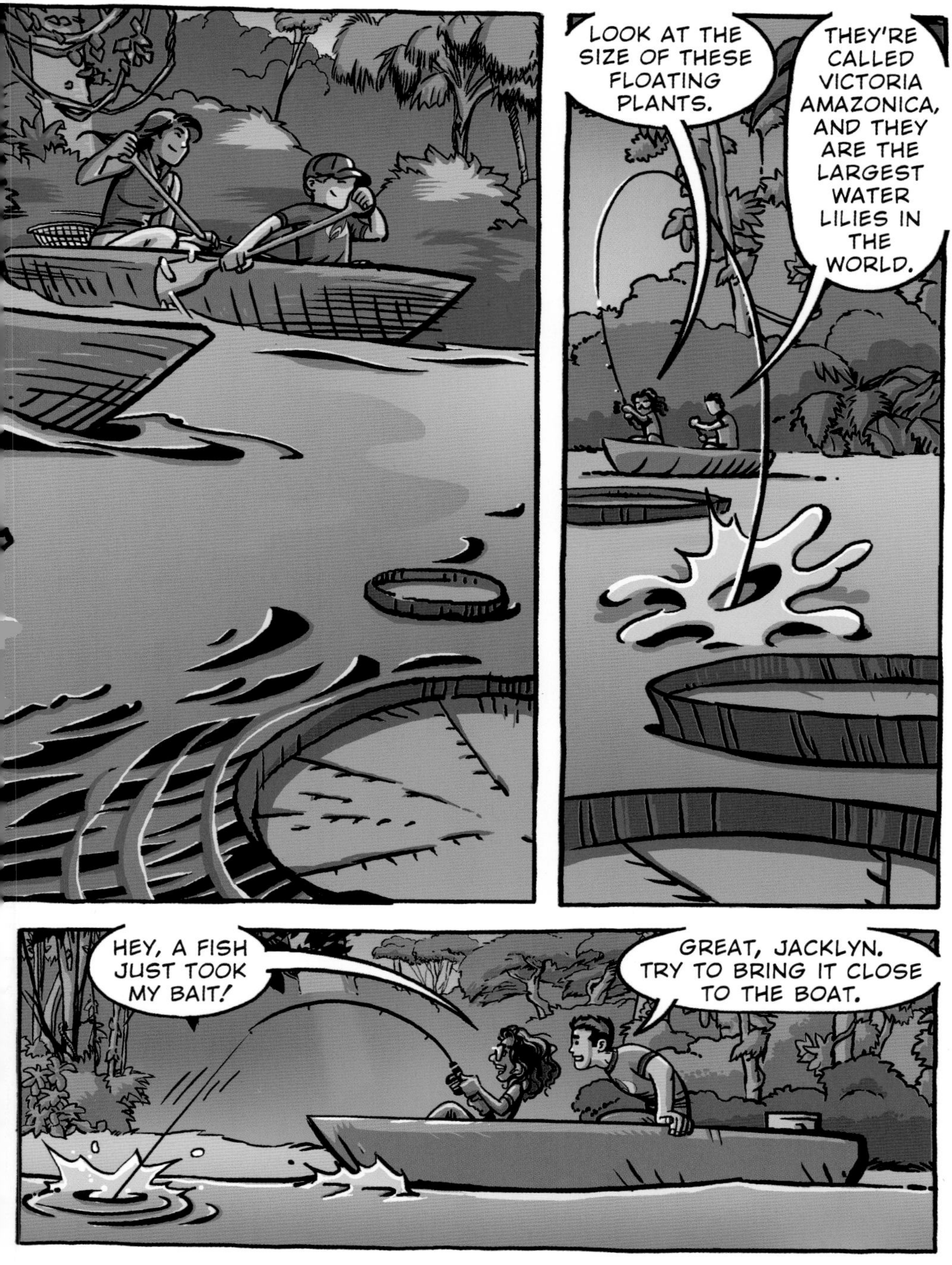
LOOK AT THE SIZE OF THESE FLOATING PLANTS.
THEY'RE CALLED VICTORIA AMAZONICA, AND THEY ARE THE LARGEST WATER LILIES IN THE WORLD.
HEY, A FISH JUST TOOK MY BAIT!
GREAT, JACKLYN. TRY TO BRING IT CLOSE TO THE BOAT.

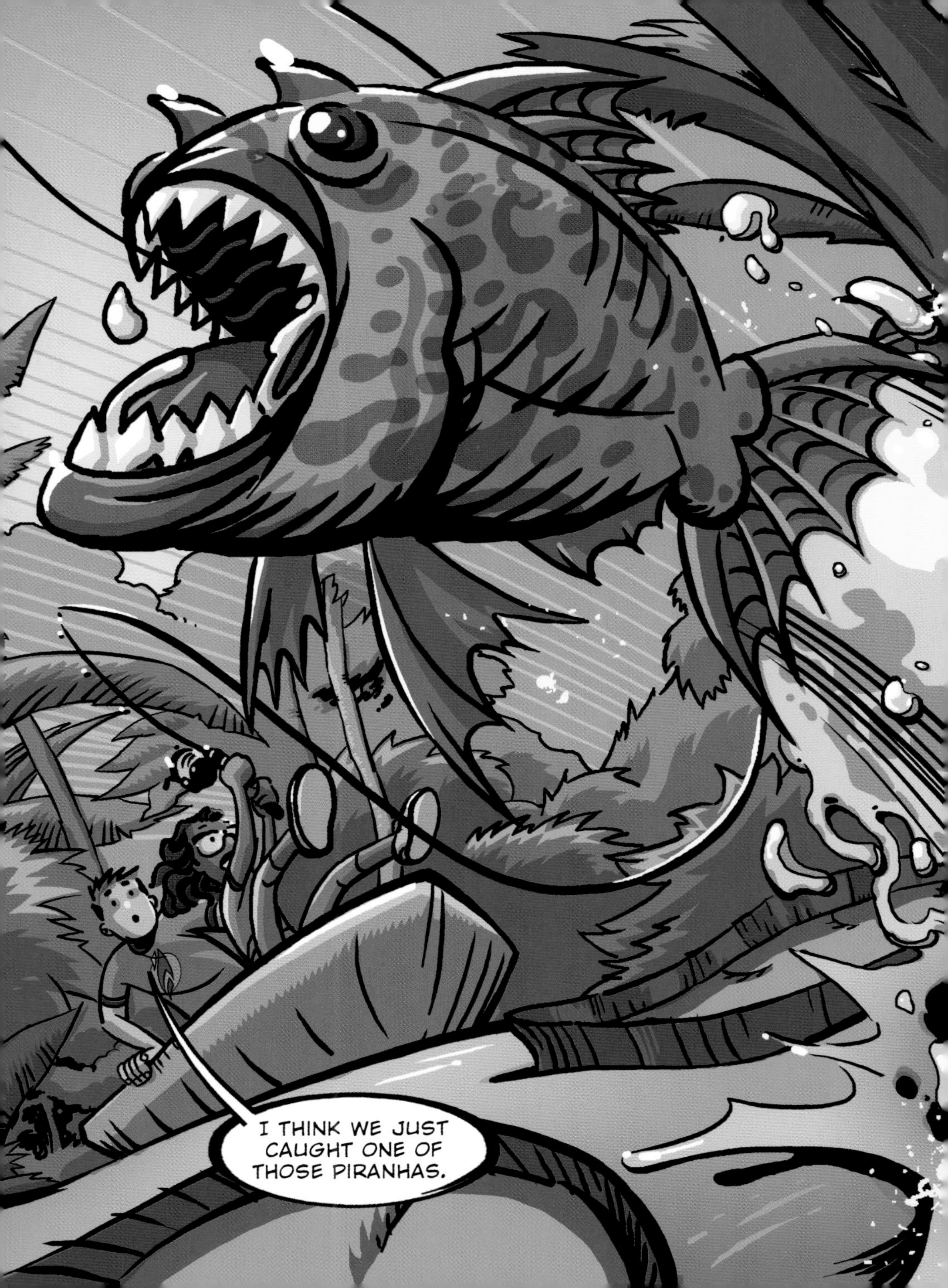
I THINK WE JUST CAUGHT ONE OF THOSE PIRANHAS.

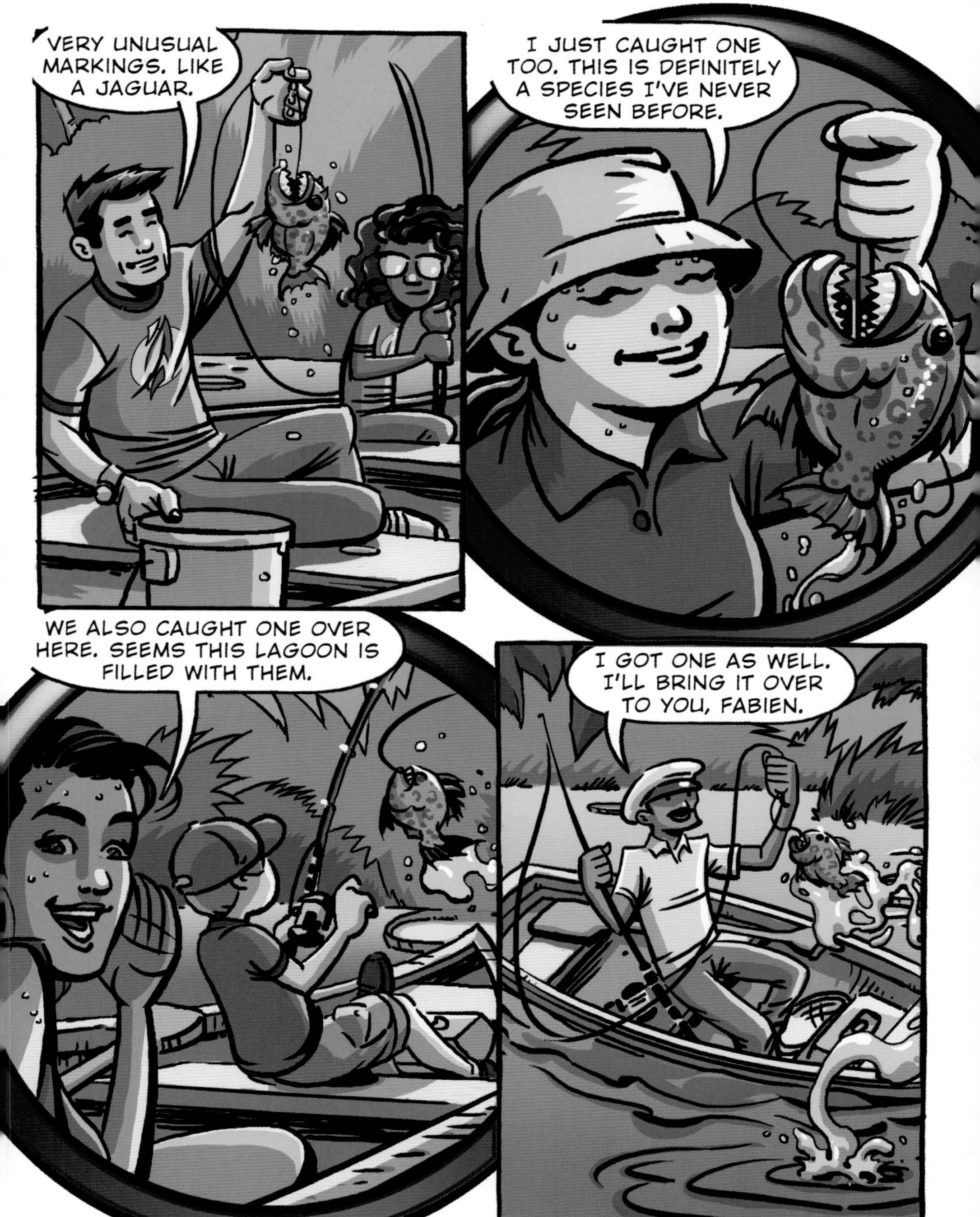
VERY UNUSUAL MARKINGS. LIKE A JAGUAR.
I JUST CAUGHT ONE TOO. THIS IS DEFINITELY A SPECIES I'VE NEVER SEEN BEFORE.
WE ALSO CAUGHT ONE OVER HERE. SEEMS THIS LAGOON IS FILLED WITH THEM.
I GOT ONE AS WELL. I'LL BRING IT OVER TO YOU, FABIEN.

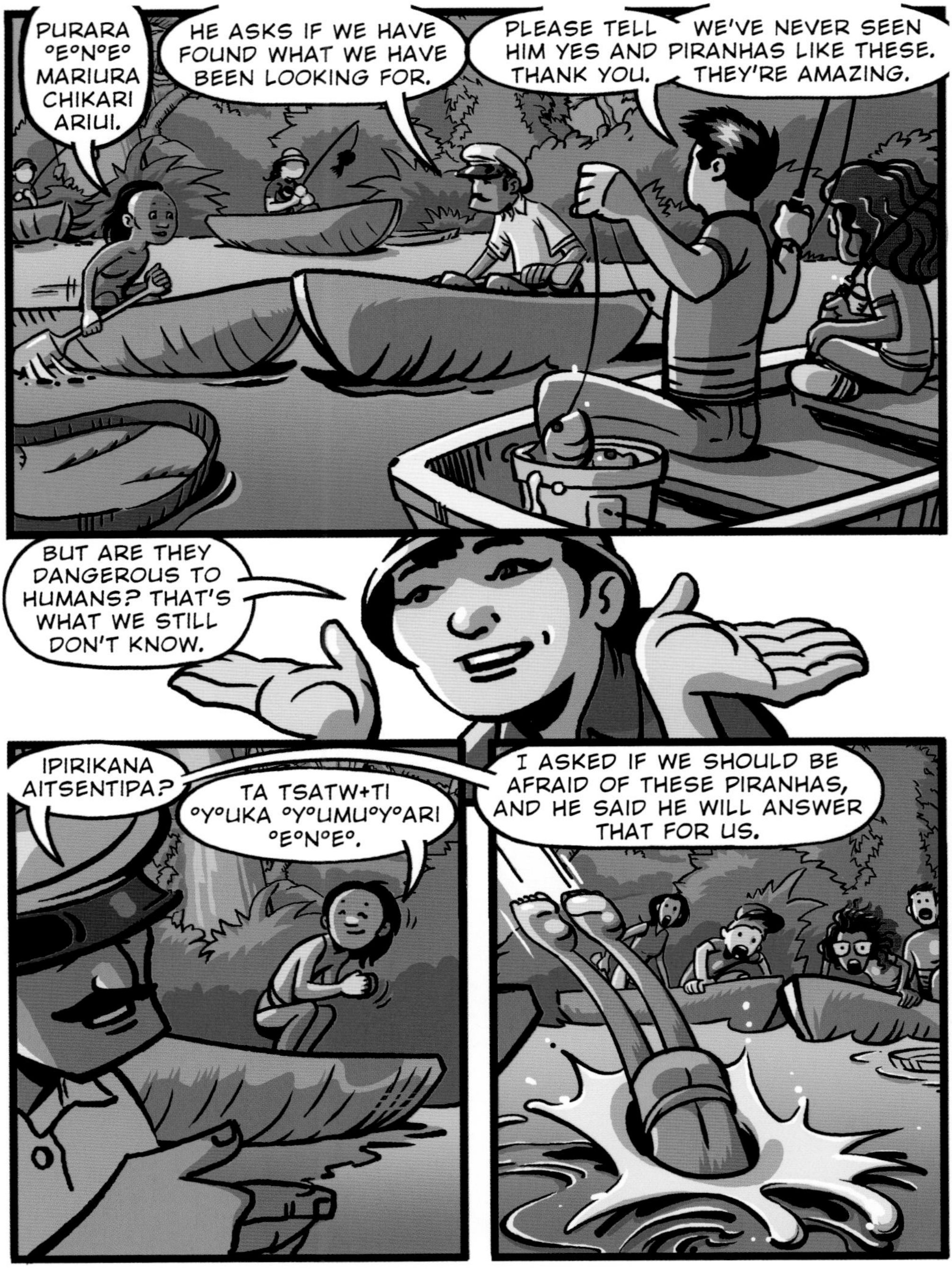
PURARA °E°N°E° MARIURA CHIKARI ARIUI.
HE ASKS IF WE HAVE FOUND WHAT WE HAVE BEEN LOOKING FOR.
PLEASE TELL HIM YES AND THANK YOU.
WE'VE NEVER SEEN PIRANHAS LIKE THESE. THEY'RE AMAZING.
BUT ARE THEY DANGEROUS TO HUMANS? THAT'S WHAT WE STILL DON'T KNOW.
IPIRIKANA AITSENTIPA?
TA TSATW+TI °Y°UKA °Y°UMU°Y°ARI °E°N°E°.
I ASKED IF WE SHOULD BE AFRAID OF THESE PIRANHAS, AND HE SAID HE WILL ANSWER THAT FOR US.

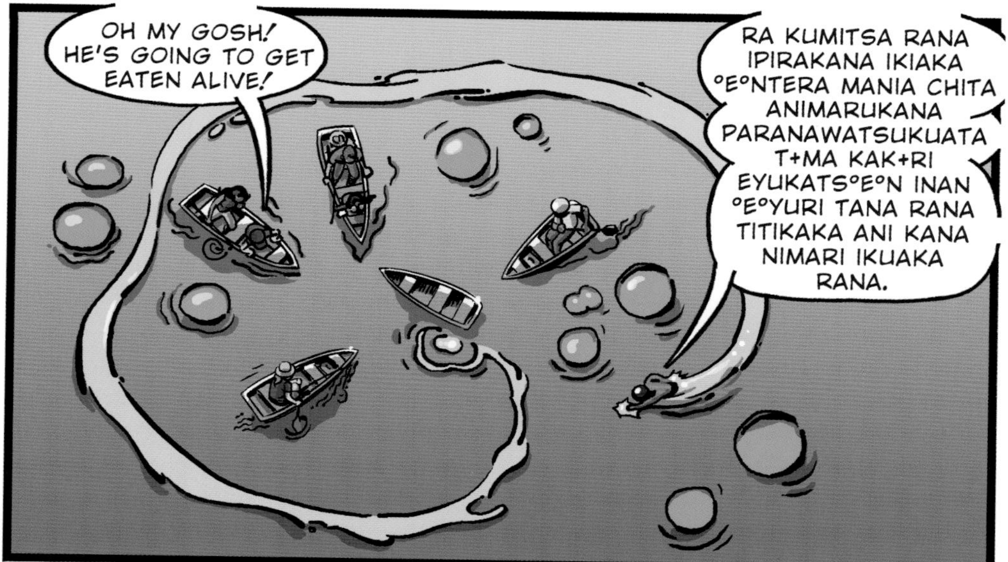
OH MY GOSH! HE'S GOING TO GET EATEN ALIVE!
RA KUMITSA RANA IPIRAKANA IKIAKA °E°NTERA MANIA CHITA ANIMARUKANA PARANAWATSUKUATA T+MA KAK+RI EYUKATS°E°N INAN °E°YURI TANA RANA TITIKAKA ANI KANA NIMARI IKUAKA RANA.

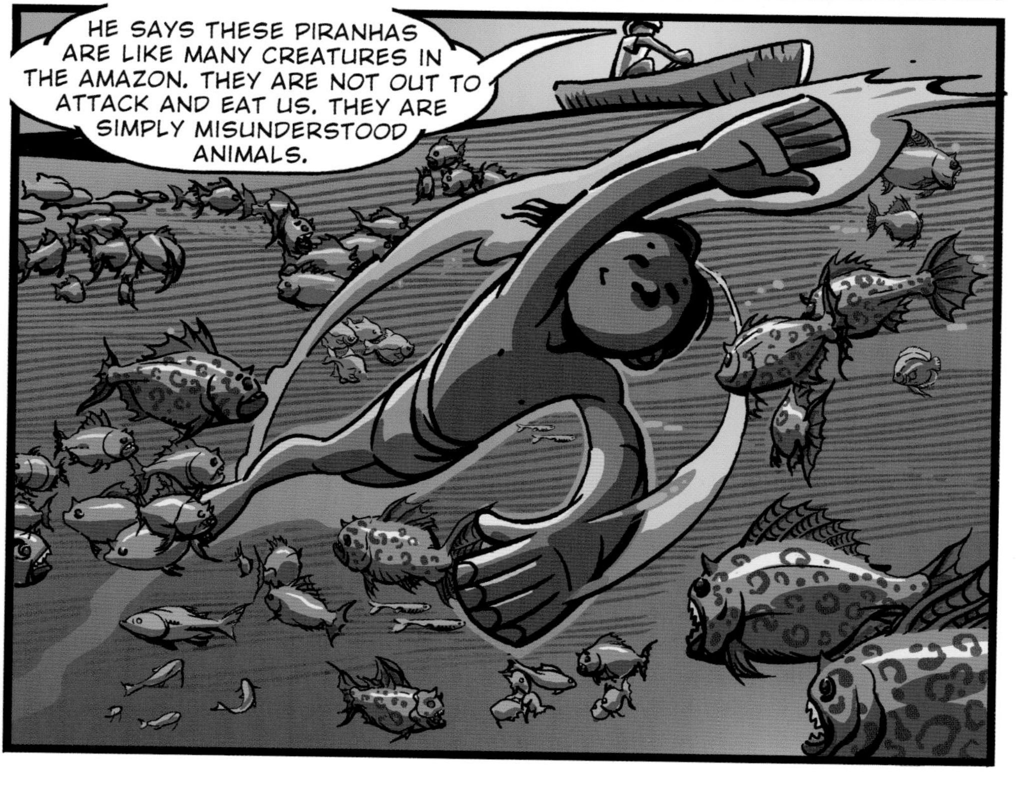
HE SAYS THESE PIRANHAS ARE LIKE MANY CREATURES IN THE AMAZON. THEY ARE NOT OUT TO ATTACK AND EAT US. THEY ARE SIMPLY MISUNDERSTOOD ANIMALS.

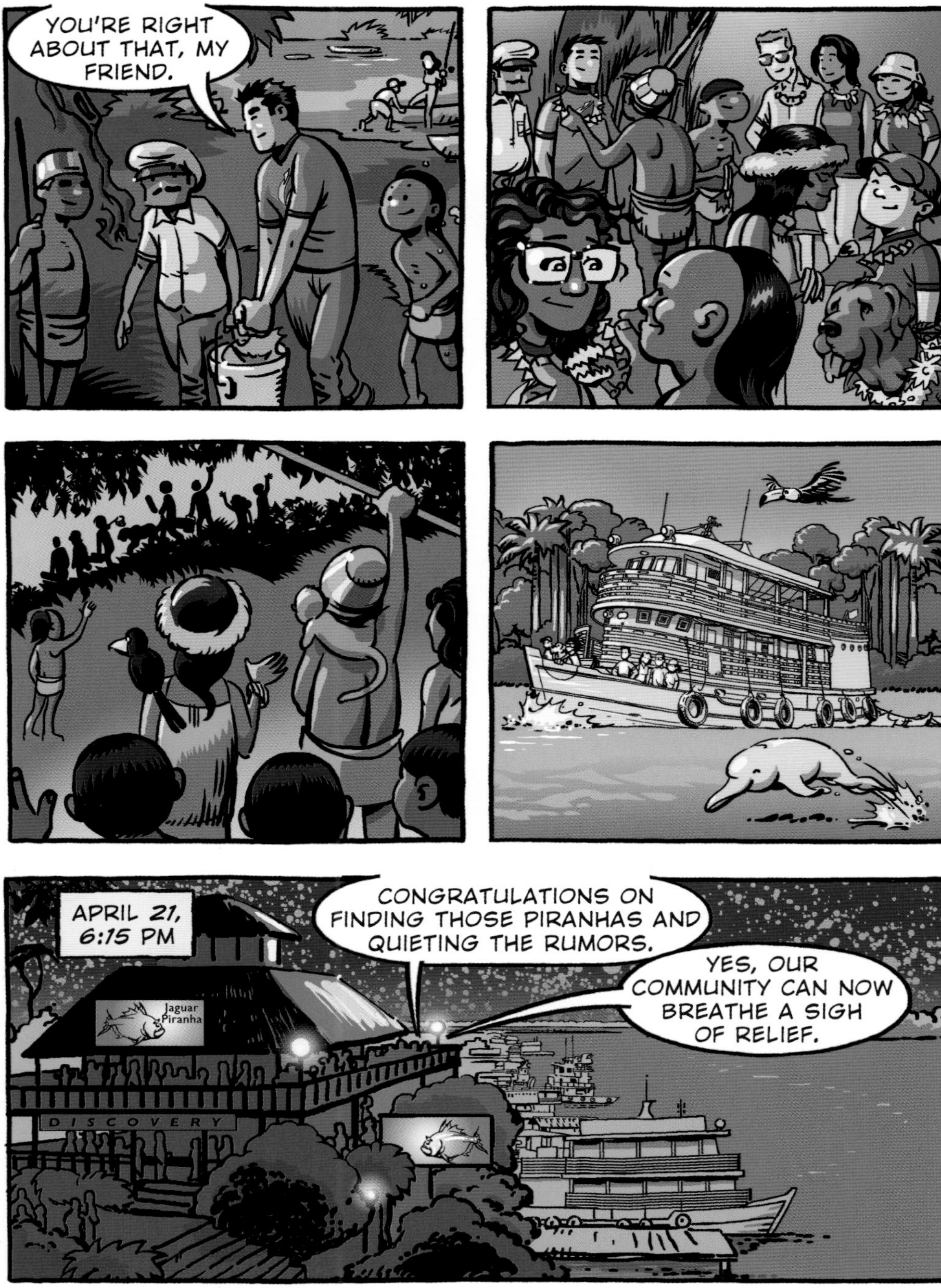
YOU'RE RIGHT ABOUT THAT, MY FRIEND.
APRIL 21, 6:15 PM
CONGRATULATIONS ON FINDING THOSE PIRANHAS AND QUIETING THE RUMORS.
YES, OUR COMMUNITY CAN NOW BREATHE A SIGH OF RELIEF.
Jaguar Piranha
DISCOVERY

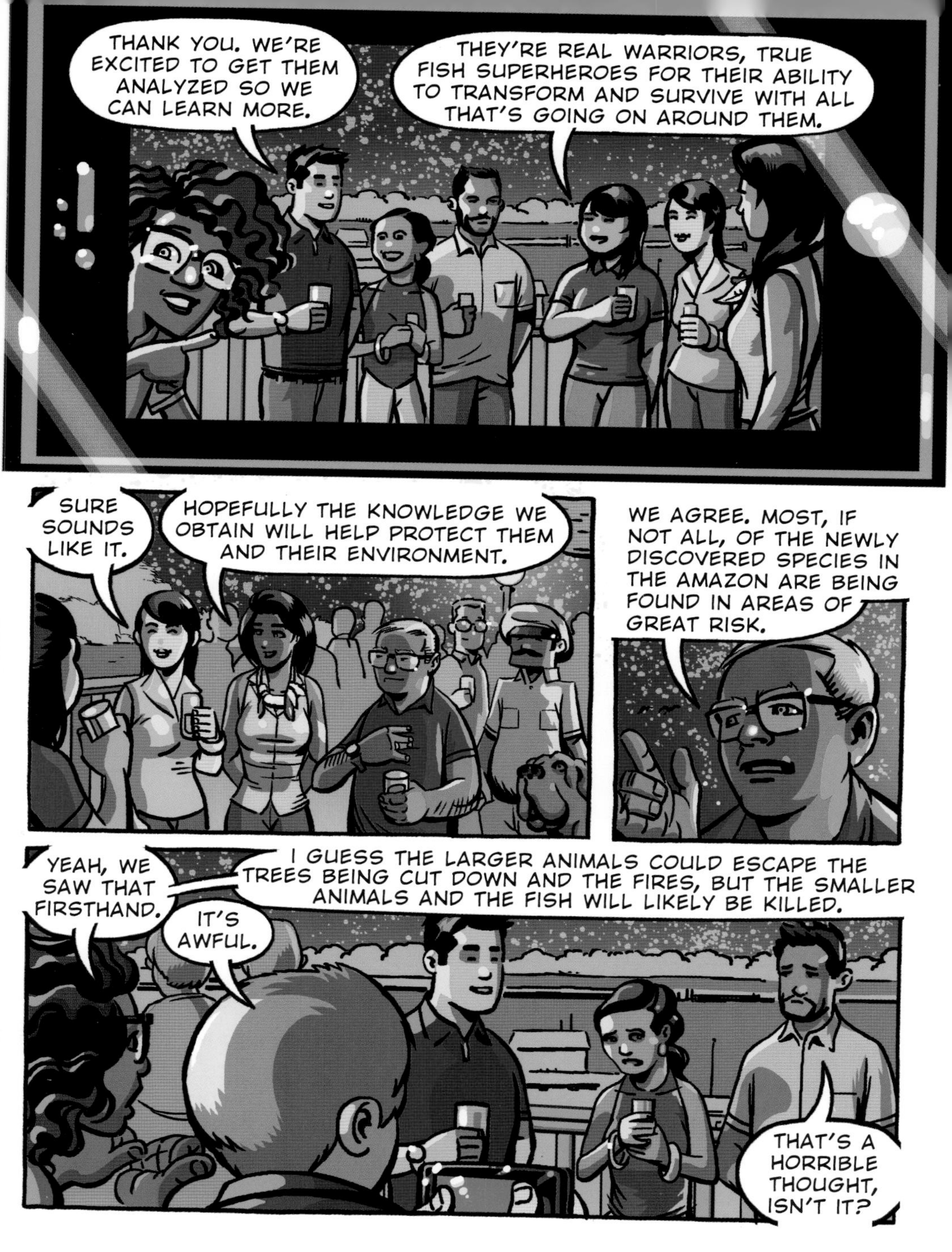
THANK YOU. WE'RE EXCITED TO GET THEM ANALYZED SO WE CAN LEARN MORE.
THEY'RE REAL WARRIORS, TRUE FISH SUPERHEROES FOR THEIR ABILITY TO TRANSFORM AND SURVIVE WITH ALL THAT'S GOING ON AROUND THEM.
SURE SOUNDS LIKE IT.
HOPEFULLY THE KNOWLEDGE WE OBTAIN WILL HELP PROTECT THEM AND THEIR ENVIRONMENT.
WE AGREE. MOST, IF NOT ALL, OF THE NEWLY DISCOVERED SPECIES IN THE AMAZON ARE BEING FOUND IN AREAS OF GREAT RISK.
YEAH, WE SAW THAT FIRSTHAND.
I GUESS THE LARGER ANIMALS COULD ESCAPE THE TREES BEING CUT DOWN AND THE FIRES, BUT THE SMALLER ANIMALS AND THE FISH WILL LIKELY BE KILLED.
IT'S AWFUL.
THAT'S A HORRIBLE THOUGHT, ISN'T IT?

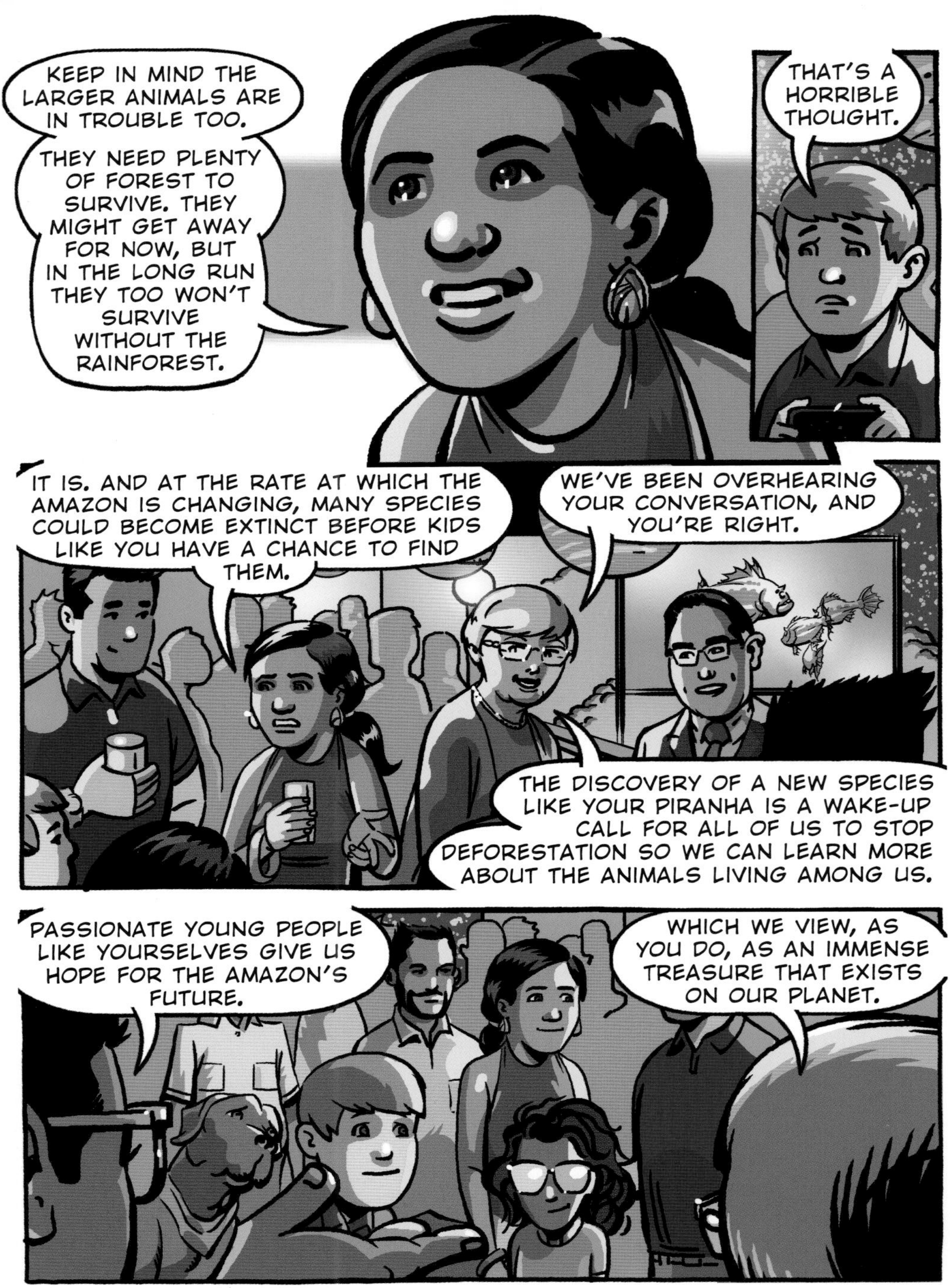
KEEP IN MIND THE LARGER ANIMALS ARE IN TROUBLE TOO.
THEY NEED PLENTY OF FOREST TO SURVIVE. THEY MIGHT GET AWAY FOR NOW, BUT IN THE LONG RUN THEY TOO WON'T SURVIVE WITHOUT THE RAINFOREST.
THAT'S A HORRIBLE THOUGHT.
IT IS. AND AT THE RATE AT WHICH THE AMAZON IS CHANGING, MANY SPECIES COULD BECOME EXTINCT BEFORE KIDS LIKE YOU HAVE A CHANCE TO FIND THEM.
WE'VE BEEN OVERHEARING YOUR CONVERSATION, AND YOU'RE RIGHT.
THE DISCOVERY OF A NEW SPECIES LIKE YOUR PIRANHA IS A WAKE-UP CALL FOR ALL OF US TO STOP DEFORESTATION SO WE CAN LEARN MORE ABOUT THE ANIMALS LIVING AMONG US.
PASSIONATE YOUNG PEOPLE LIKE YOURSELVES GIVE US HOPE FOR THE AMAZON'S FUTURE.
WHICH WE VIEW, AS YOU DO, AS AN IMMENSE TREASURE THAT EXISTS ON OUR PLANET.

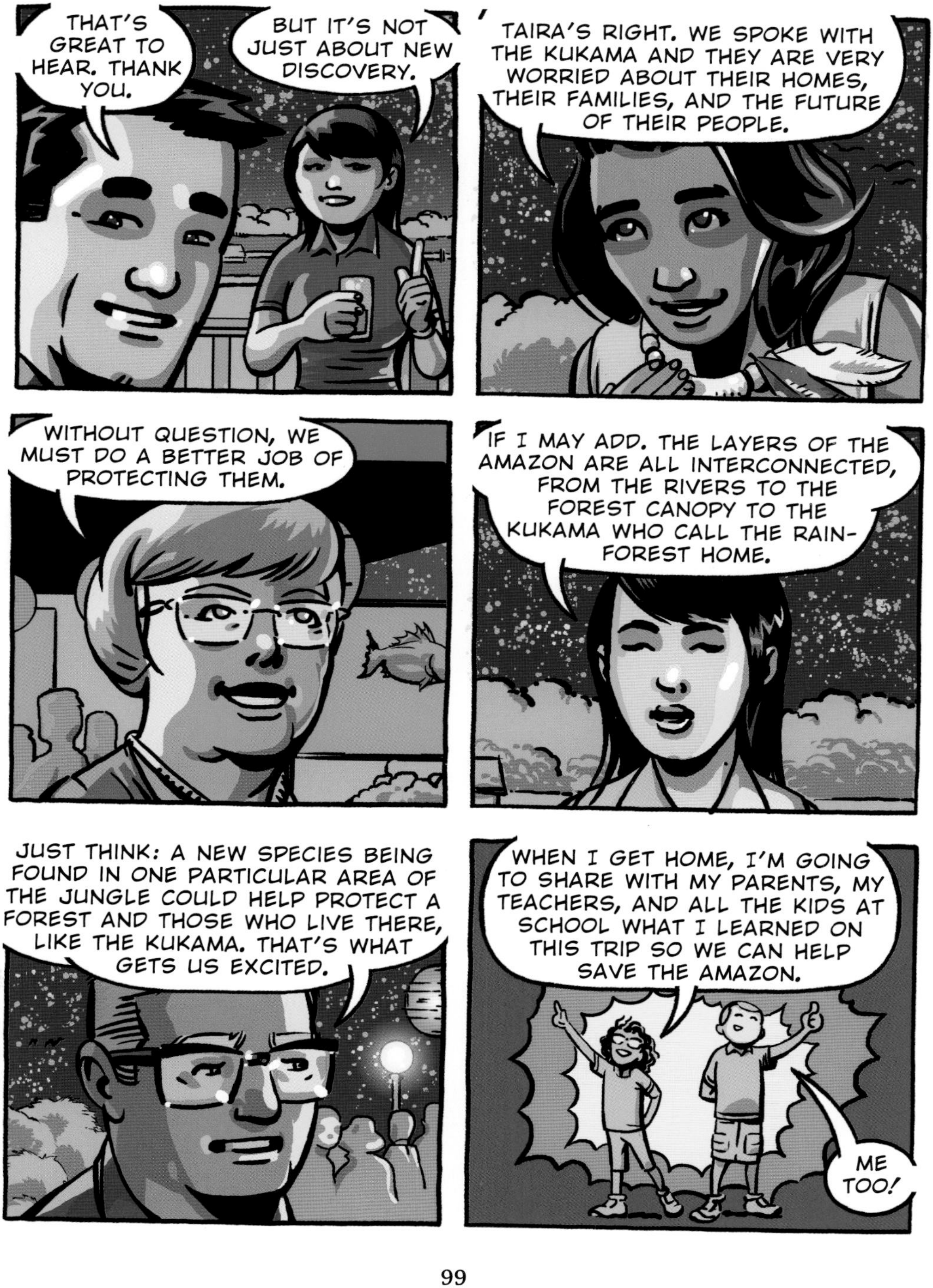
THAT'S GREAT TO HEAR. THANK YOU.
BUT IT'S NOT JUST ABOUT NEW DISCOVERY.
TAIRA'S RIGHT. WE SPOKE WITH THE KUKAMA AND THEY ARE VERY WORRIED ABOUT THEIR HOMES, THEIR FAMILIES, AND THE FUTURE OF THEIR PEOPLE.
WITHOUT QUESTION, WE MUST DO A BETTER JOB OF PROTECTING THEM.
IF I MAY ADD. THE LAYERS OF THE AMAZON ARE ALL INTERCONNECTED, FROM THE RIVERS TO THE FOREST CANOPY TO THE KUKAMA WHO CALL THE RAIN-FOREST HOME.
JUST THINK: A NEW SPECIES BEING FOUND IN ONE PARTICULAR AREA OF THE JUNGLE COULD HELP PROTECT A FOREST AND THOSE WHO LIVE THERE, LIKE THE KUKAMA. THAT'S WHAT GETS US EXCITED.
WHEN I GET HOME, I'M GOING TO SHARE WITH MY PARENTS, MY TEACHERS, AND ALL THE KIDS AT SCHOOL WHAT I LEARNED ON THIS TRIP SO WE CAN HELP SAVE THE AMAZON.
ME TOO!

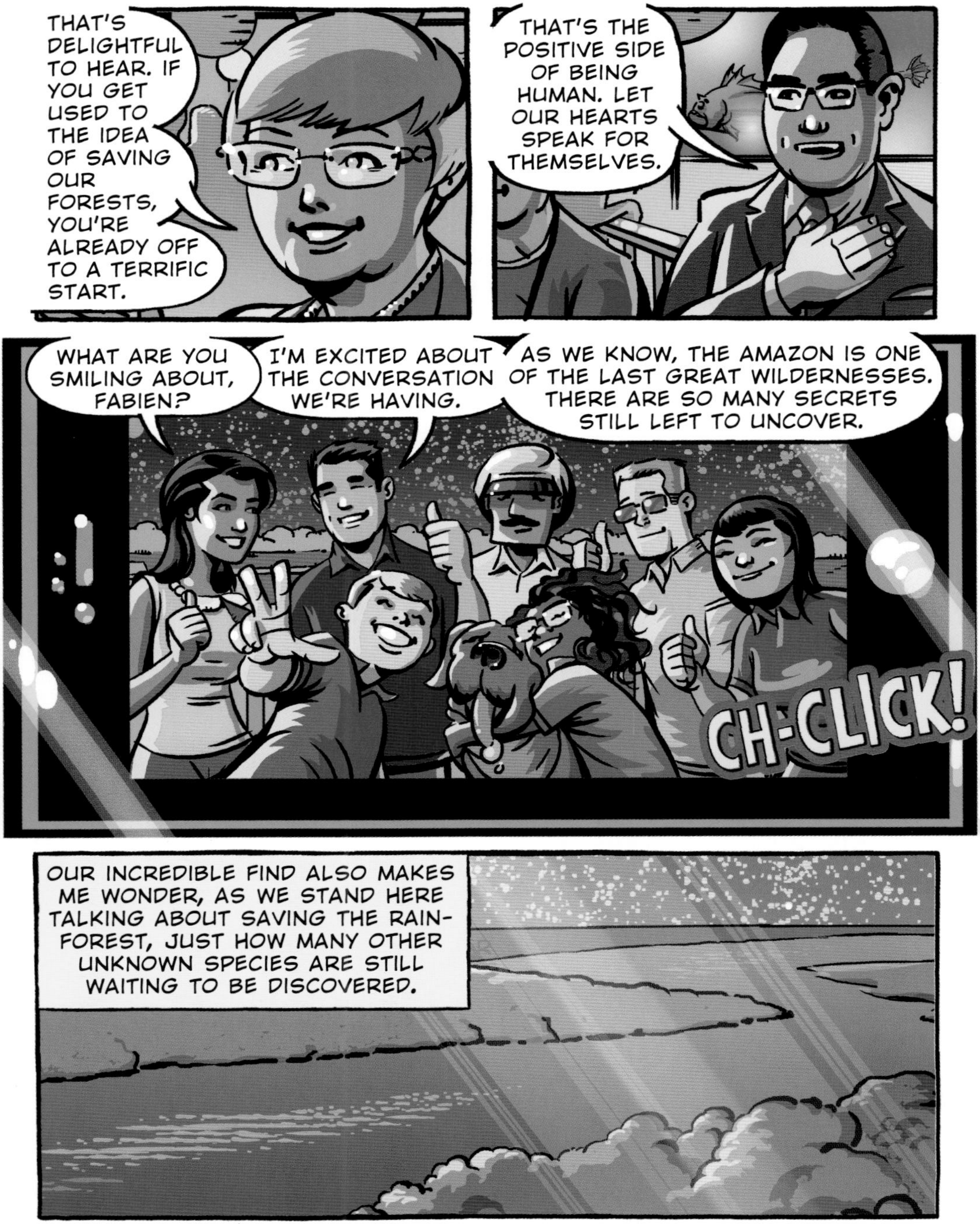
THAT'S DELIGHTFUL TO HEAR. IF YOU GET USED TO THE IDEA OF SAVING OUR FORESTS, YOU'RE ALREADY OFF TO A TERRIFIC START.
THAT'S THE POSITIVE SIDE OF BEING HUMAN. LET OUR HEARTS SPEAK FOR THEMSELVES.
WHAT ARE YOU SMILING ABOUT, FABIEN?
I'M EXCITED ABOUT THE CONVERSATION WE'RE HAVING.
AS WE KNOW, THE AMAZON IS ONE OF THE LAST GREAT WILDERNESSES. THERE ARE SO MANY SECRETS STILL LEFT TO UNCOVER.
CH-CLICK!
OUR INCREDIBLE FIND ALSO MAKES ME WONDER, AS WE STAND HERE TALKING ABOUT SAVING THE RAIN-FOREST, JUST HOW MANY OTHER UNKNOWN SPECIES ARE STILL WAITING TO BE DISCOVERED.

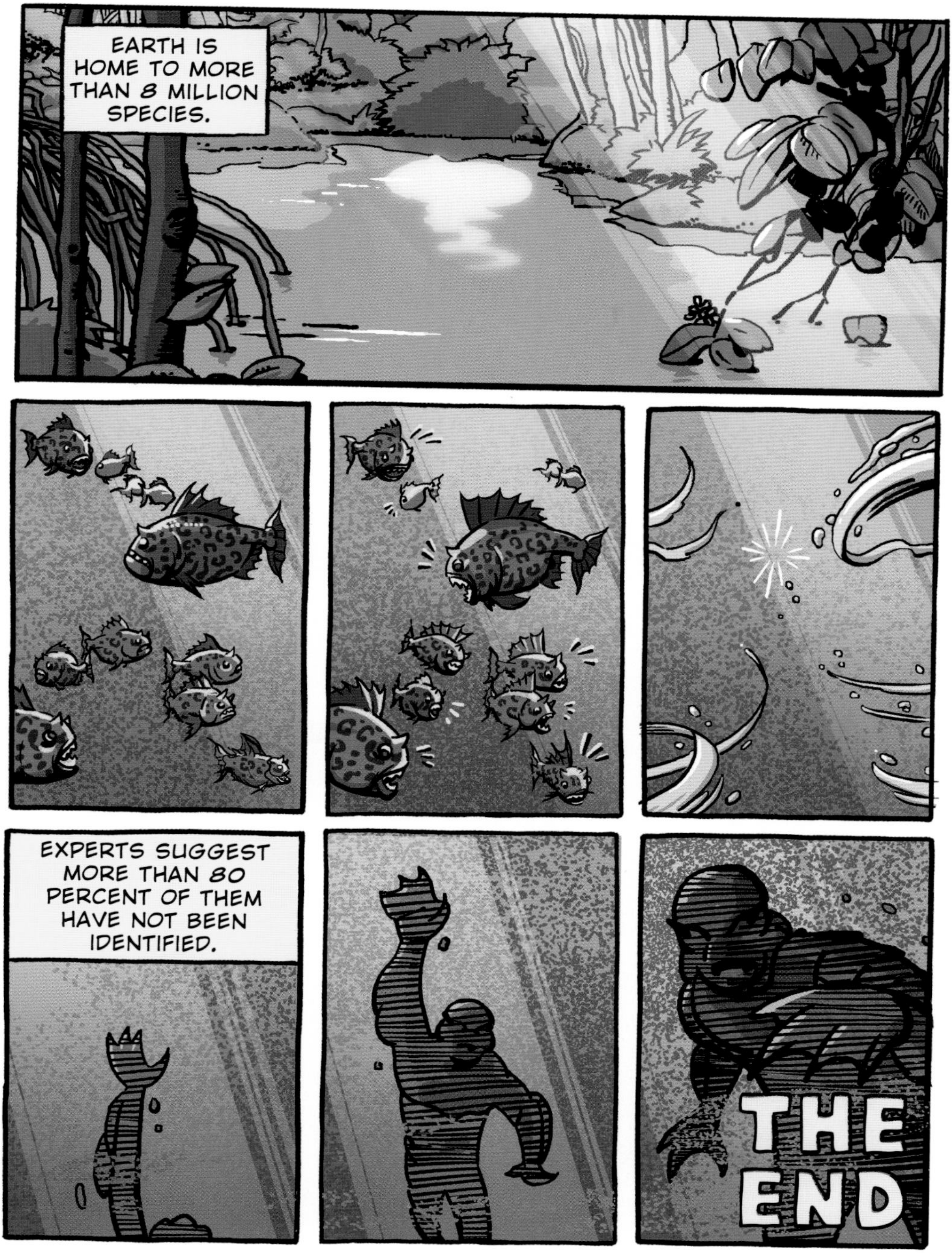
EARTH IS HOME TO MORE THAN 8 MILLION SPECIES.
EXPERTS SUGGEST MORE THAN 80 PERCENT OF THEM HAVE NOT BEEN IDENTIFIED.
THE END

The authors would like to personally thank:

Karen Wojtyla and the editorial publishing team at Margaret K. McElderry Books and Simon & Schuster Children's Publishing; Paul Beaver at Amazonia Expeditions and Angels of the Amazon; Celeste Taricuarima; Devon Graham, PhD, and Jim Lovins at Project Amazonas Inc.; Tiffany Armstrong; and William Rudd. Special thanks to David Tanguay and Sonya Pelletier for their coloring assistance.

FABIEN COUSTEAU is the grandson of famed sea explorer Jacques Cousteau and champions the family legacy as a third-generation ocean explorer and filmmaker. Learn more about his work at fabiencousteauolc.org.

JAMES O. FRAIOLI is the author of twenty-five books and is an award-winning filmmaker. He has served on the board of directors for the Seattle Aquarium and works with many environmental organizations. Learn more about his work at vesperentertainment.com.

JOE ST.PIERRE has sold more than two million comic books, illustrating and writing for Marvel, DC, and Valiant Comics, as well as his own properties published through his company, Astronaut Ink. Learn more at astronautink.com and popartproperties.com.